Totally Spies!™

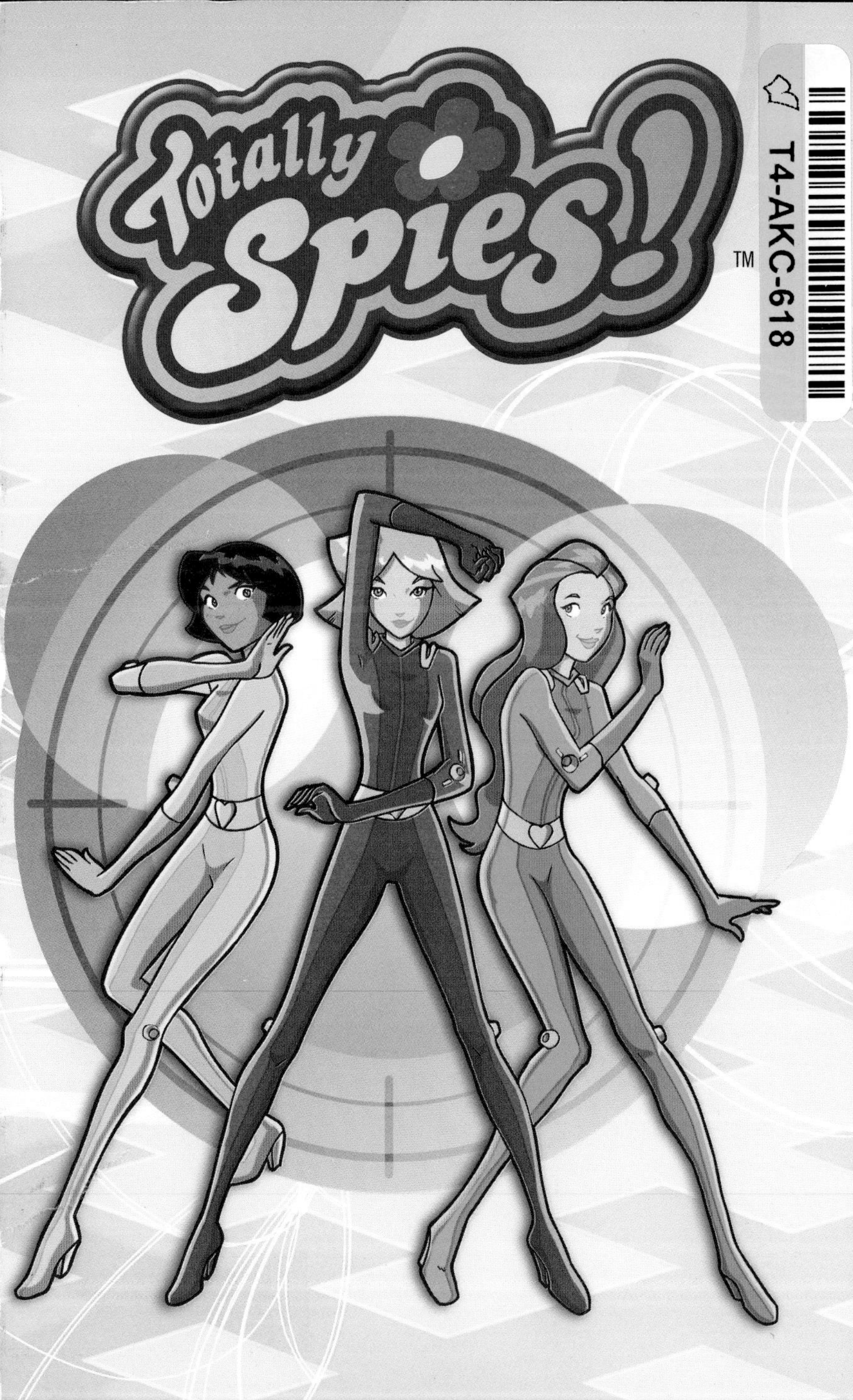

Contributing Editors - Ian Mayer and Amy Court Kaemon
Graphic Design and Lettering - Anna Kernbaum
Cover Layout - Kyle Plummer

Editor - Erin Stein
Digital Imaging Manager - Chris Buford
Pre-Press Manager - Antonio DePietro
Production Managers - Jennifer Miller and Mutsumi Miyazaki
Art Director - Matt Alford
Managing Editor - Jill Freshney
VP of Production - Ron Klamert
President & C.O.O. - John Parker
Publisher & C.E.O. - Stuart Levy

E-mail: info@tokyopop.com
Come visit us online at www.TOKYOPOP.com

A **TOKYOPOP** Cine-Manga® Book
TOKYOPOP Inc.
5900 Wilshire Blvd., Suite 2000
Los Angeles, CA 90036

Totally Spies!: Spies in Disguise

ISBN: 1-59532-286-8

First TOKYOPOP® printing: November 2004

10 9 8 7 6 5 4 3 2

Printed in the USA

Totally **SPIES!** ™

TOKYOPOP®

LOS ANGELES • TOKYO • LONDON • HAMBURG

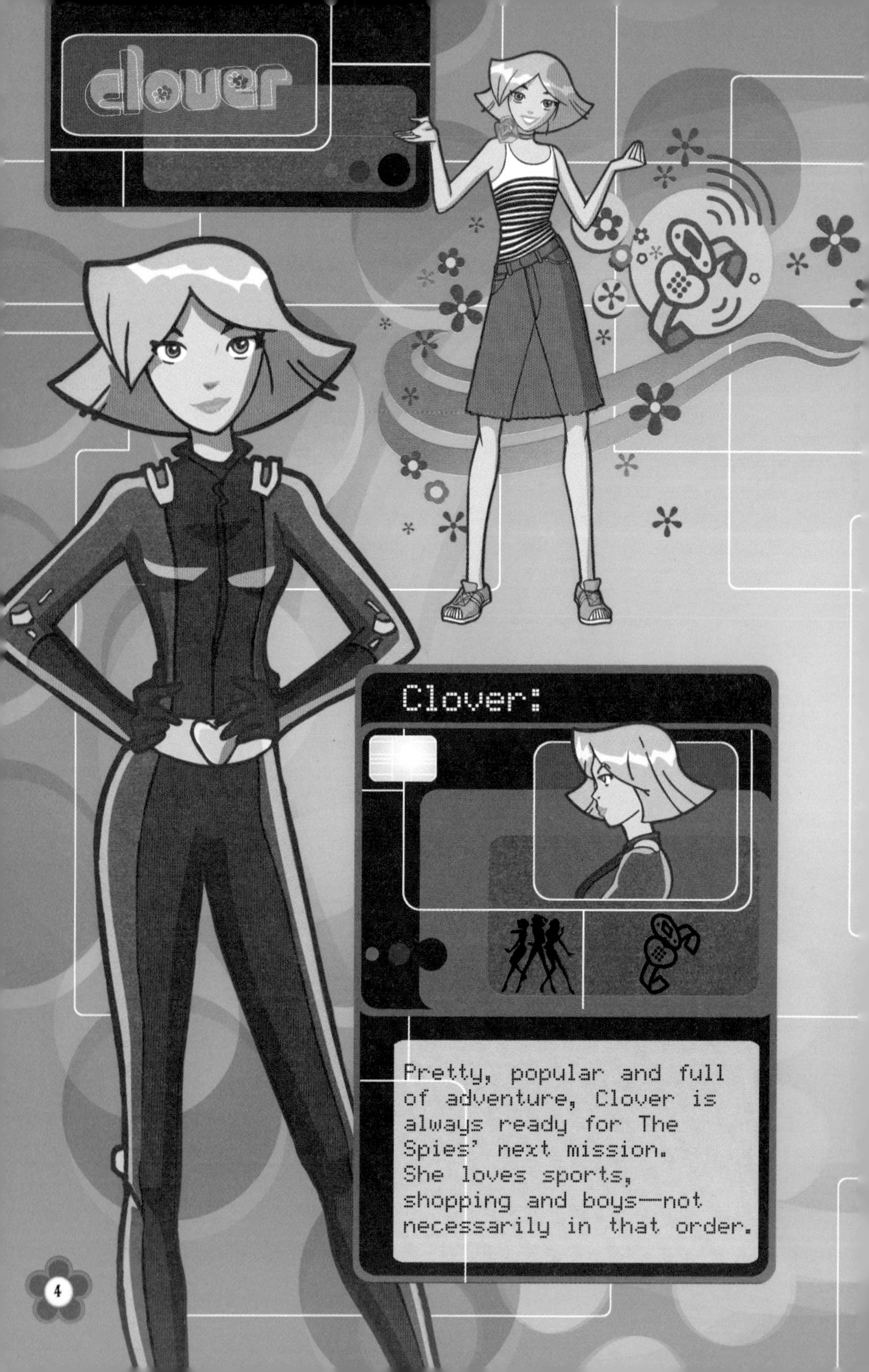
clover
Clover:
Pretty, popular and full of adventure, Clover is always ready for The Spies' next mission. She loves sports, shopping and boys—not necessarily in that order.

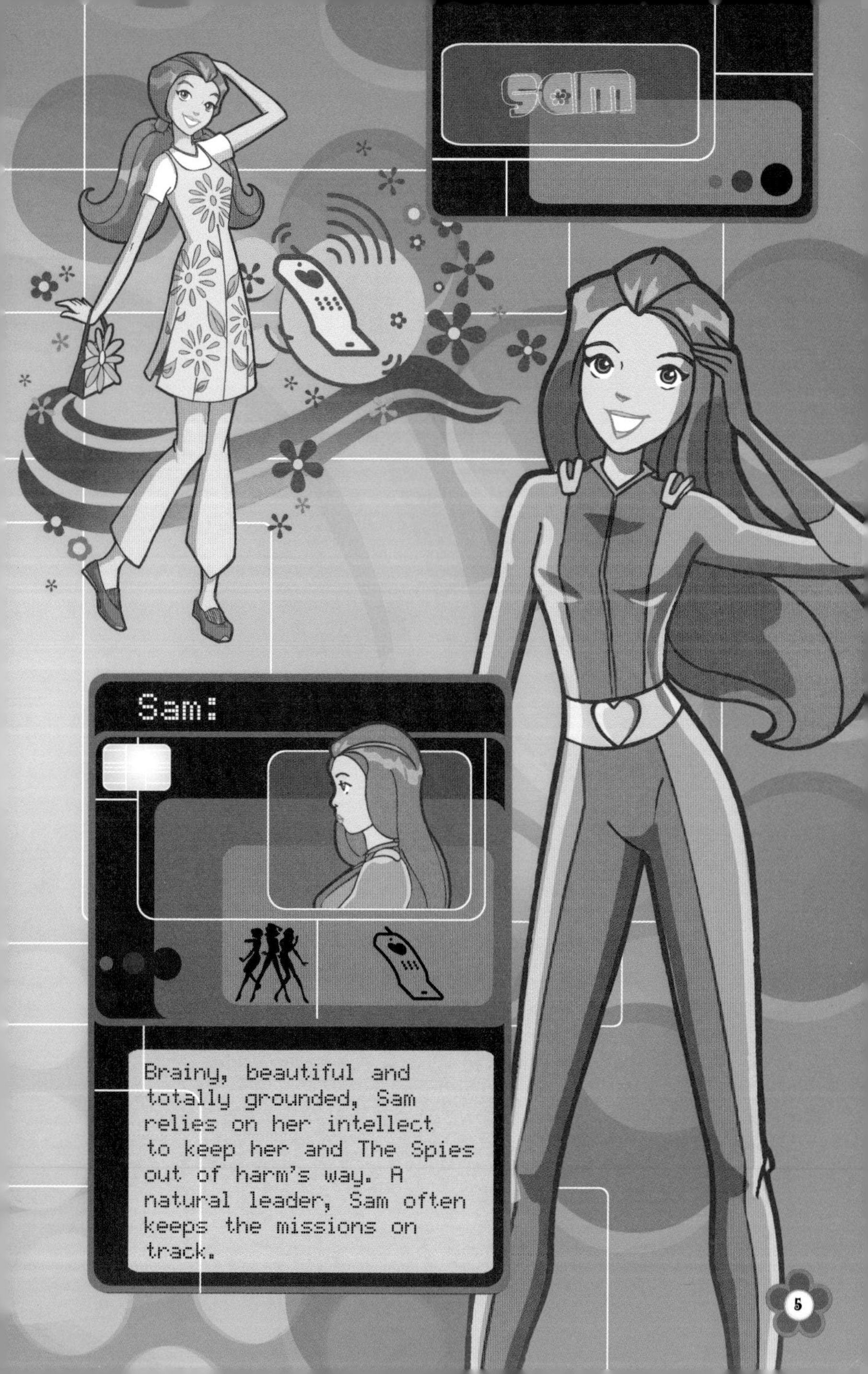
sam
Sam:
Brainy, beautiful and totally grounded, Sam relies on her intellect to keep her and The Spies out of harm's way. A natural leader, Sam often keeps the missions on track.

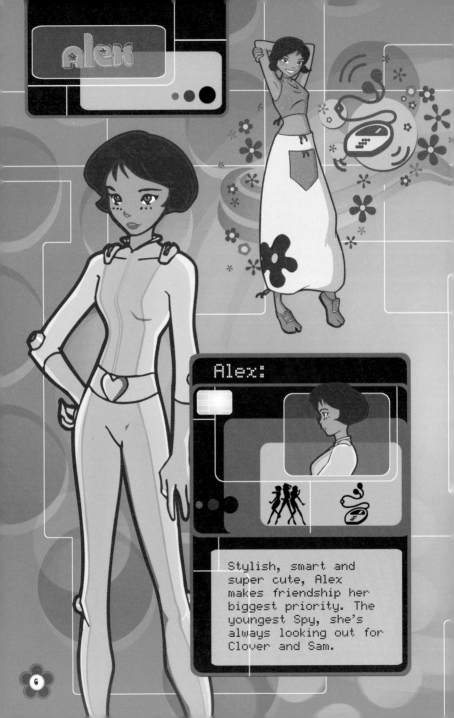

alex

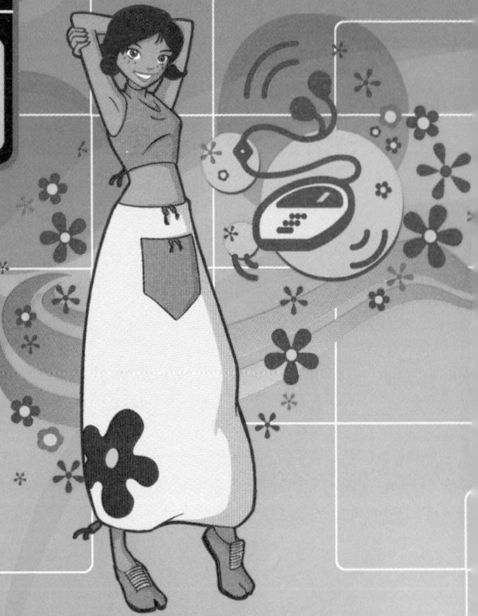

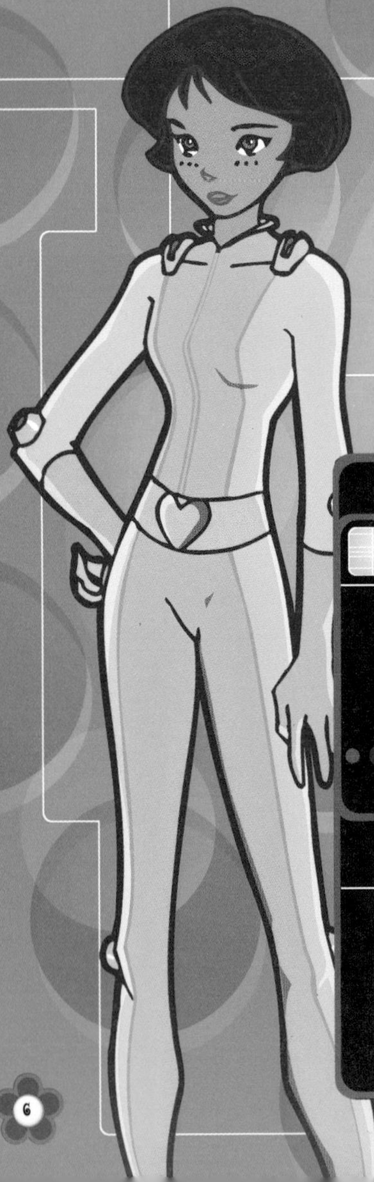

Alex:

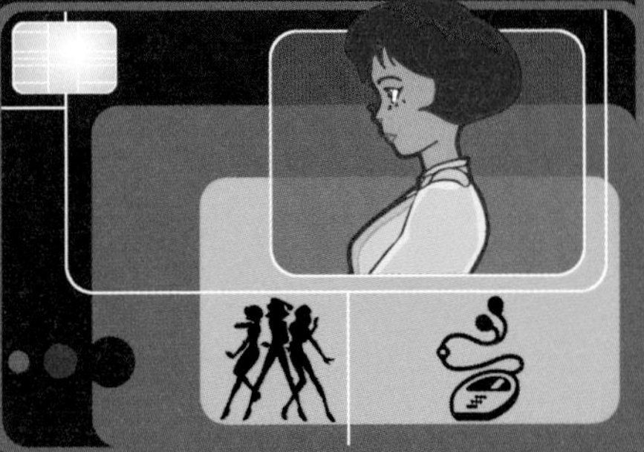

Stylish, smart and super cute, Alex makes friendship her biggest priority. The youngest Spy, she's always looking out for Clover and Sam.

Jerry:

The Spies' contact at WOOHP, the World Organization of Human Protection.

Ricky Mathis:

Pop music's latest overnight sensation.

Phil Jenkins:

Ricky's tour manager.

Mr. Sebastian:

The owner of Ricky's record label.

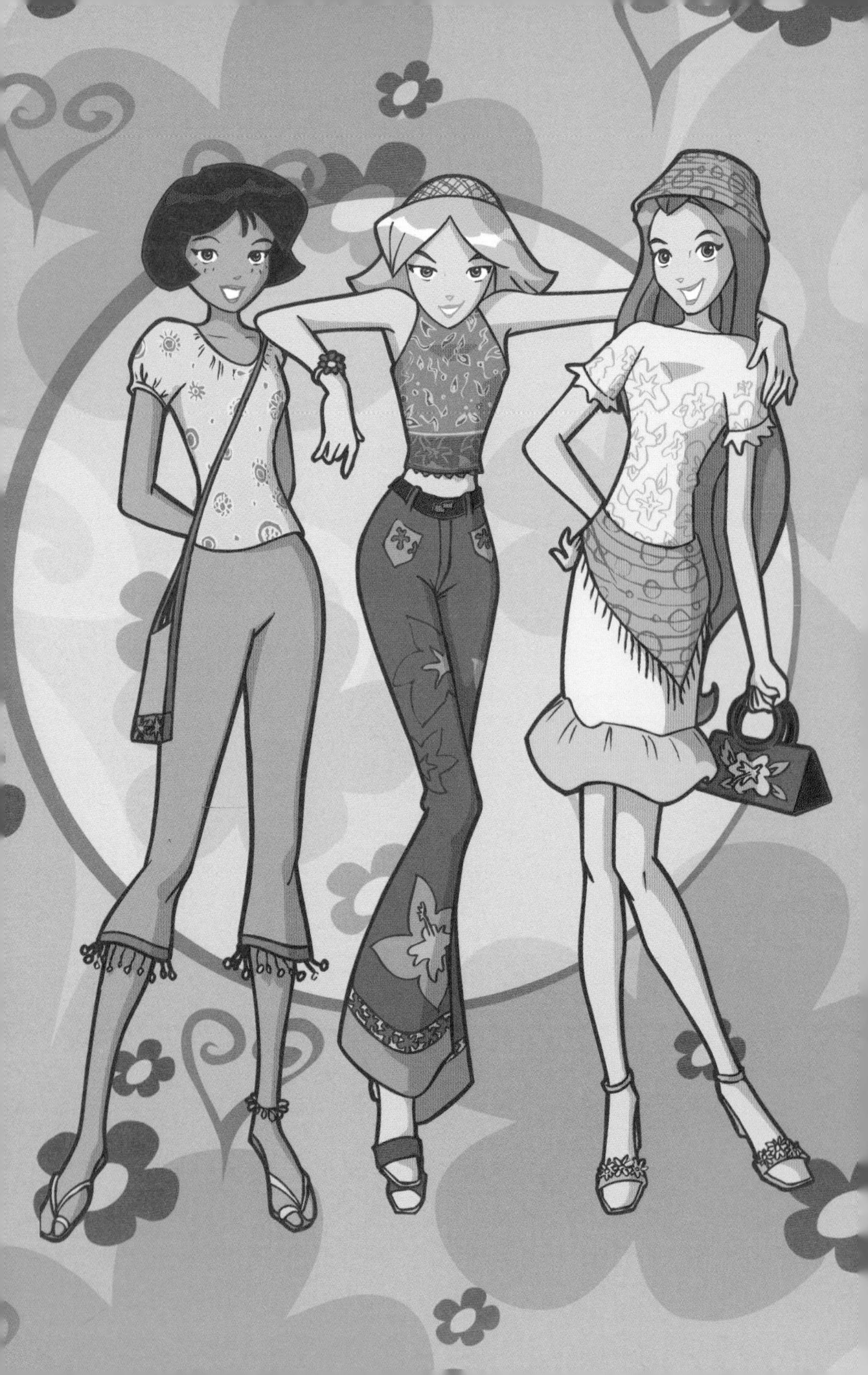

Totally Spies!™

A Thing for Musicians

by
michelle and robert lamoreaux

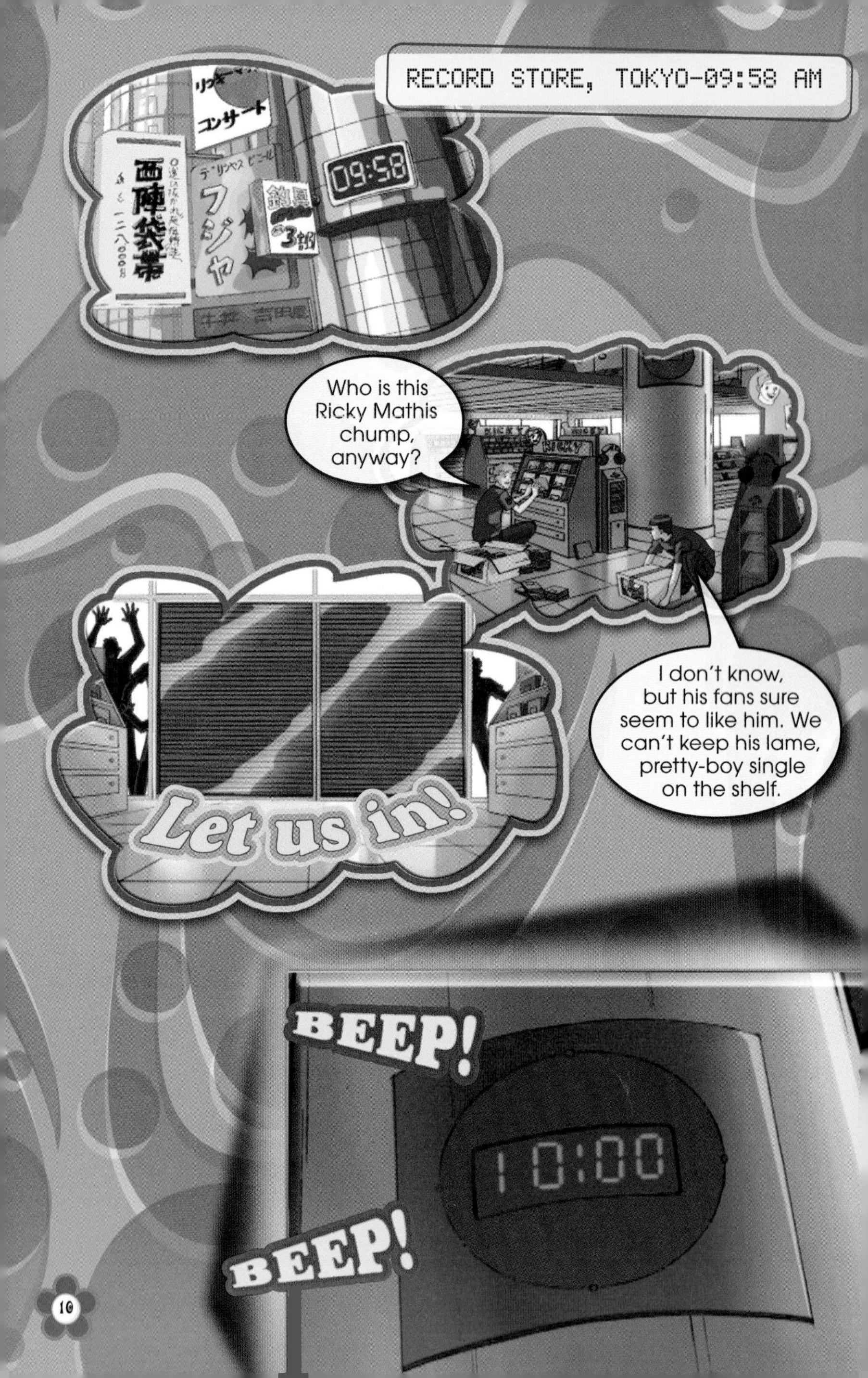

RECORD STORE, TOKYO-09:58 AM
コンサート
09:58
Who is this Ricky Mathis chump, anyway?
I don't know, but his fans sure seem to like him. We can't keep his lame, pretty-boy single on the shelf.
Let us in!
BEEP!
BEEP!
10:00

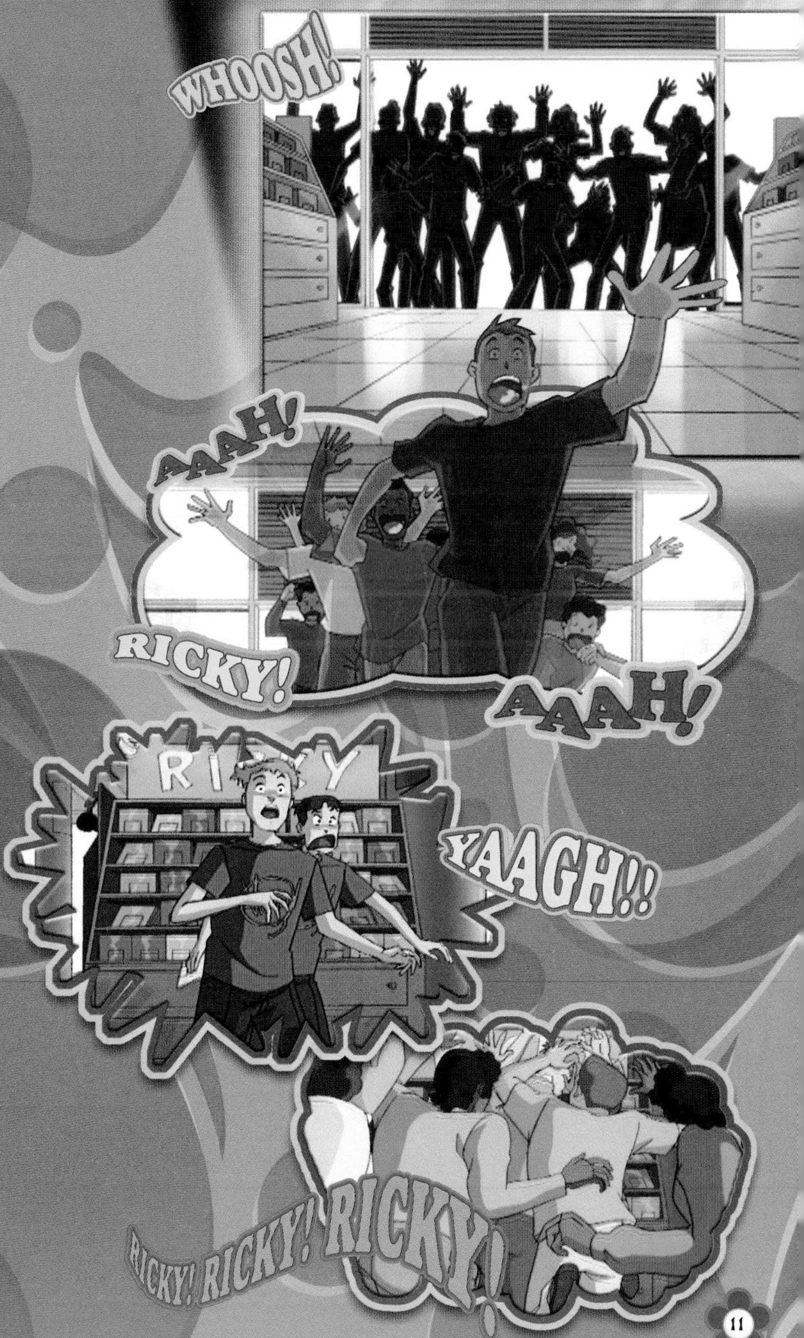
WHOOSH!
AAAH!
RICKY!
AAAH!
YAAGH!!
RICKY! RICKY! RICKY!

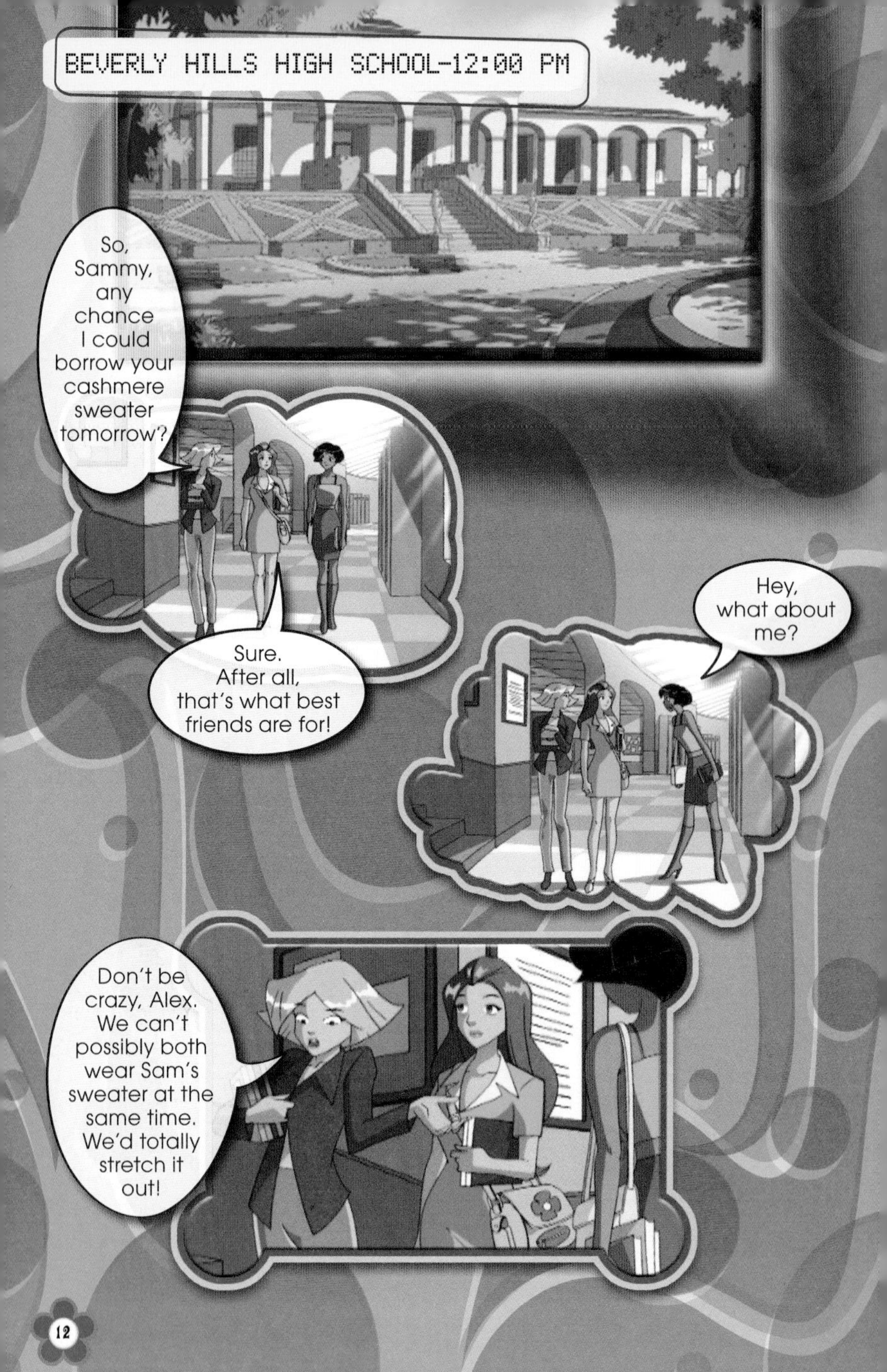
BEVERLY HILLS HIGH SCHOOL-12:00 PM
So, Sammy, any chance I could borrow your cashmere sweater tomorrow?
Sure. After all, that's what best friends are for!
Hey, what about me?
Don't be crazy, Alex. We can't possibly both wear Sam's sweater at the same time. We'd totally stretch it out!

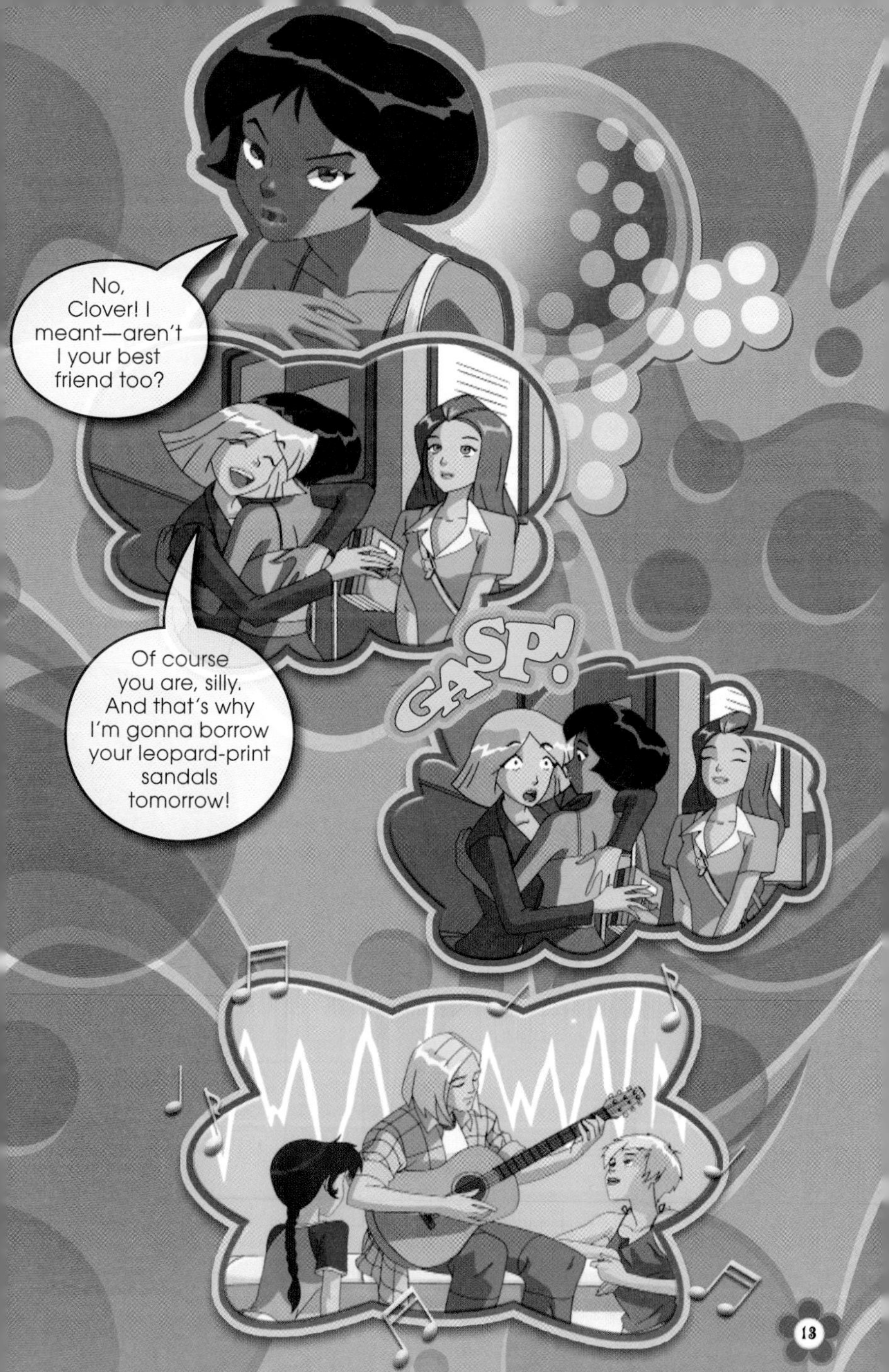
No, Clover! I meant—aren't I your best friend too?
Of course you are, silly. And that's why I'm gonna borrow your leopard-print sandals tomorrow!
GASP!

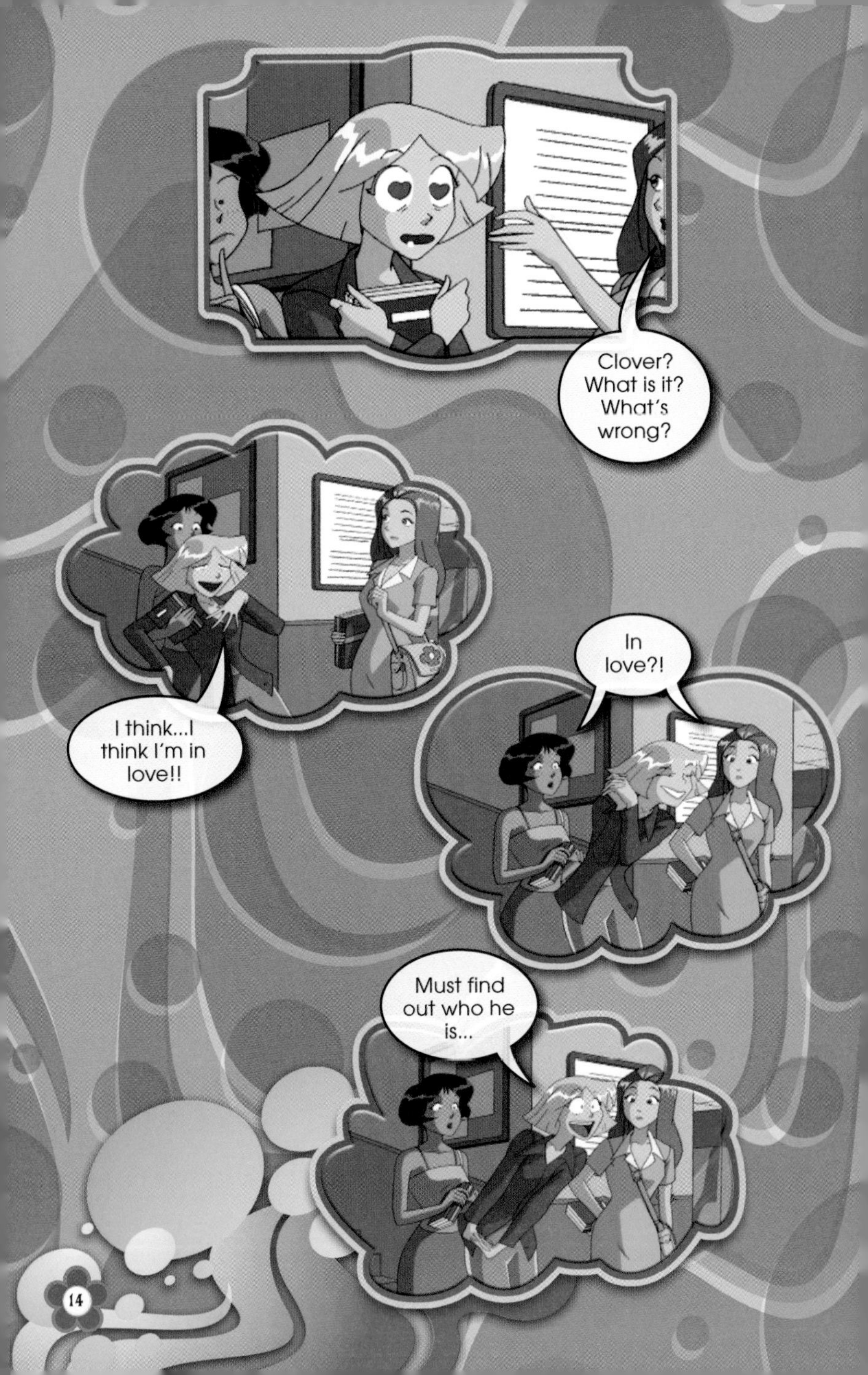
Clover? What is it? What's wrong?
I think...I think I'm in love!!
In love?!
Must find out who he is...

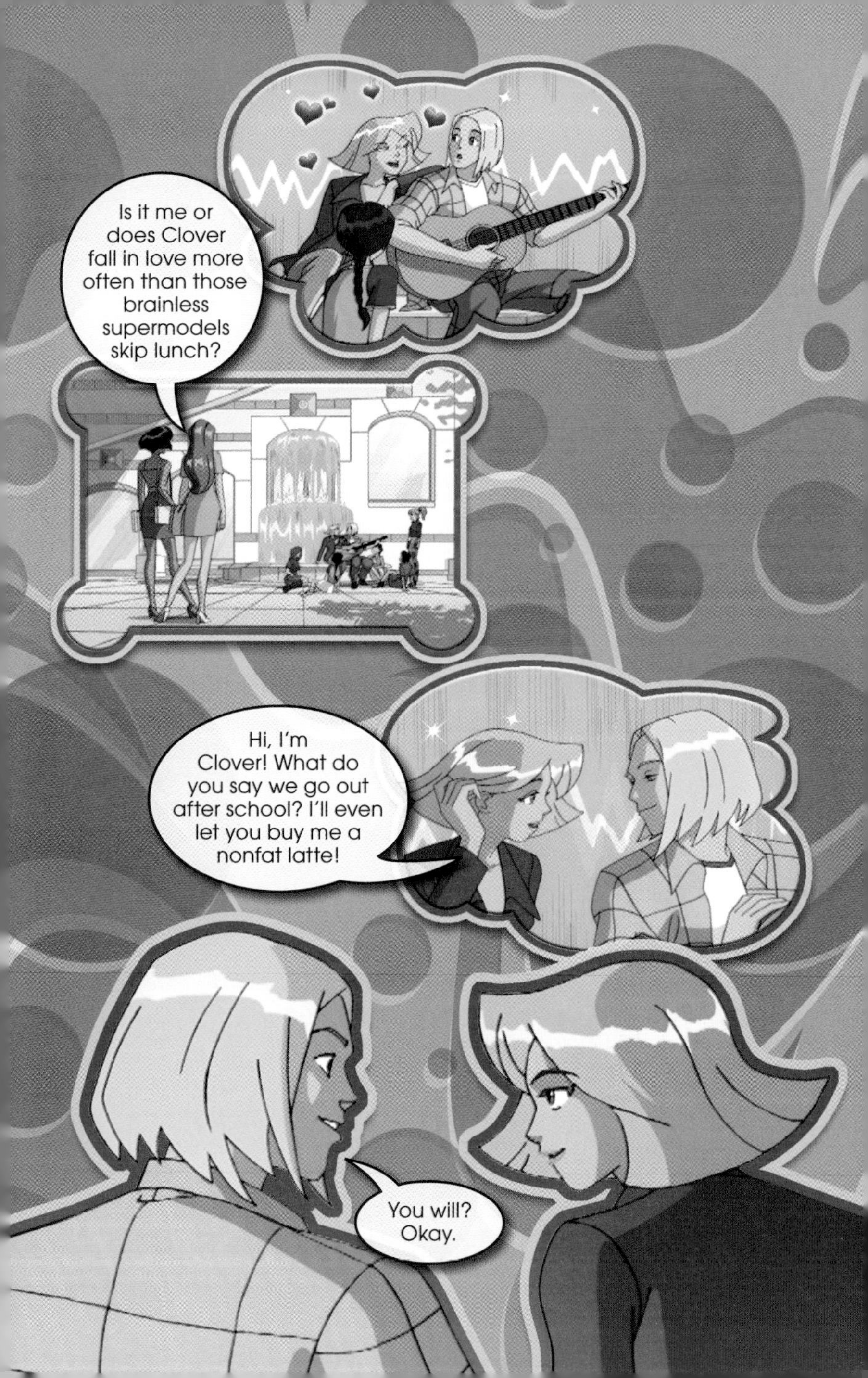
Is it me or does Clover fall in love more often than those brainless supermodels skip lunch?
Hi, I'm Clover! What do you say we go out after school? I'll even let you buy me a nonfat latte!
You will? Okay.

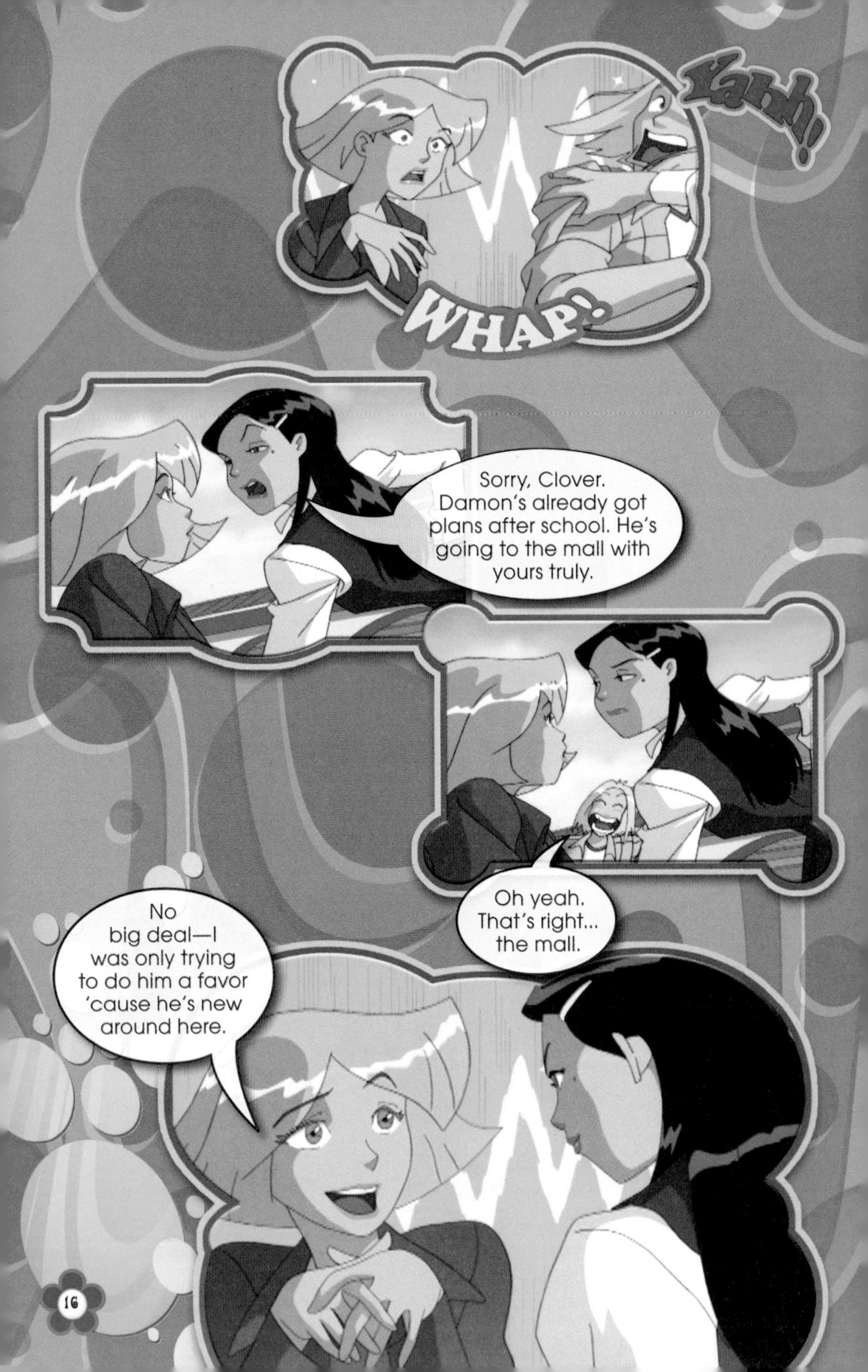
Yahh!!
WHAP!
Sorry, Clover. Damon's already got plans after school. He's going to the mall with yours truly.
Oh yeah. That's right... the mall.
No big deal—I was only trying to do him a favor 'cause he's new around here.

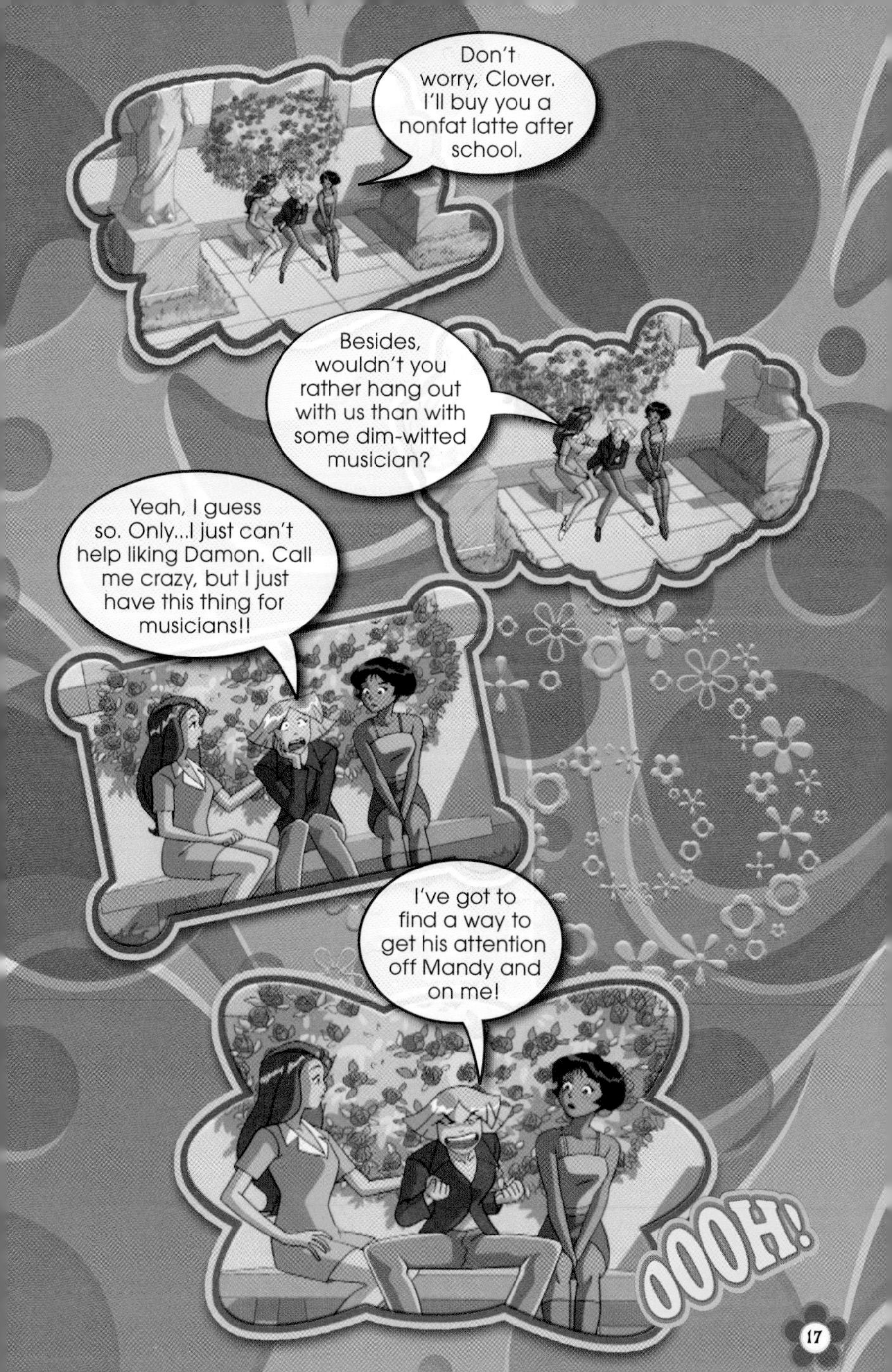

Don't worry, Clover. I'll buy you a nonfat latte after school.
Besides, wouldn't you rather hang out with us than with some dim-witted musician?
Yeah, I guess so. Only...I just can't help liking Damon. Call me crazy, but I just have this thing for musicians!!
I've got to find a way to get his attention off Mandy and on me!
OOOH!

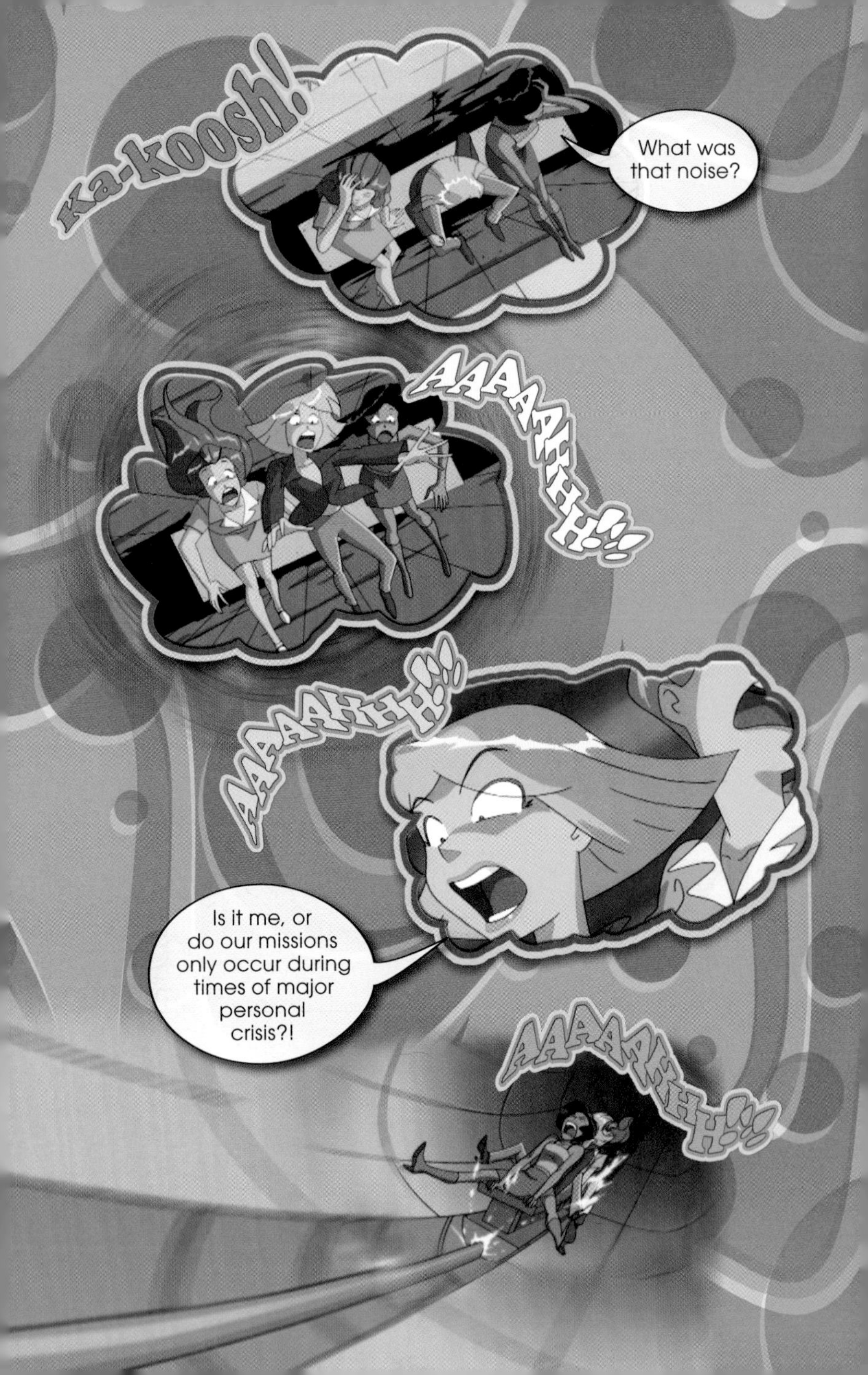
Ka-KOOSH!
What was that noise?
AAAAHHH!!!
AAAAHHH!!!
Is it me, or do our missions only occur during times of major personal crisis?!
AAAAHHH!!!

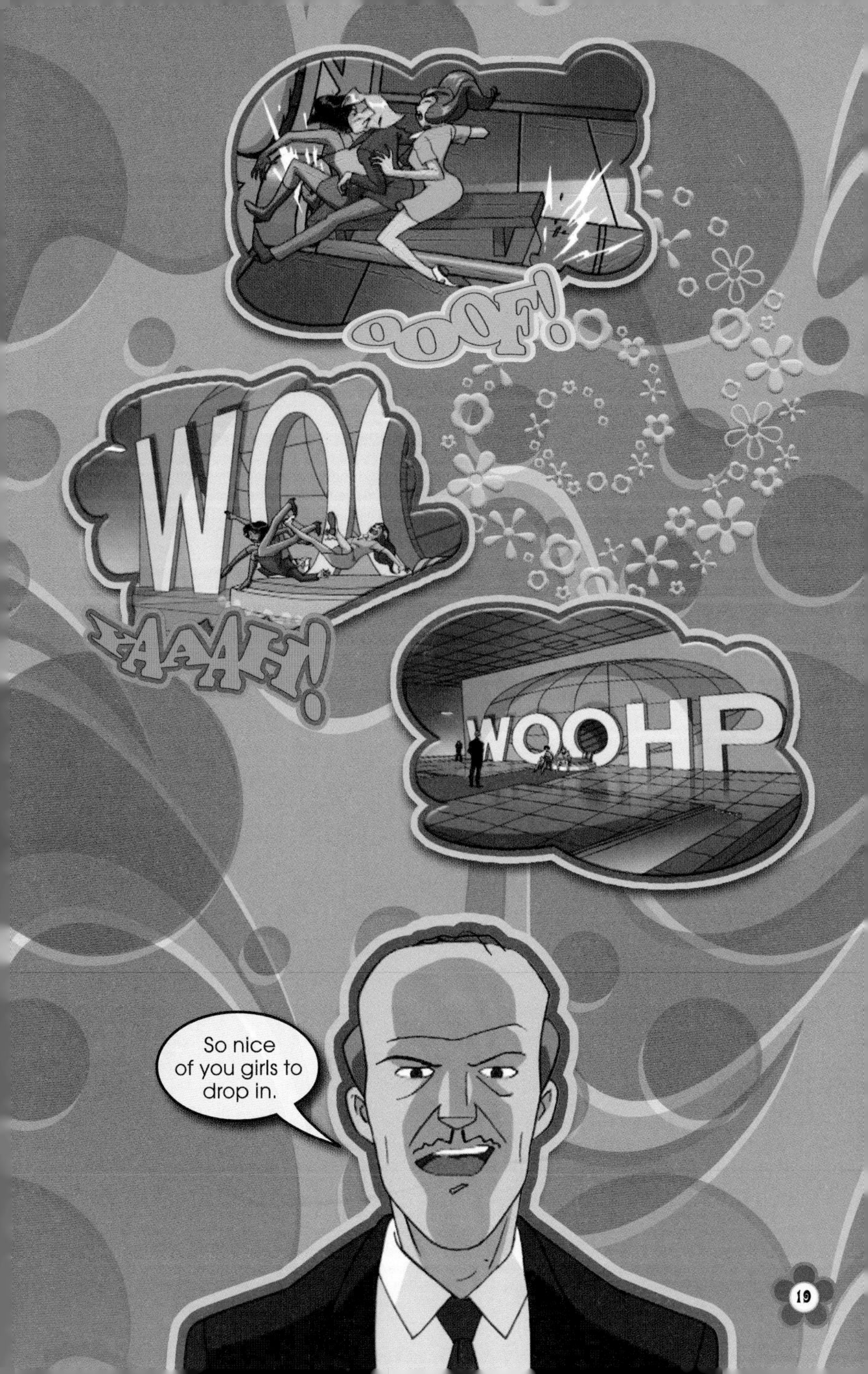
OOOF!
WO
YAAAH!
WOOHP
So nice of you girls to drop in.

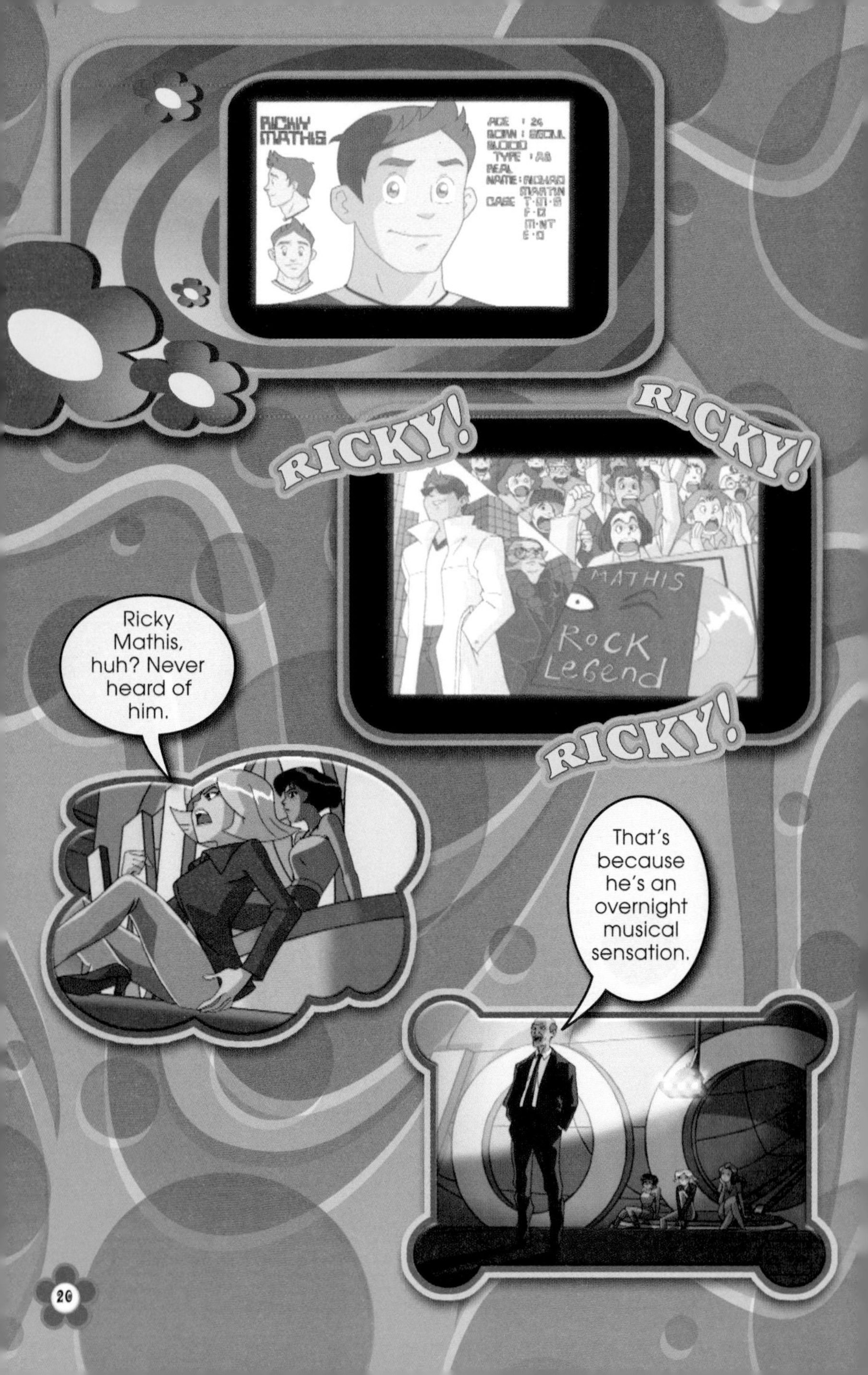
RICKY MATHIS
AGE : 24
RICKY!
RICKY!
MATHIS
ROCK LEGEND
RICKY!
Ricky Mathis, huh? Never heard of him.
That's because he's an overnight musical sensation.

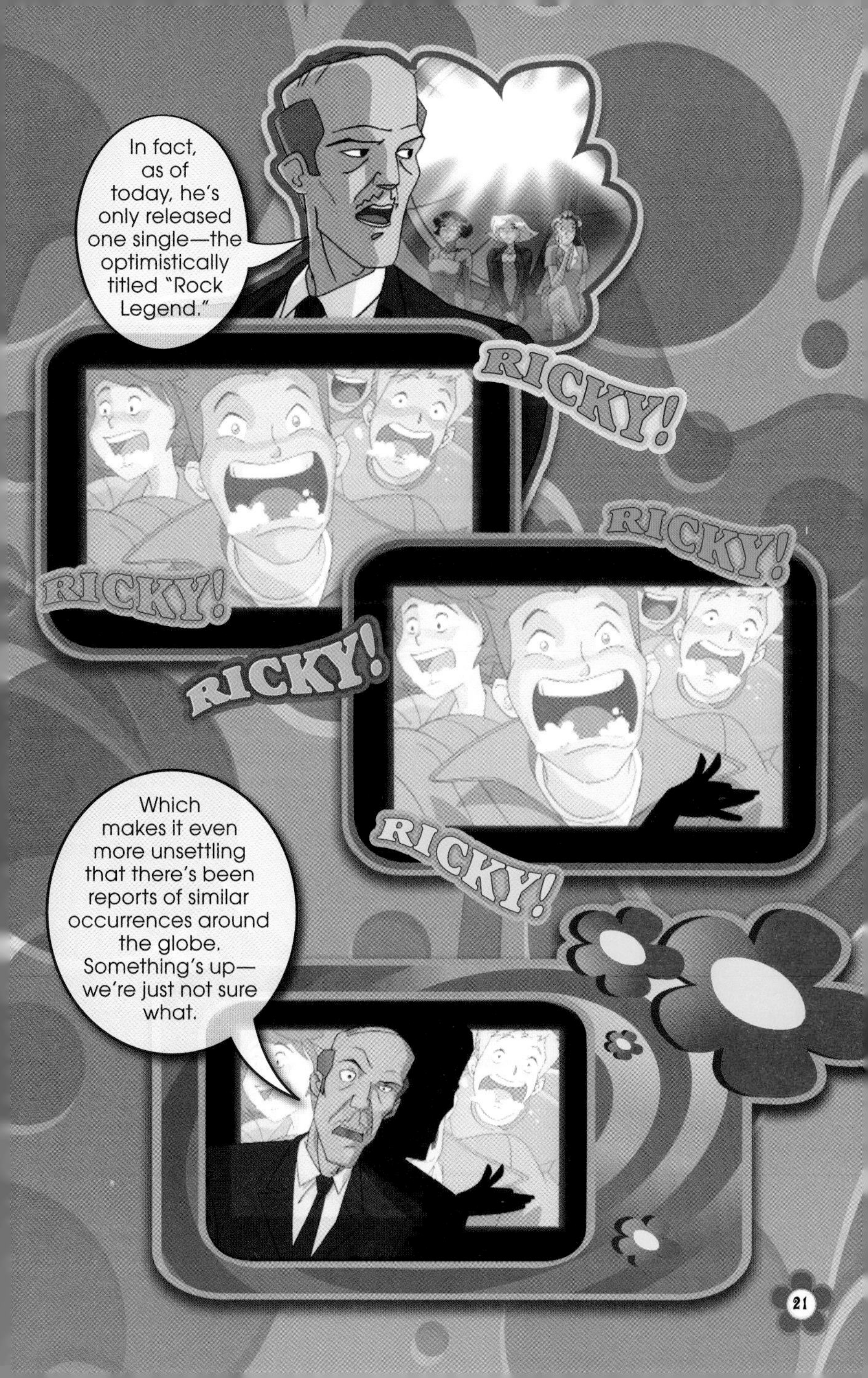

In fact, as of today, he's only released one single—the optimistically titled "Rock Legend."
RICKY!
RICKY!
RICKY!
RICKY!
RICKY!
Which makes it even more unsettling that there's been reports of similar occurrences around the globe. Something's up—we're just not sure what.

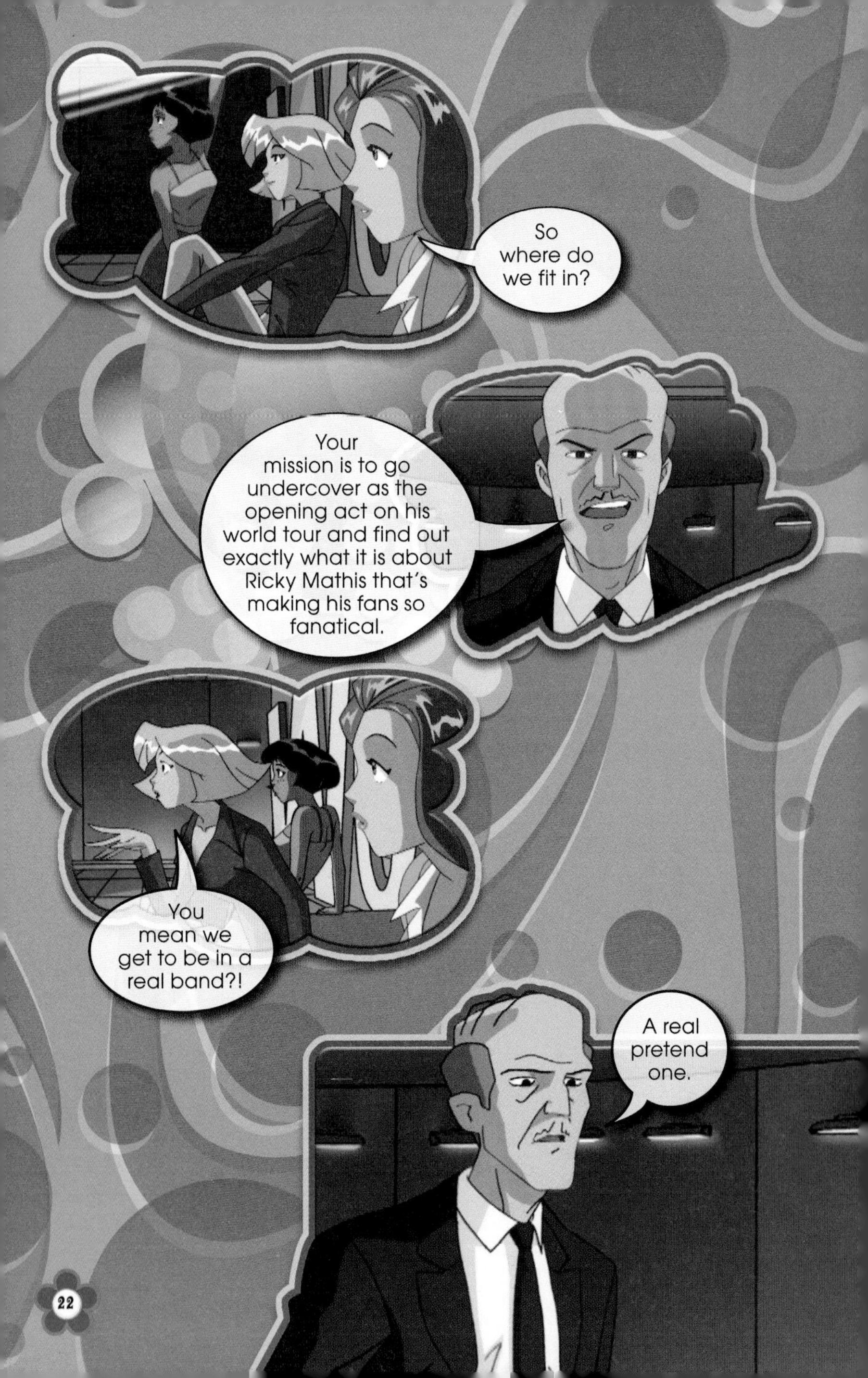
So where do we fit in?
Your mission is to go undercover as the opening act on his world tour and find out exactly what it is about Ricky Mathis that's making his fans so fanatical.
You mean we get to be in a real band?!
A real pretend one.

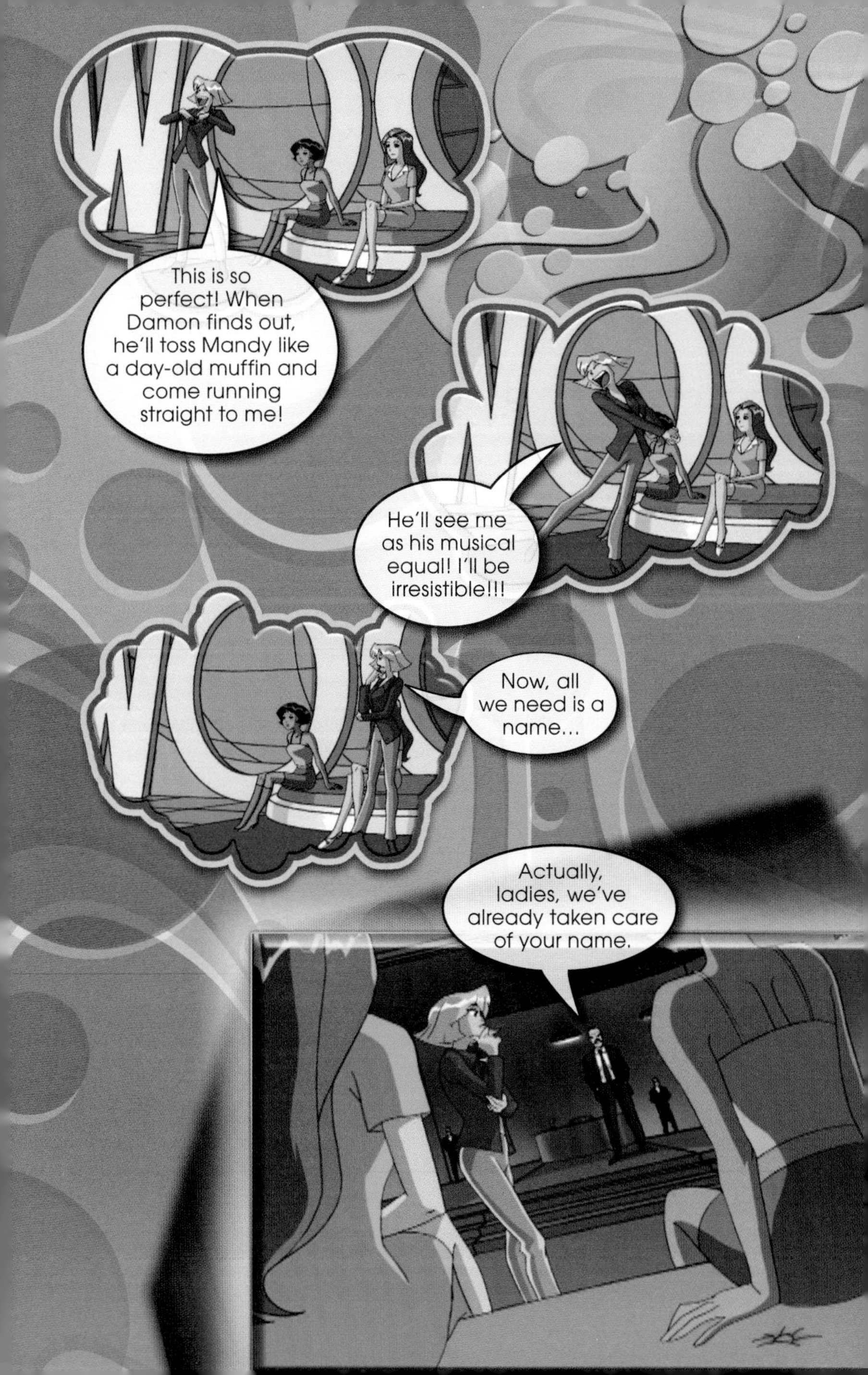
This is so perfect! When Damon finds out, he'll toss Mandy like a day-old muffin and come running straight to me!
He'll see me as his musical equal! I'll be irresistible!!!
Now, all we need is a name...
Actually, ladies, we've already taken care of your name.

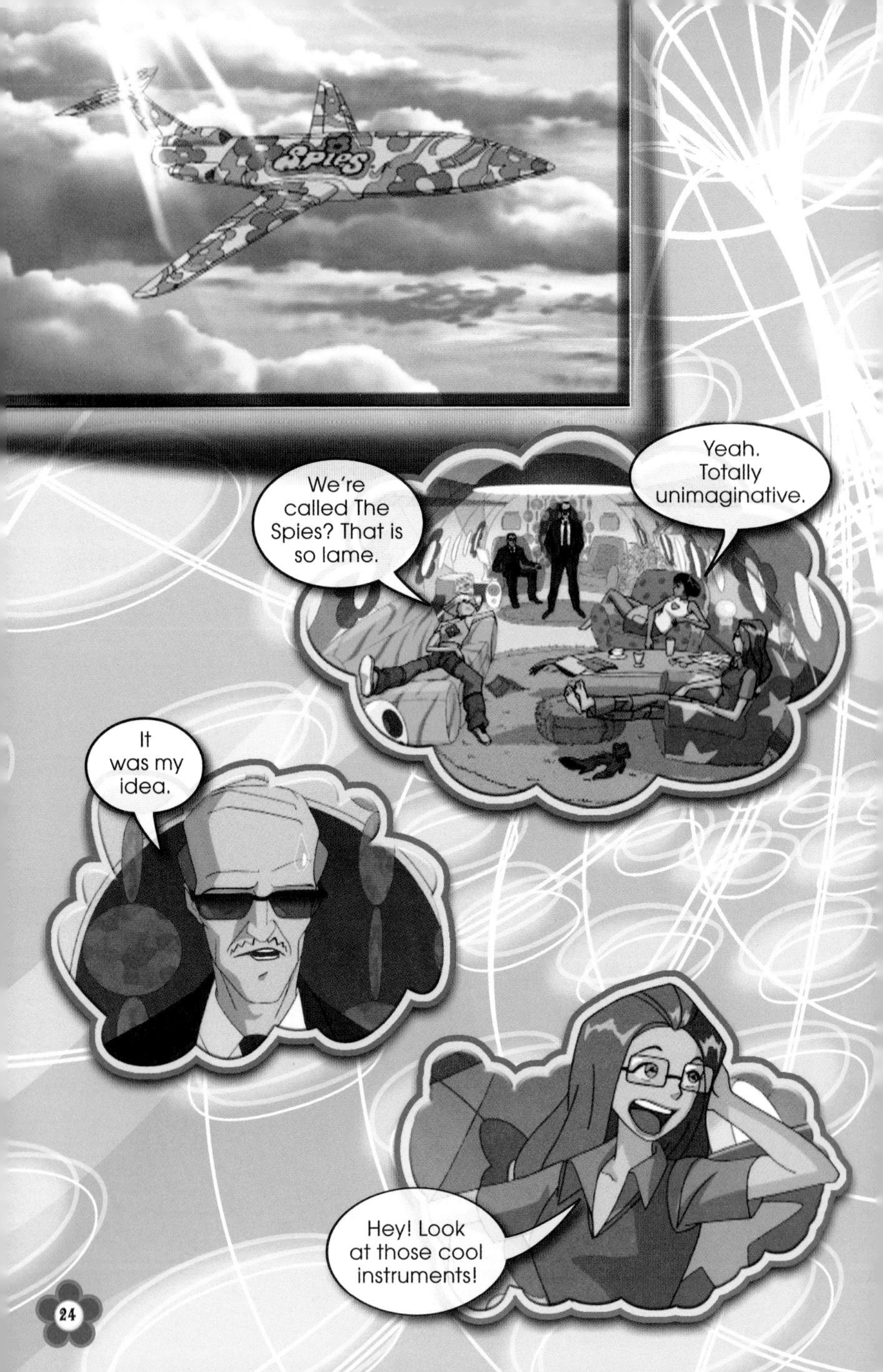
SPIES
We're called The Spies? That is so lame.
Yeah. Totally unimaginative.
It was my idea.
Hey! Look at those cool instruments!

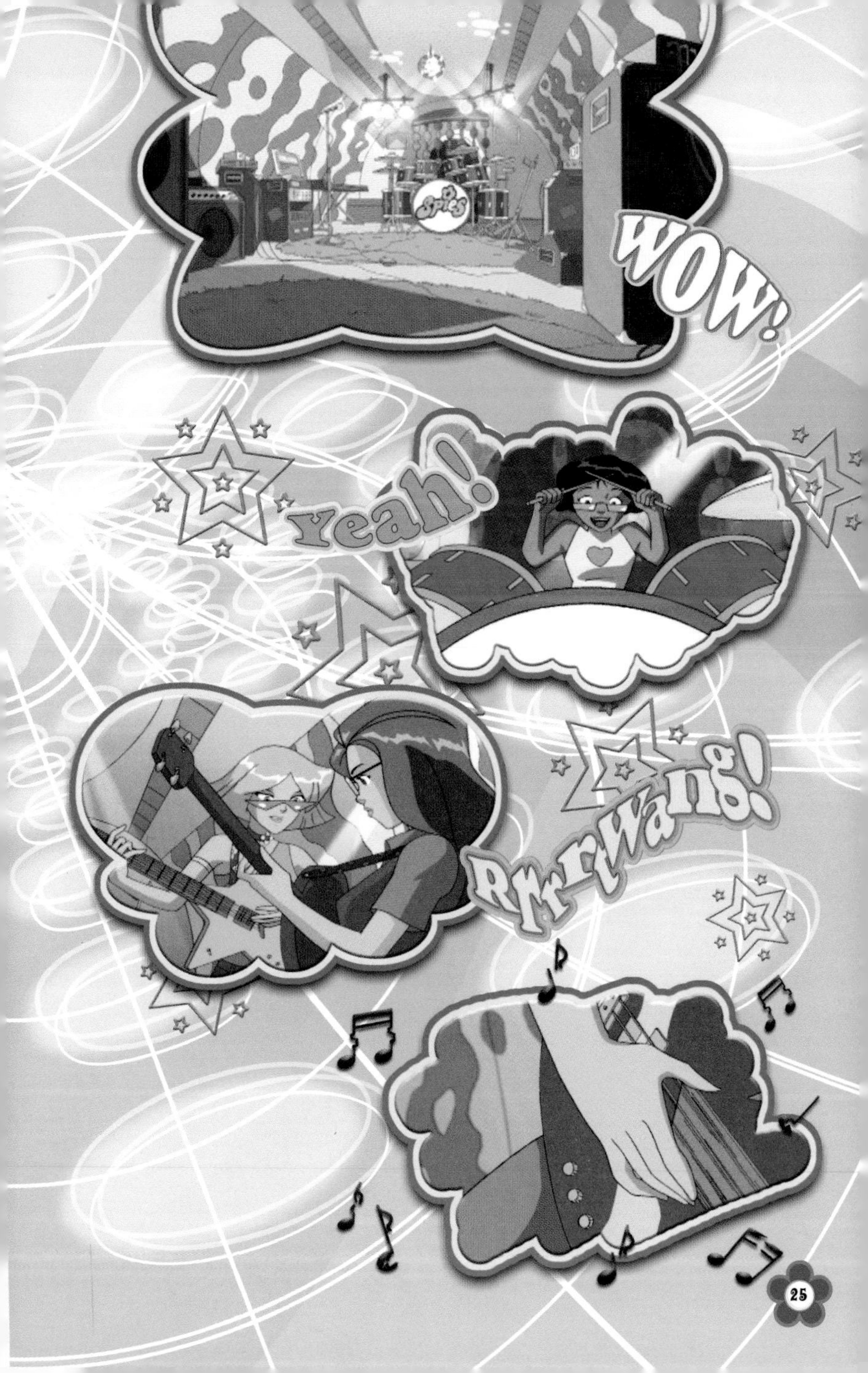
Spies
WOW!
Yeah!
Rrrrwang!

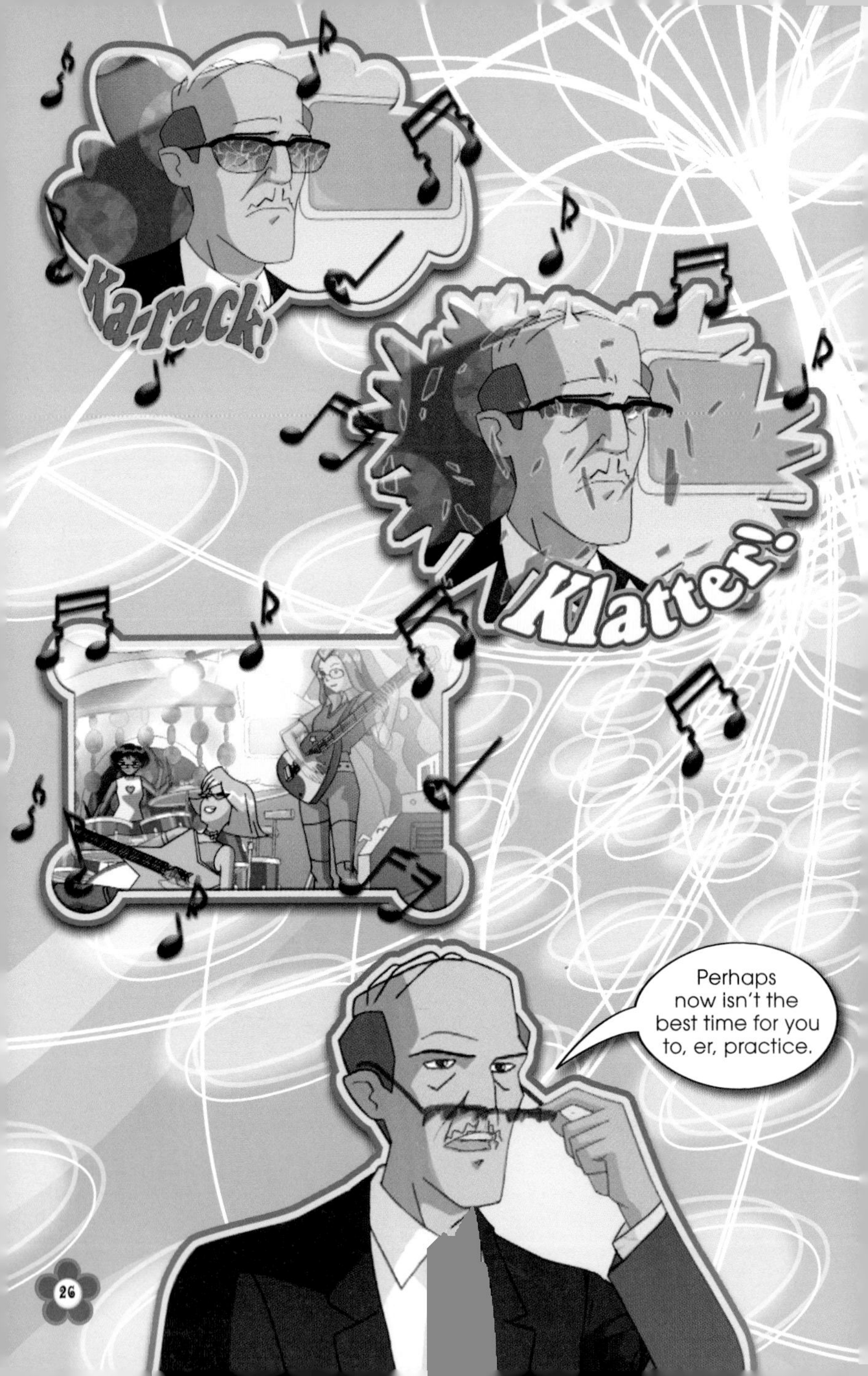
Ka-rack!
Klatter!
Perhaps now isn't the best time for you to, er, practice.

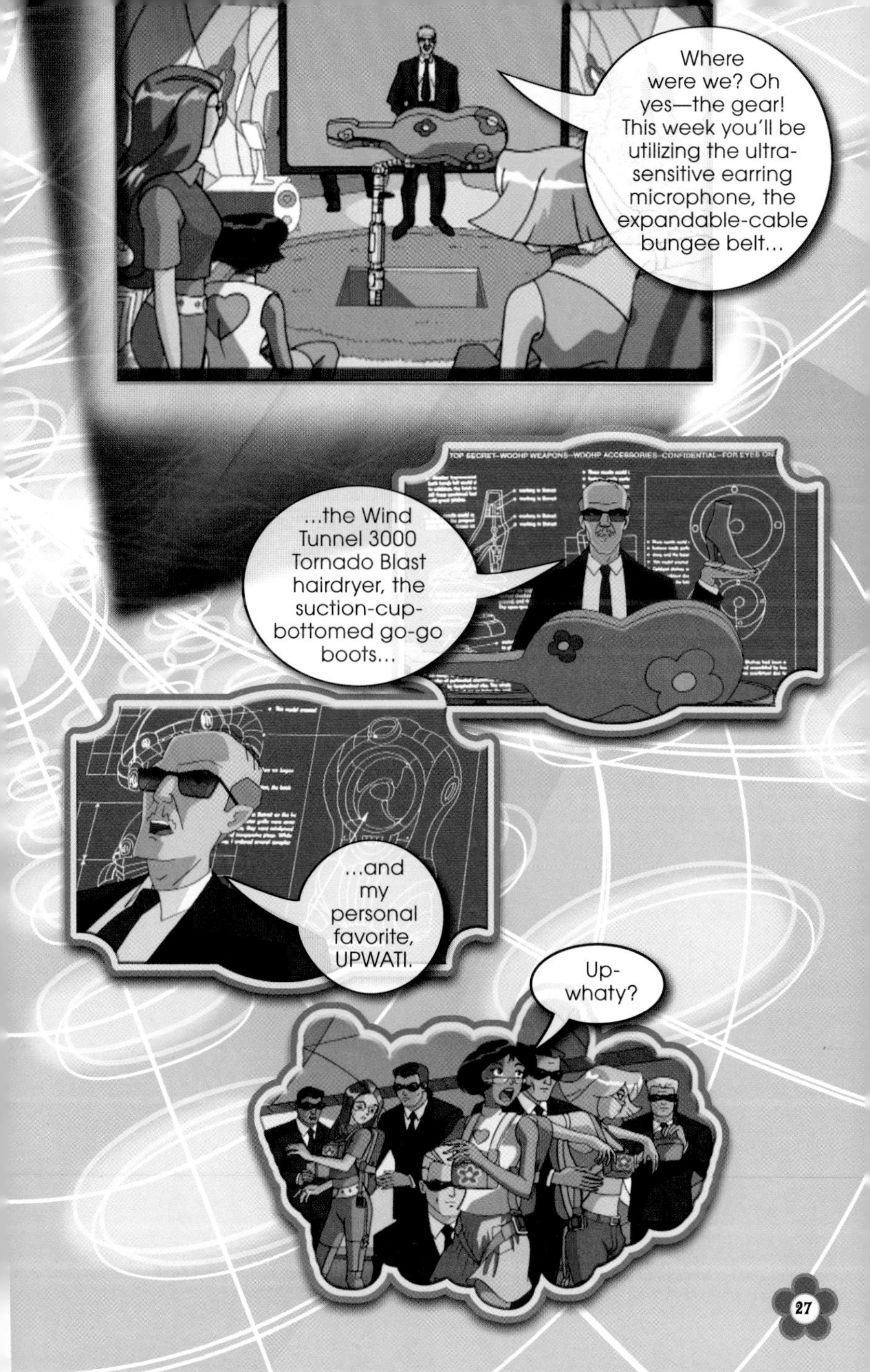
Where were we? Oh yes—the gear! This week you'll be utilizing the ultra-sensitive earring microphone, the expandable-cable bungee belt...
TOP SECRET—WOOHP WEAPONS—WOOHP ACCESSORIES—CONFIDENTIAL
...the Wind Tunnel 3000 Tornado Blast hairdryer, the suction-cup-bottomed go-go boots...
...and my personal favorite, UPWATI.
Up-whaty?

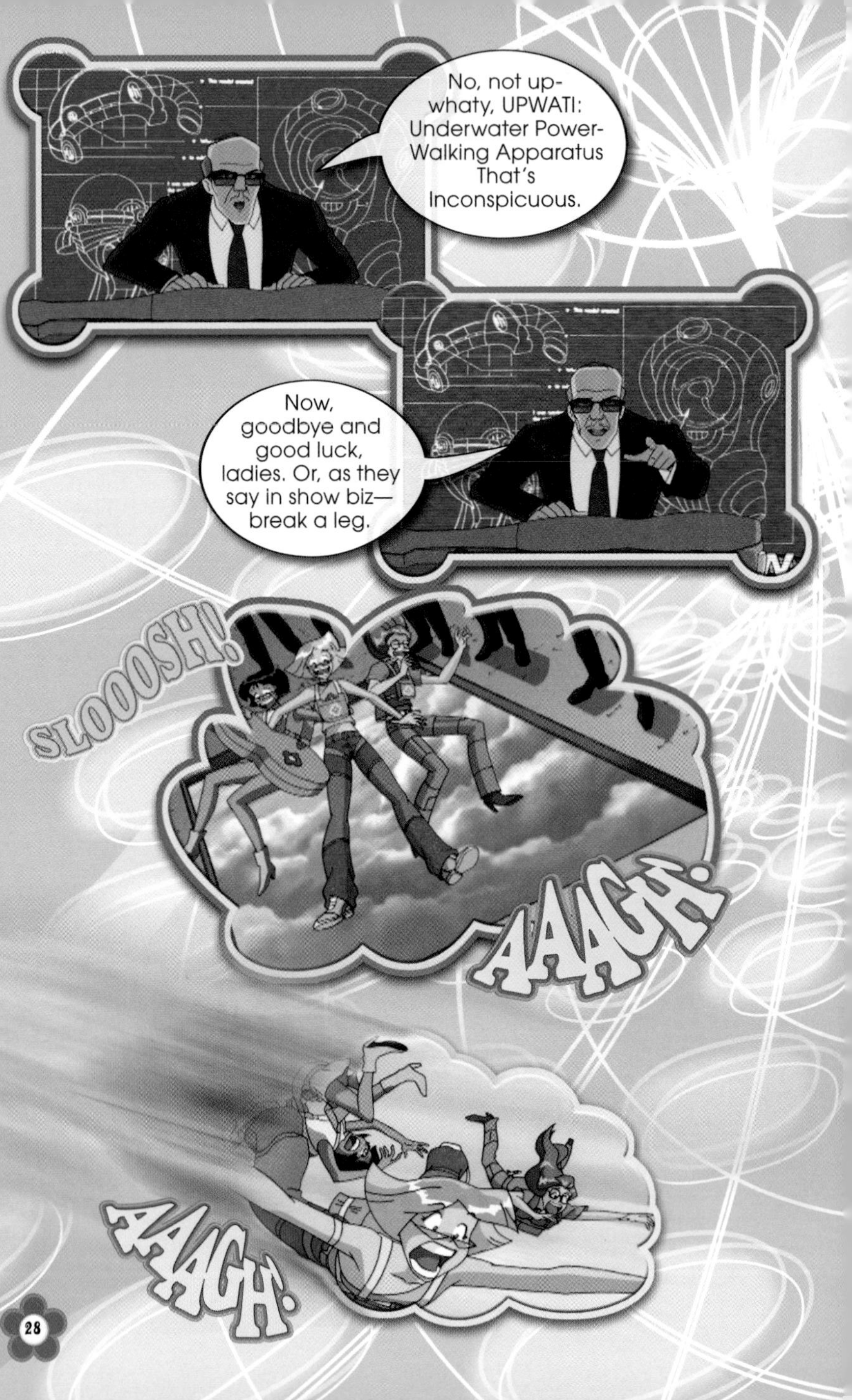
No, not up-whaty, UPWATI: Underwater Power-Walking Apparatus That's Inconspicuous.
Now, goodbye and good luck, ladies. Or, as they say in show biz—break a leg.
SLOOOSH!
AAAGH!
AAAGH!

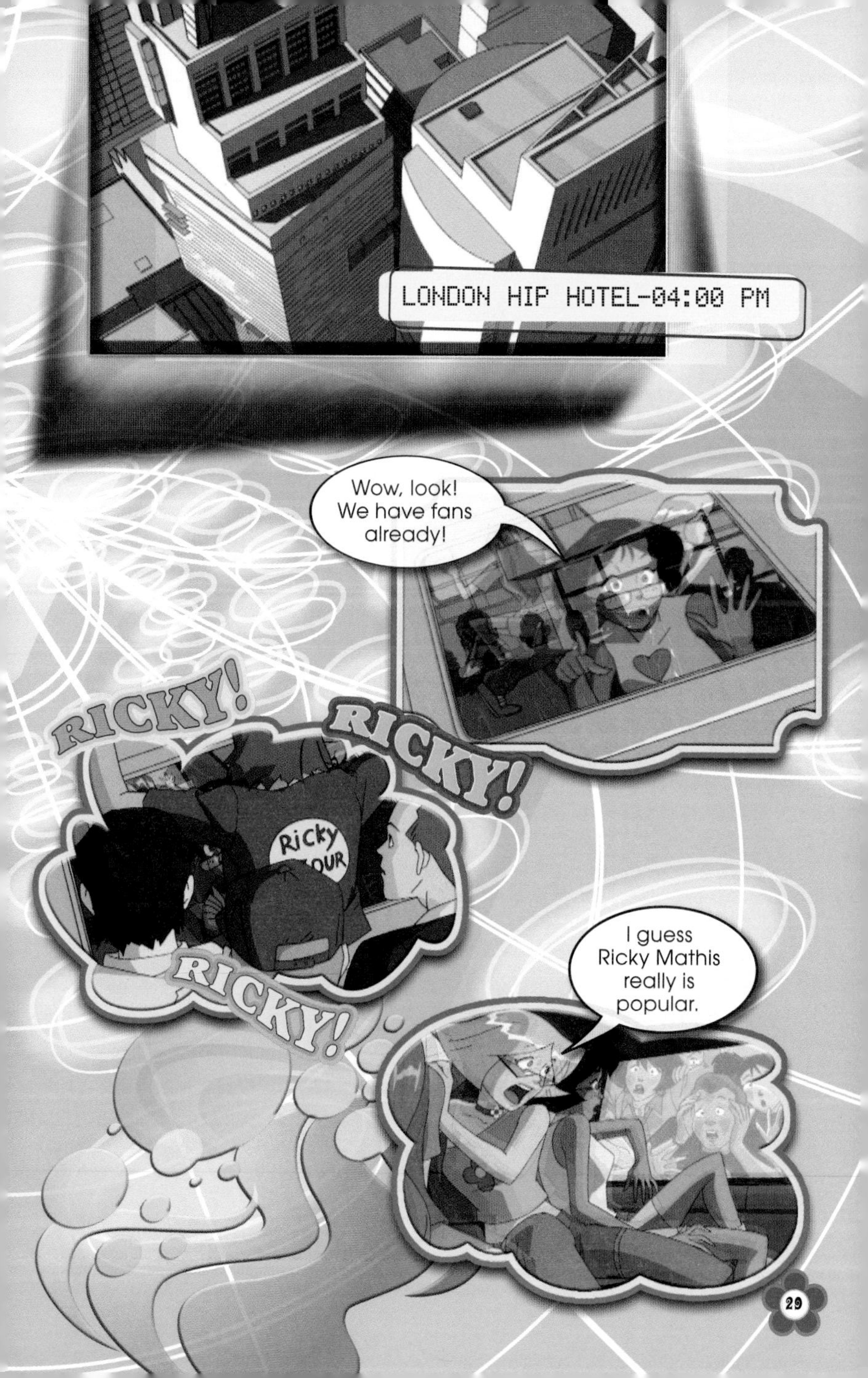
LONDON HIP HOTEL–04:00 PM
Wow, look! We have fans already!
RICKY!
RICKY!
Ricky
RICKY!
I guess Ricky Mathis really is popular.

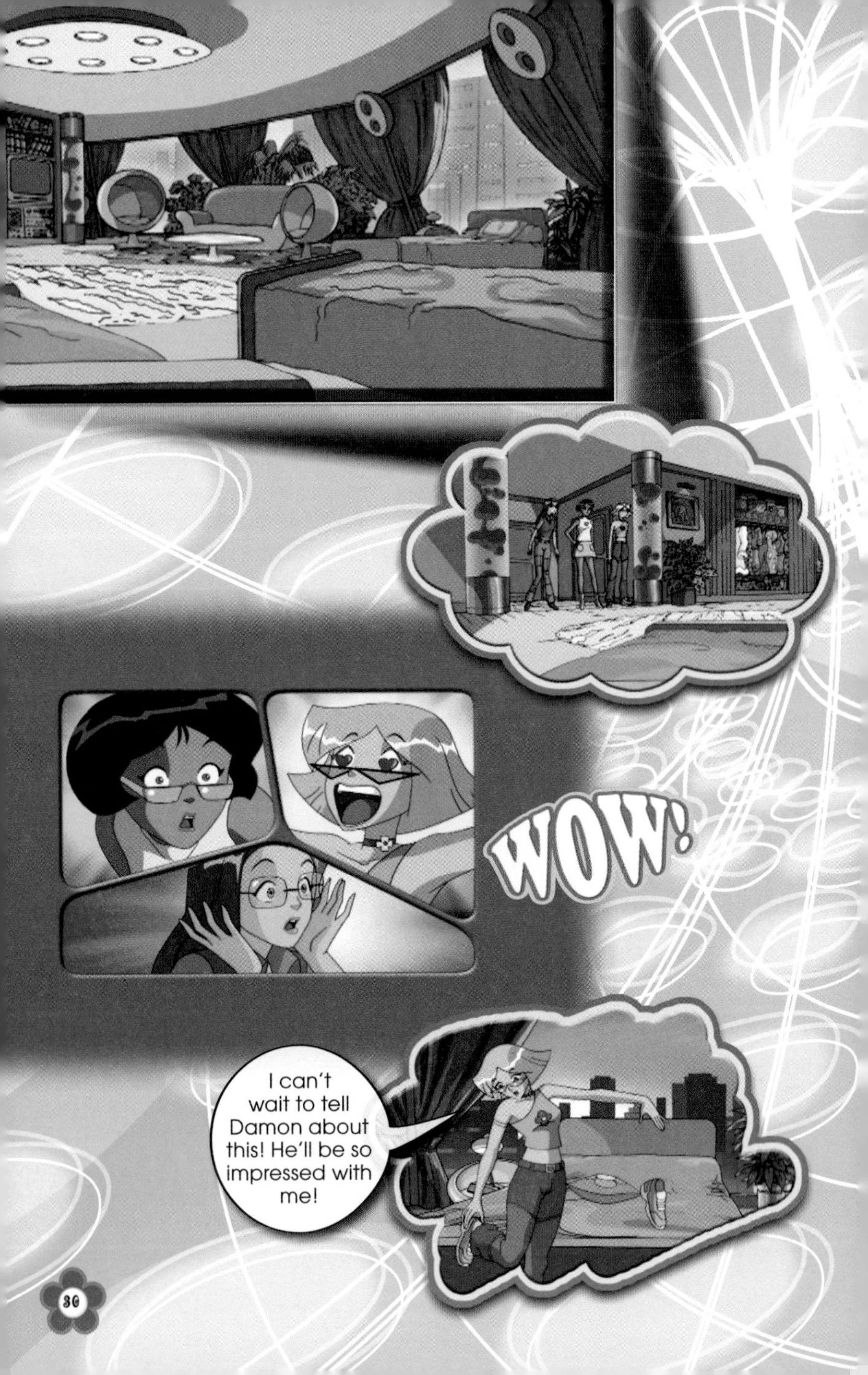
WOW!
I can't wait to tell Damon about this! He'll be so impressed with me!

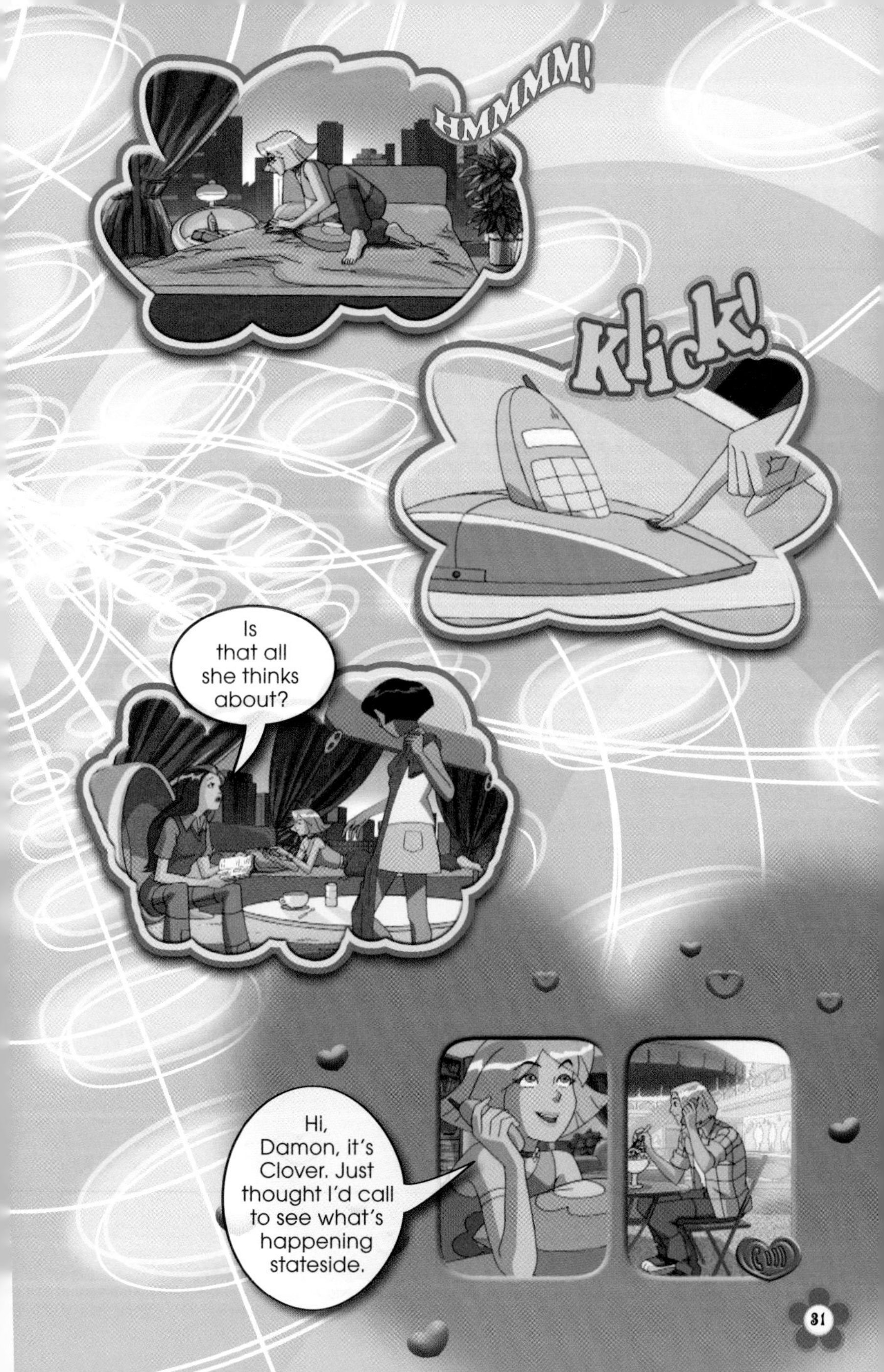
HMMMMM!
Klick!
Is that all she thinks about?
Hi, Damon, it's Clover. Just thought I'd call to see what's happening stateside.

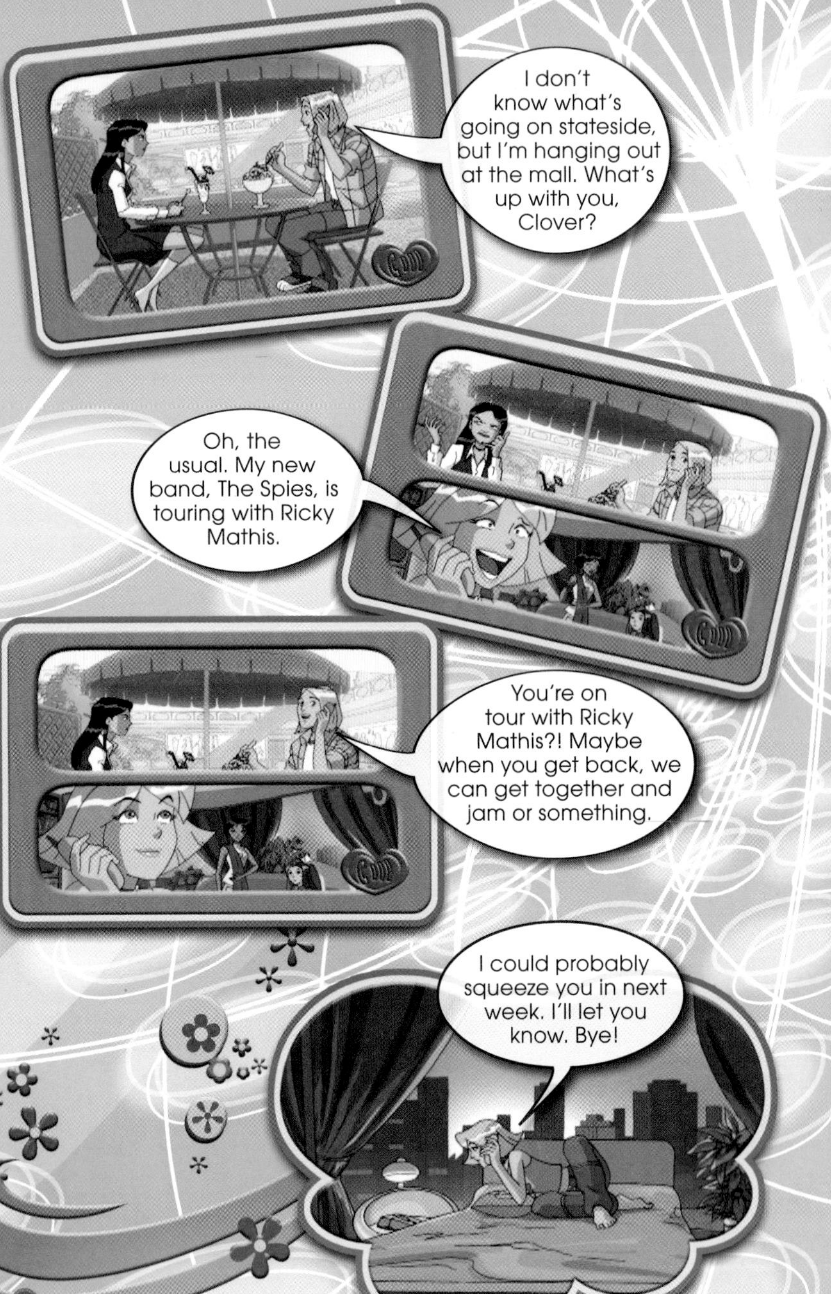
I don't know what's going on stateside, but I'm hanging out at the mall. What's up with you, Clover?
Oh, the usual. My new band, The Spies, is touring with Ricky Mathis.
You're on tour with Ricky Mathis?! Maybe when you get back, we can get together and jam or something.
I could probably squeeze you in next week. I'll let you know. Bye!

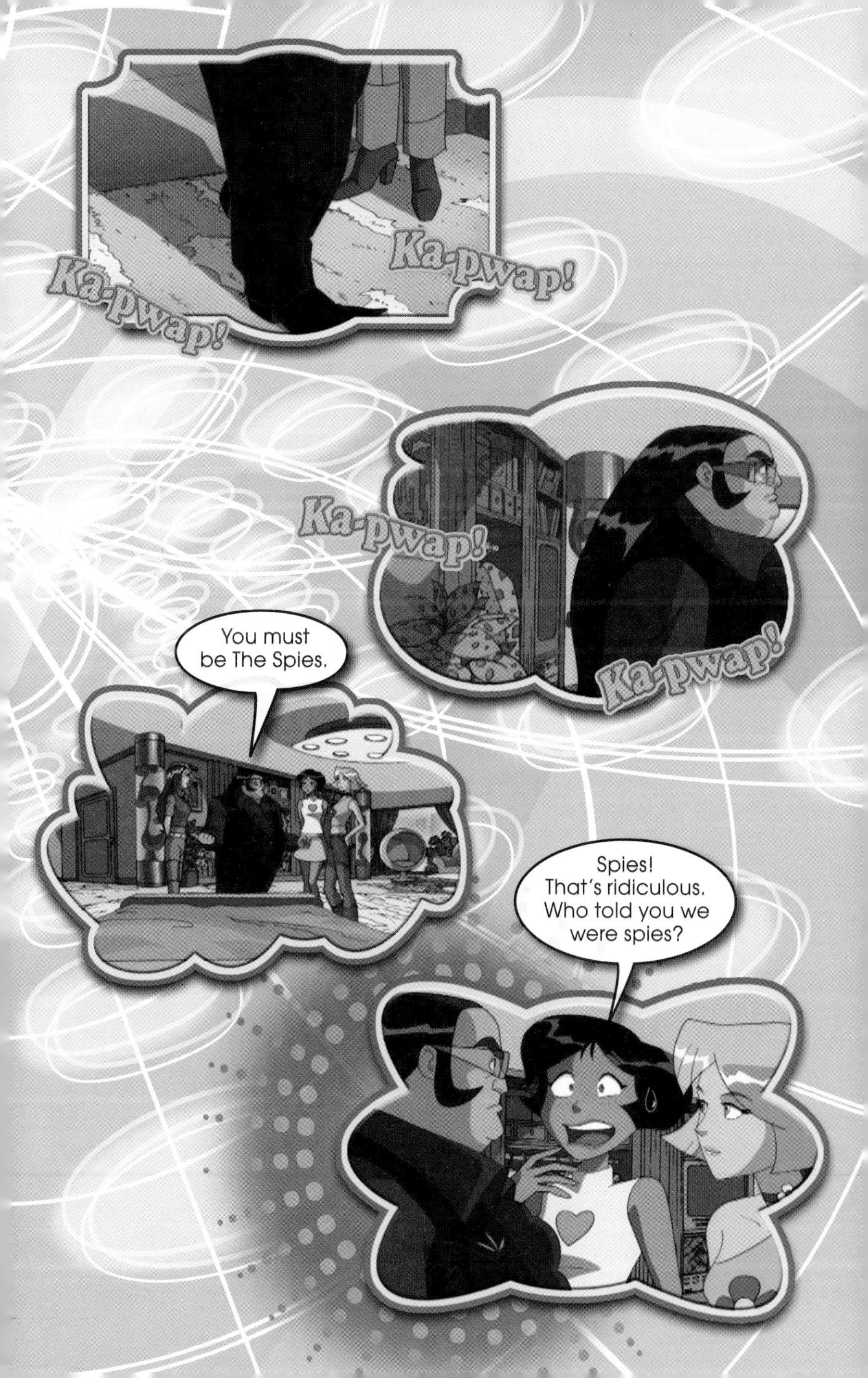

Ka-pwap!
Ka-pwap!
Ka-pwap!
Ka-pwap!
You must be The Spies.
Spies! That's ridiculous. Who told you we were spies?

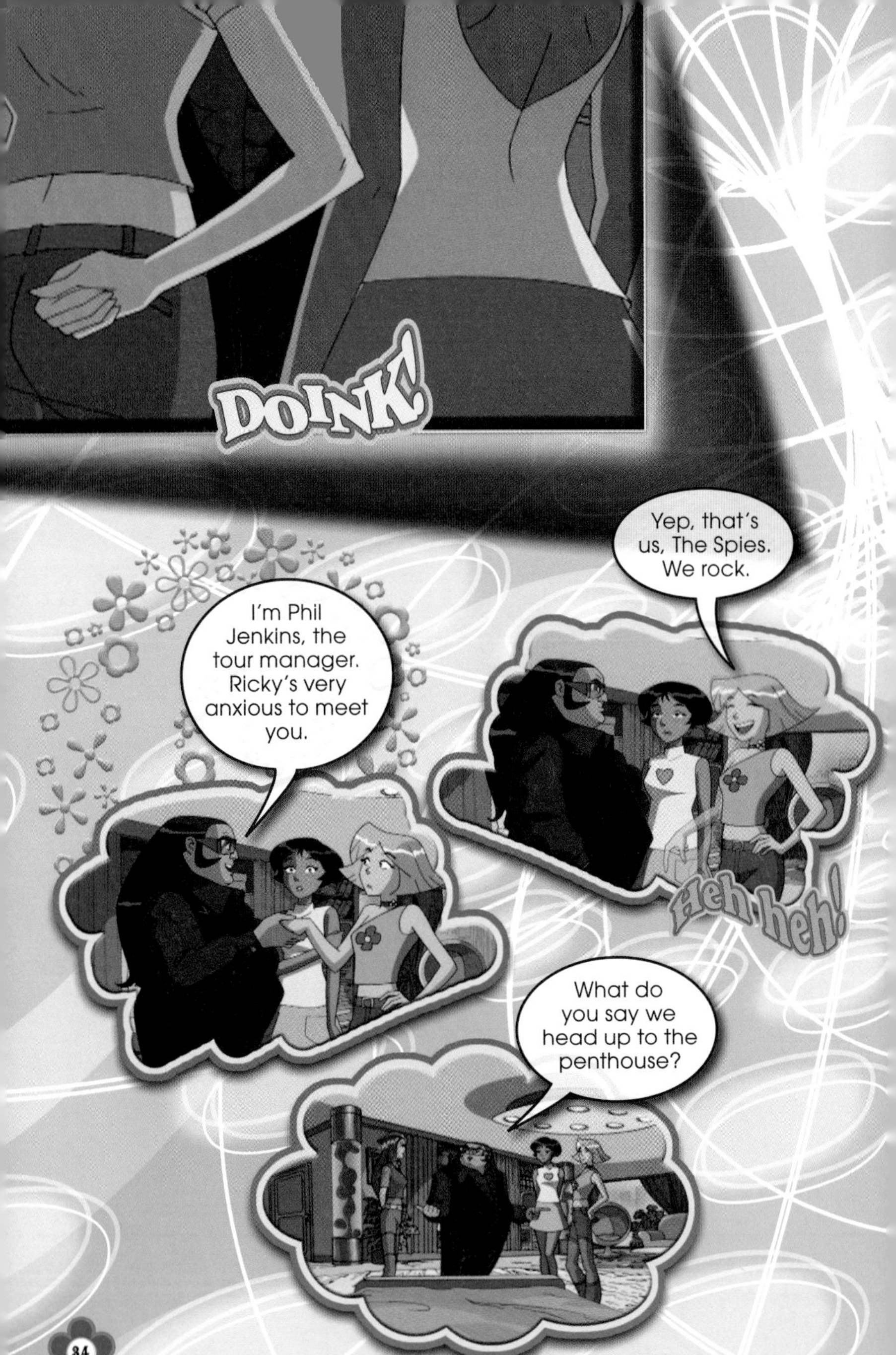
DOINK!
I'm Phil Jenkins, the tour manager. Ricky's very anxious to meet you.
Yep, that's us, The Spies. We rock.
Heh heh!
What do you say we head up to the penthouse?

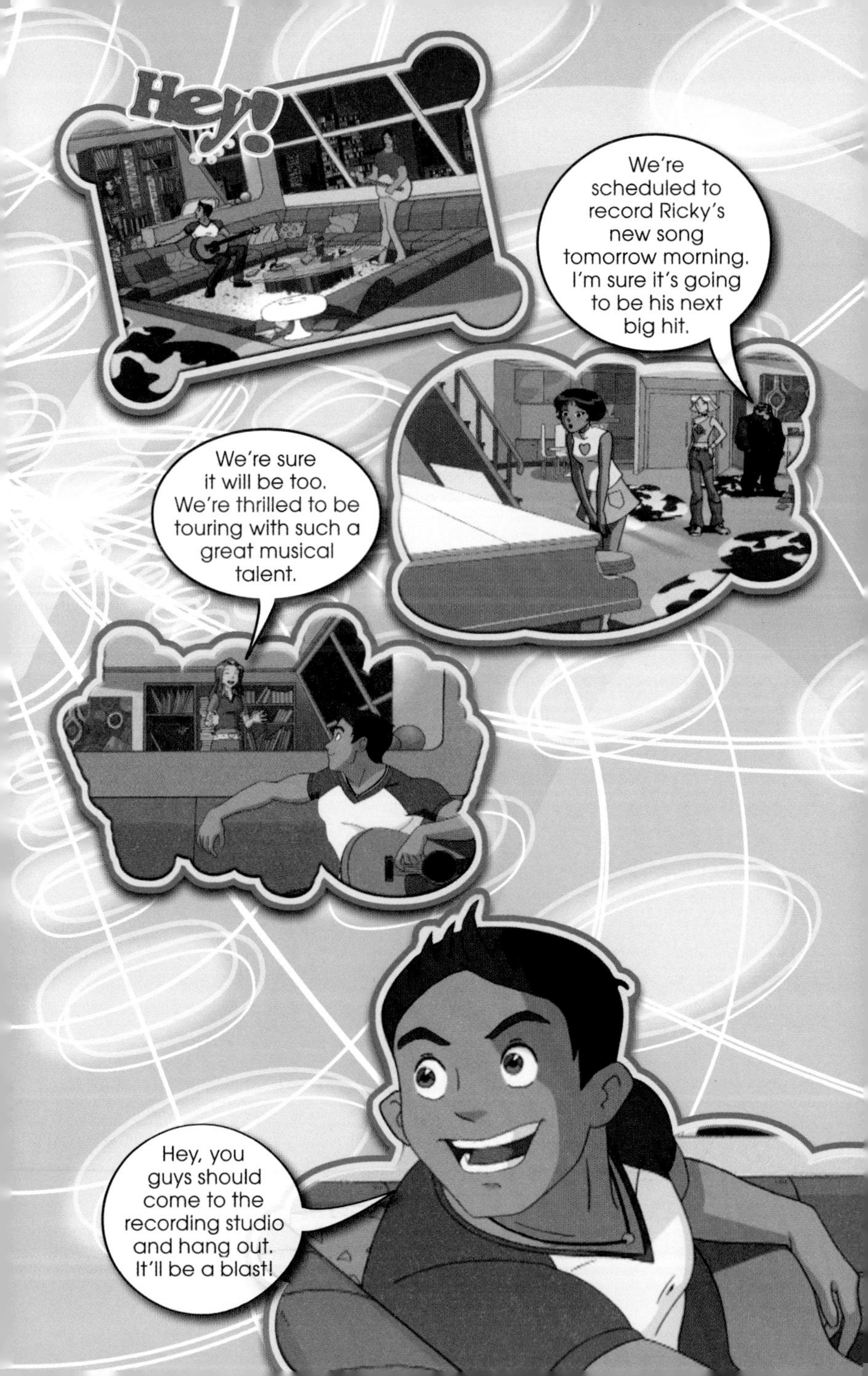
Hey!
We're scheduled to record Ricky's new song tomorrow morning. I'm sure it's going to be his next big hit.
We're sure it will be too. We're thrilled to be touring with such a great musical talent.
Hey, you guys should come to the recording studio and hang out. It'll be a blast!

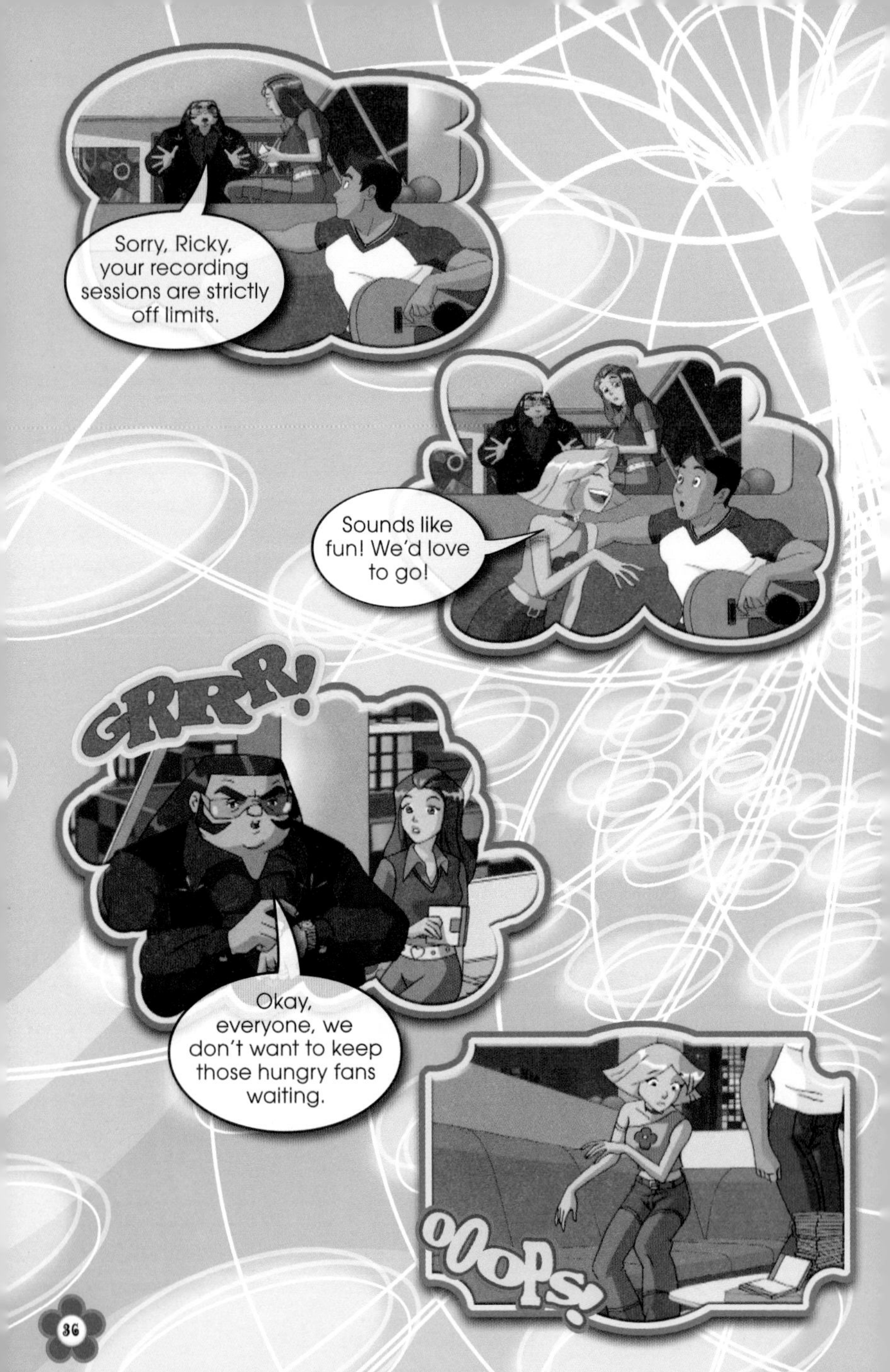
Sorry, Ricky, your recording sessions are strictly off limits.
Sounds like fun! We'd love to go!
GRRR!
Okay, everyone, we don't want to keep those hungry fans waiting.
oOOPS!

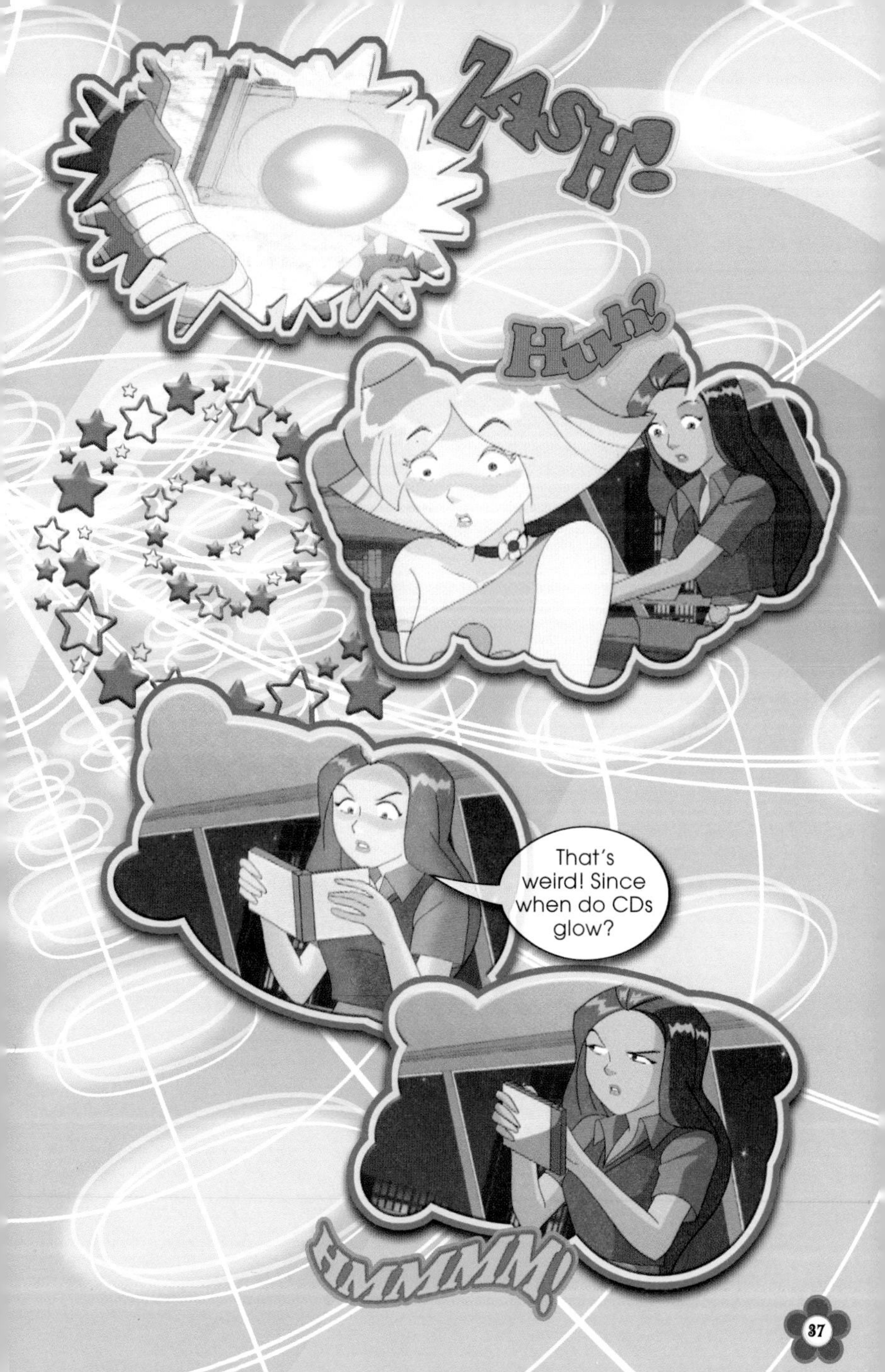
ZASH!
Huh?
That's weird! Since when do CDs glow?
HMMMM!

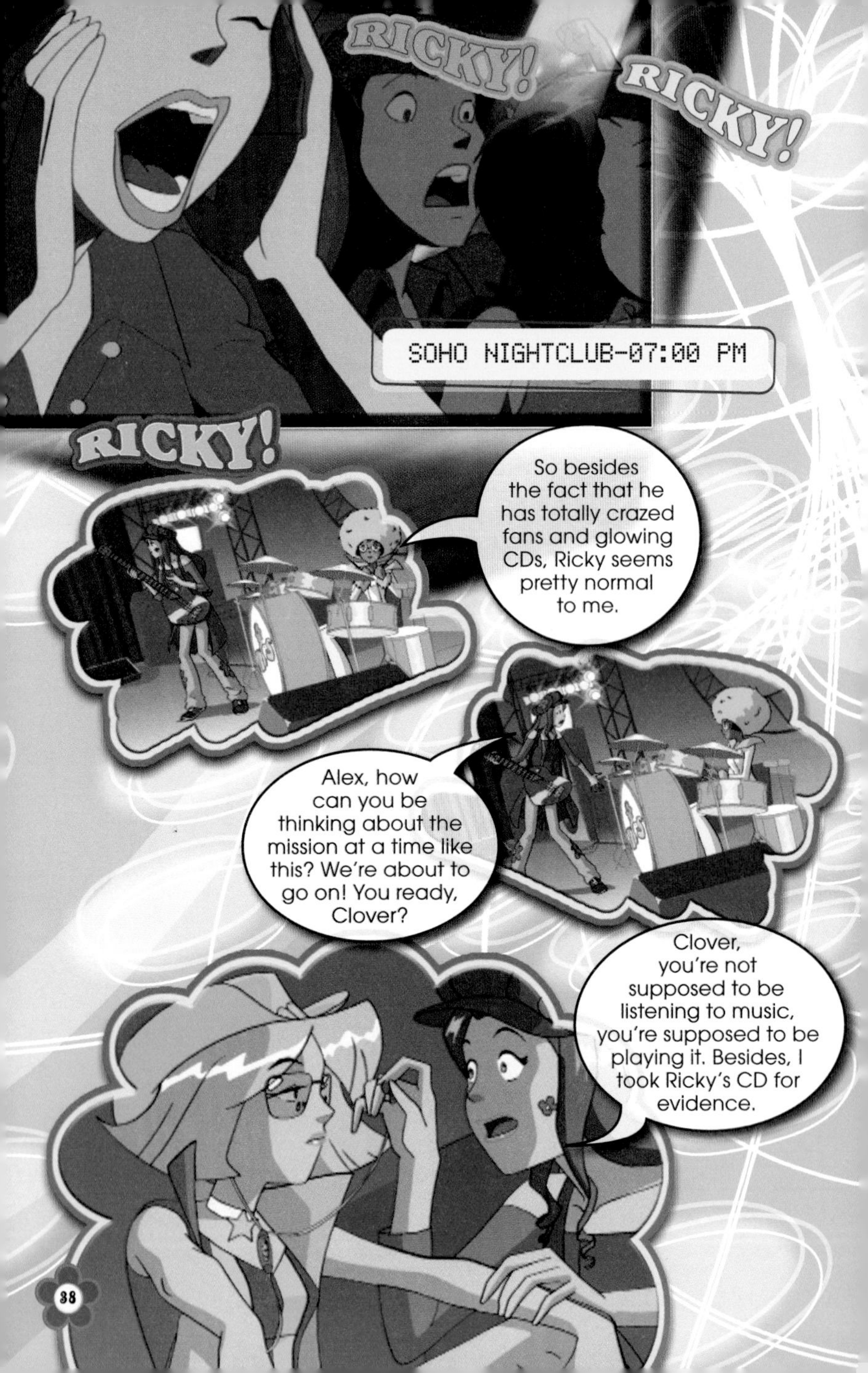
RICKY!
RICKY!
SOHO NIGHTCLUB–07:00 PM
RICKY!
So besides the fact that he has totally crazed fans and glowing CDs, Ricky seems pretty normal to me.
Alex, how can you be thinking about the mission at a time like this? We're about to go on! You ready, Clover?
Clover, you're not supposed to be listening to music, you're supposed to be playing it. Besides, I took Ricky's CD for evidence.

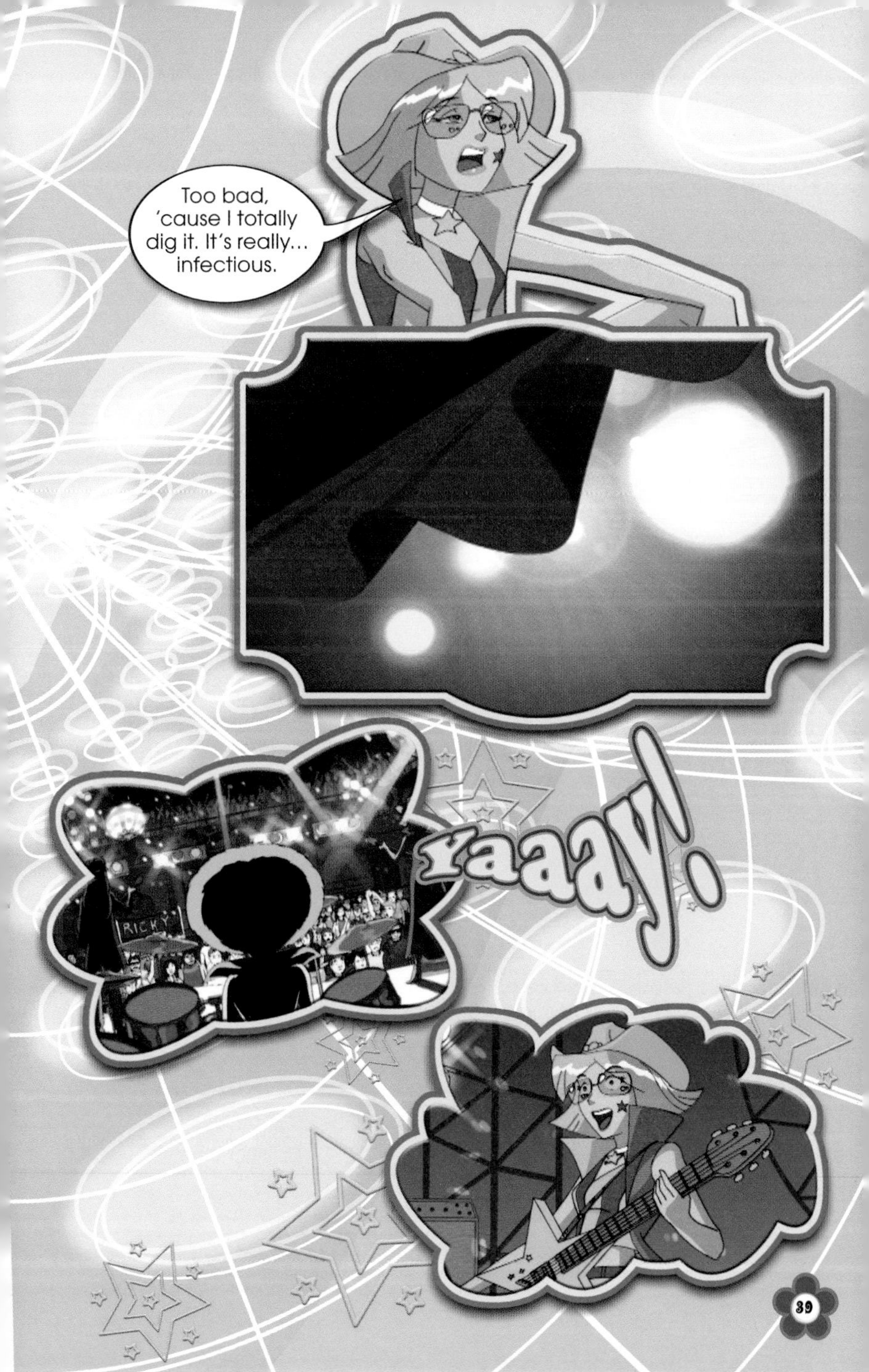
Too bad, 'cause I totally dig it. It's really... infectious.
Yaaay!
RICKY

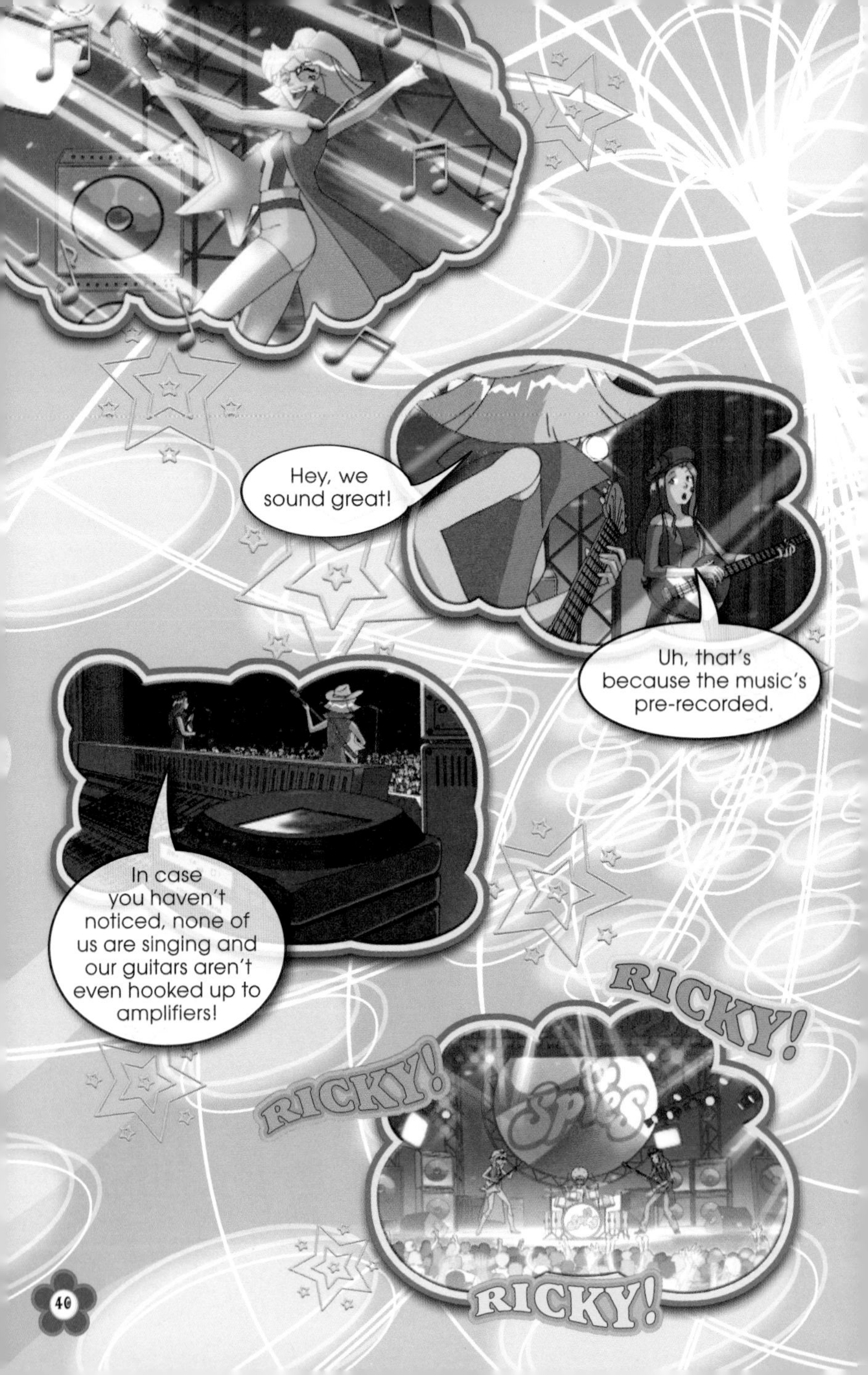
Hey, we sound great!
Uh, that's because the music's pre-recorded.
In case you haven't noticed, none of us are singing and our guitars aren't even hooked up to amplifiers!
RICKY!
RICKY!
RICKY!

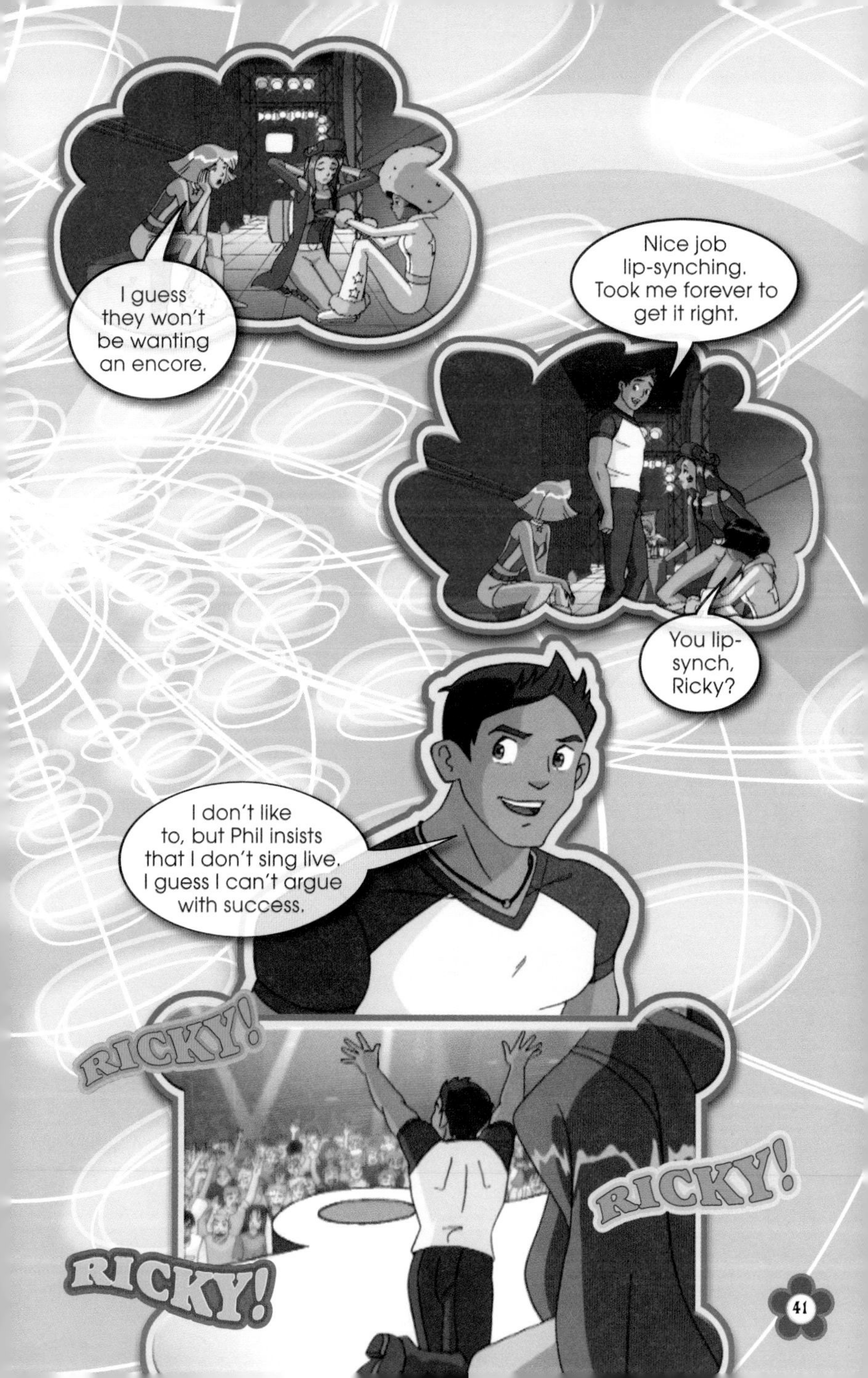
I guess they won't be wanting an encore.
Nice job lip-synching. Took me forever to get it right.
You lip-synch, Ricky?
I don't like to, but Phil insists that I don't sing live. I guess I can't argue with success.
RICKY!
RICKY!
RICKY!

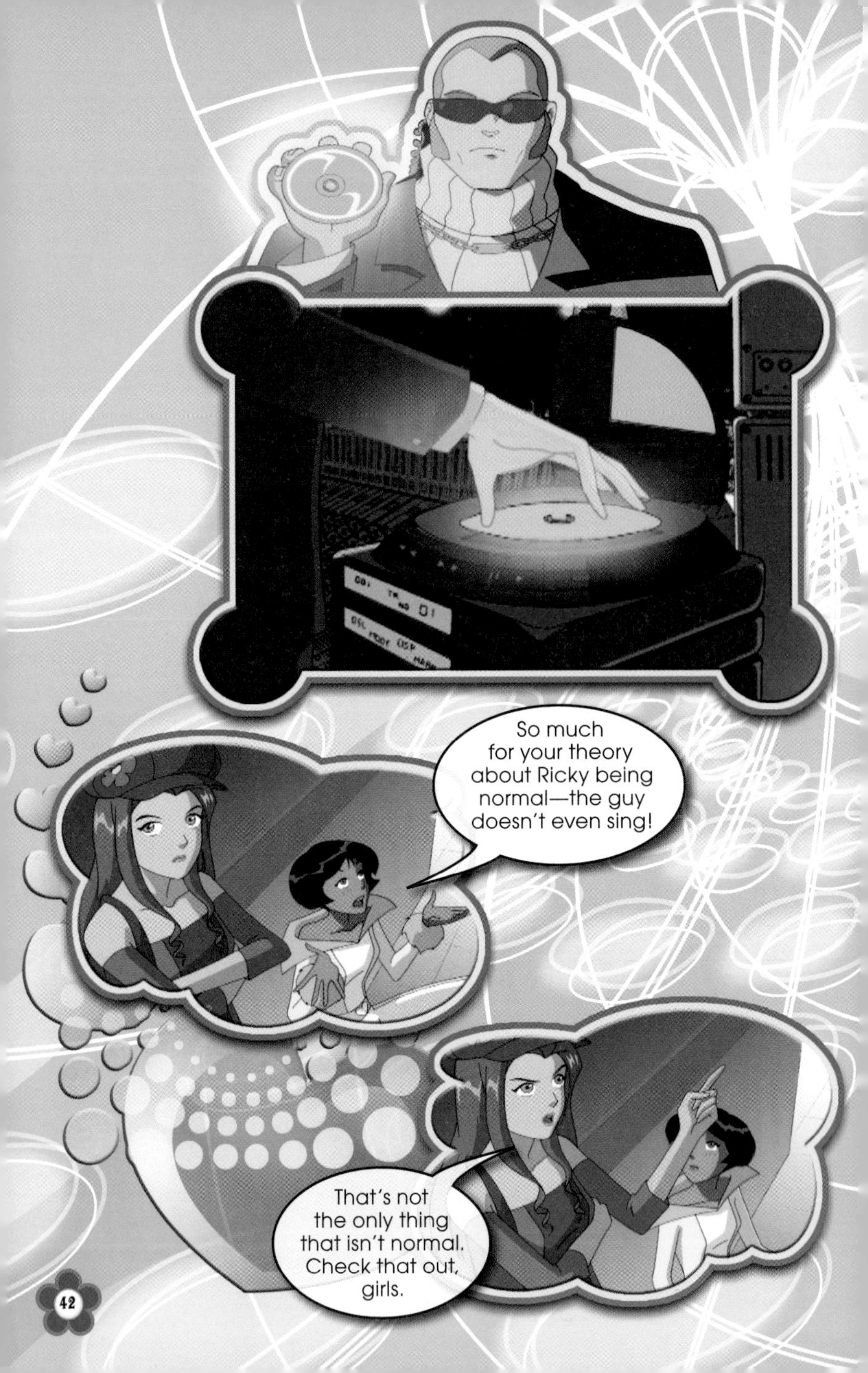
So much for your theory about Ricky being normal—the guy doesn't even sing!
That's not the only thing that isn't normal. Check that out, girls.

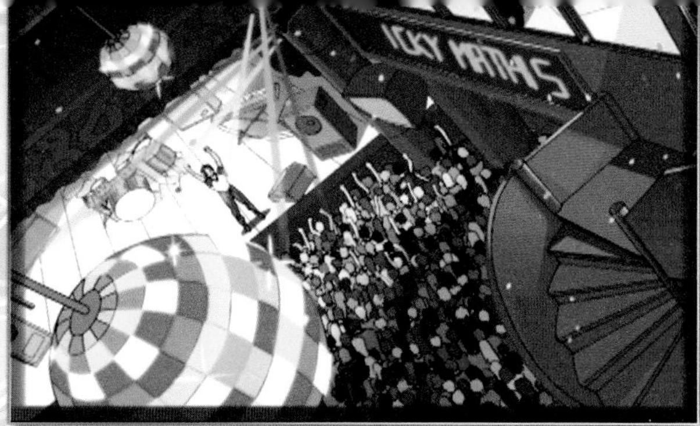
ICKY MATHIS

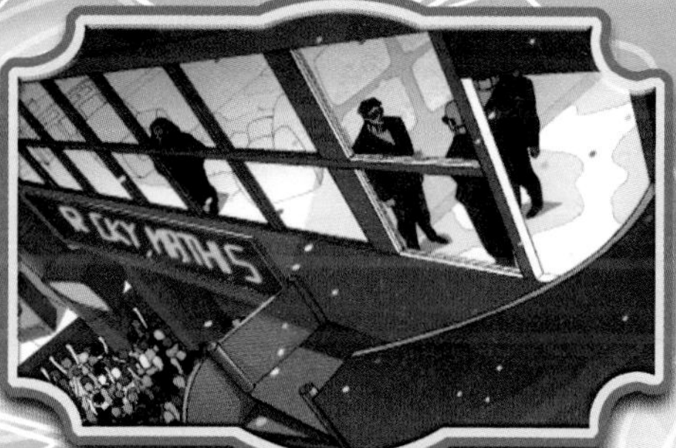

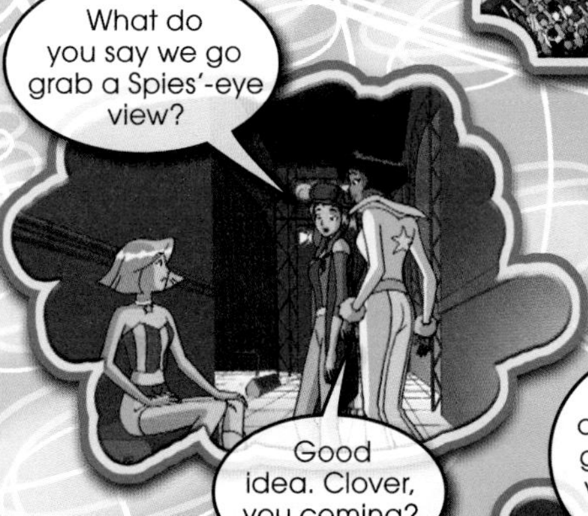
What do you say we go grab a Spies'-eye view?
Good idea. Clover, you coming?

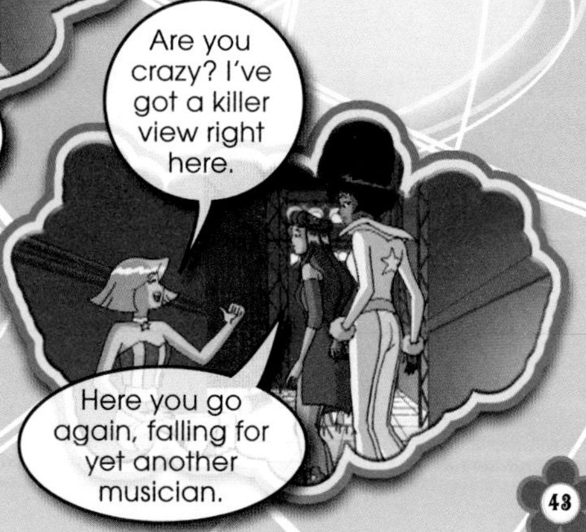
Are you crazy? I've got a killer view right here.
Here you go again, falling for yet another musician.

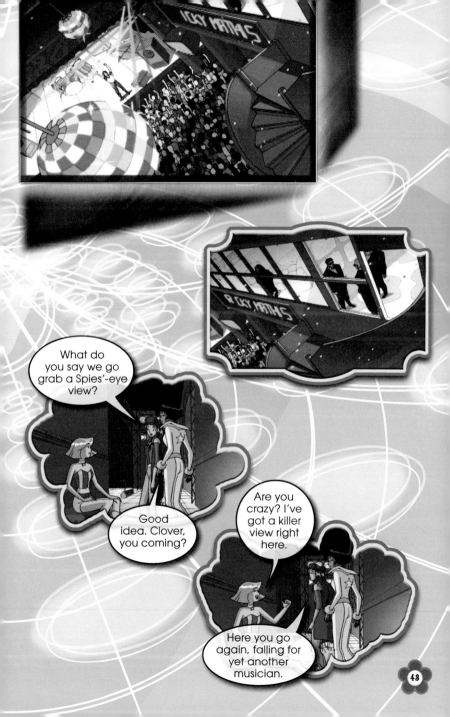

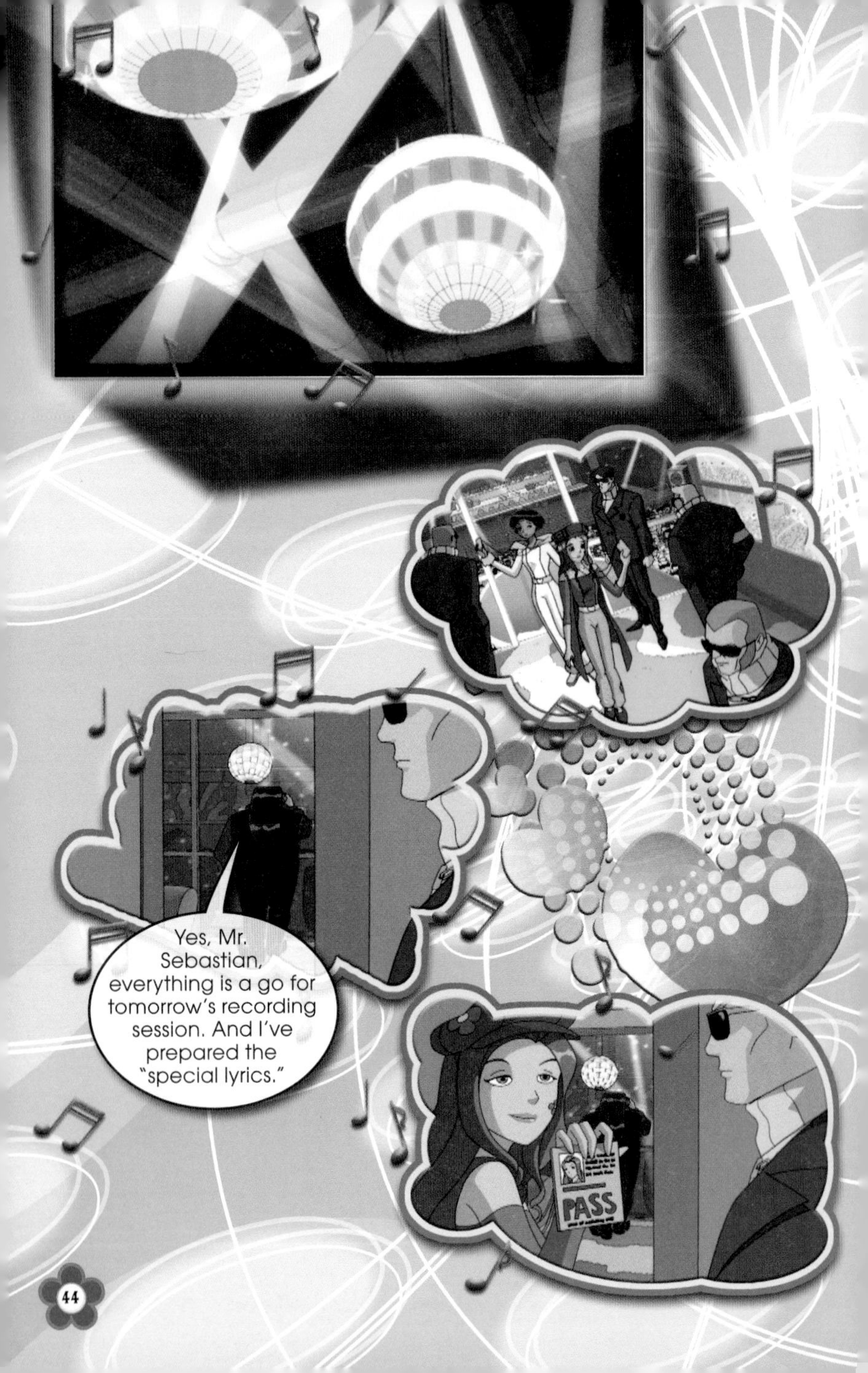
Yes, Mr. Sebastian, everything is a go for tomorrow's recording session. And I've prepared the "special lyrics."
PASS

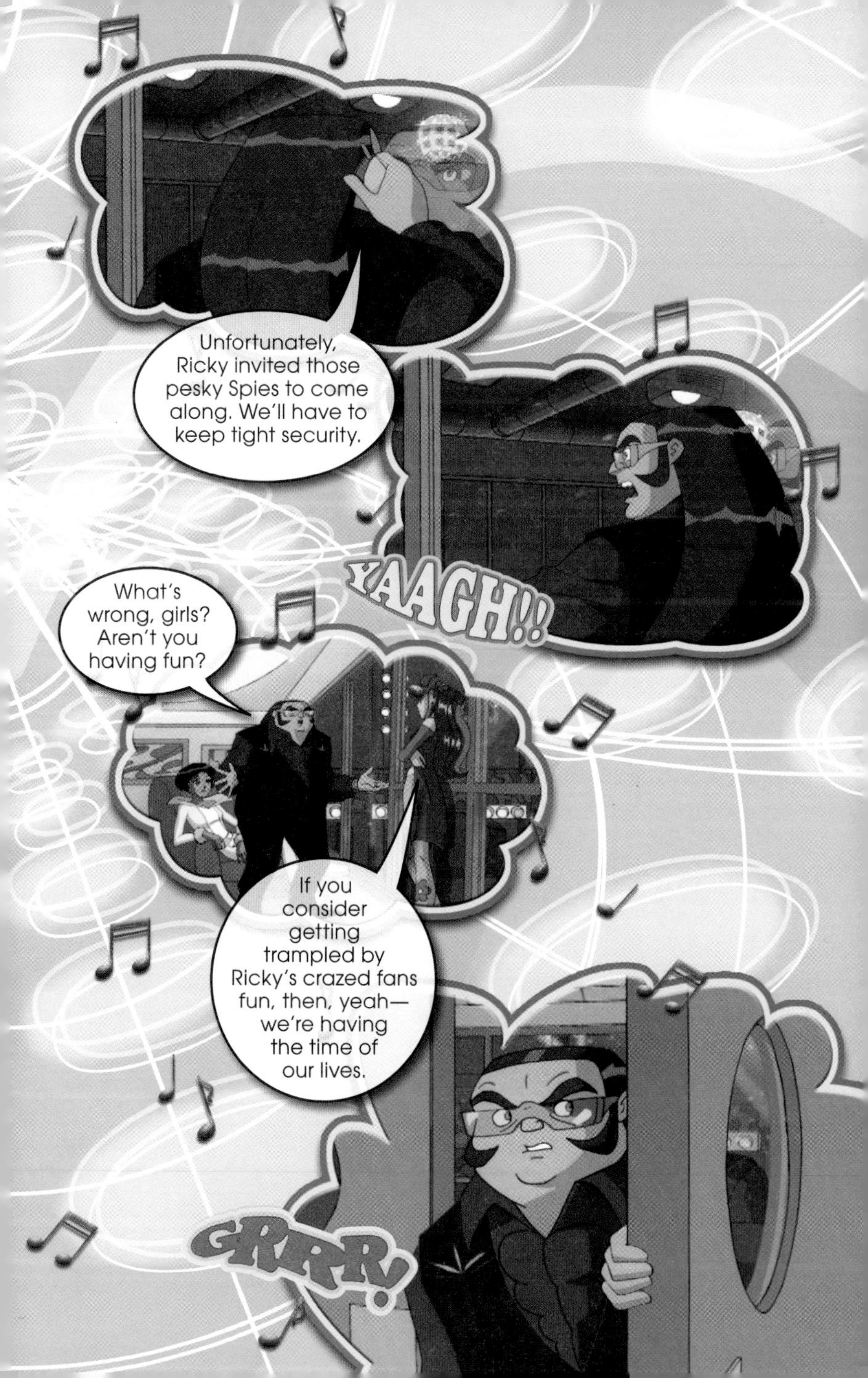
Unfortunately, Ricky invited those pesky Spies to come along. We'll have to keep tight security.
YAAGH!!
What's wrong, girls? Aren't you having fun?
If you consider getting trampled by Ricky's crazed fans fun, then, yeah—we're having the time of our lives.
GRRR!

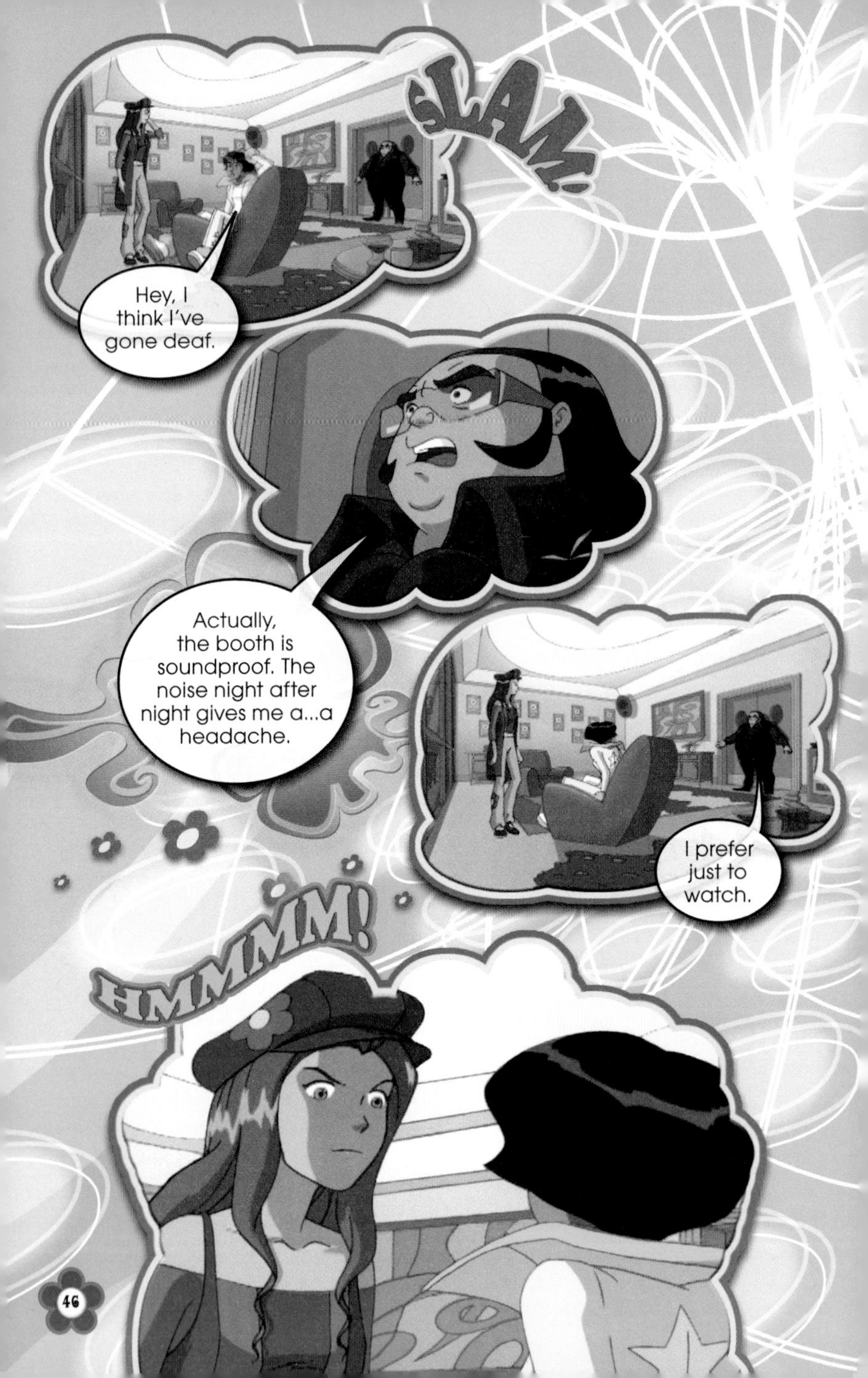
SLAM!
Hey, I think I've gone deaf.
Actually, the booth is soundproof. The noise night after night gives me a...a headache.
I prefer just to watch.
HMMMMM!

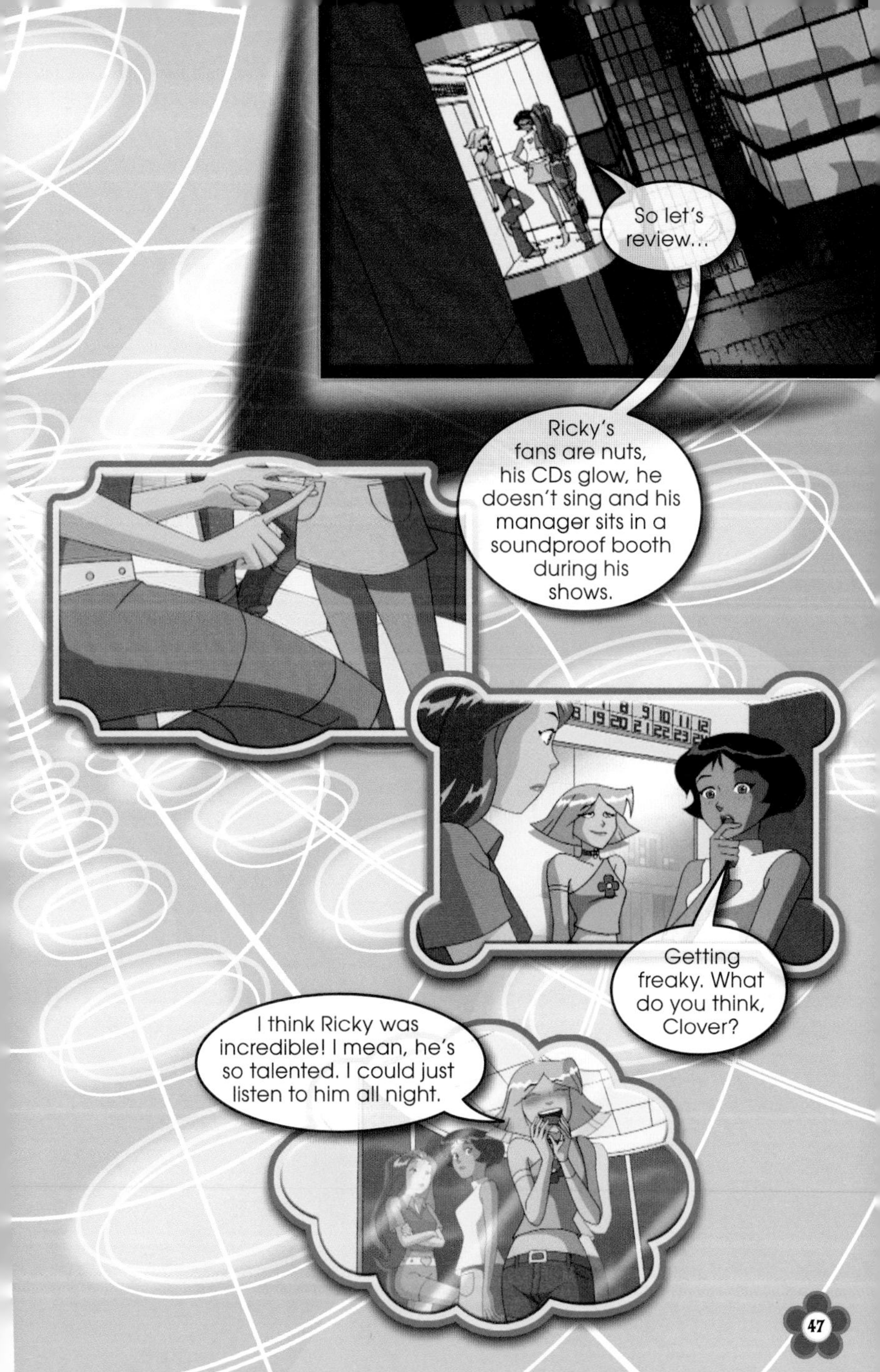
So let's review...
Ricky's fans are nuts, his CDs glow, he doesn't sing and his manager sits in a soundproof booth during his shows.
Getting freaky. What do you think, Clover?
I think Ricky was incredible! I mean, he's so talented. I could just listen to him all night.

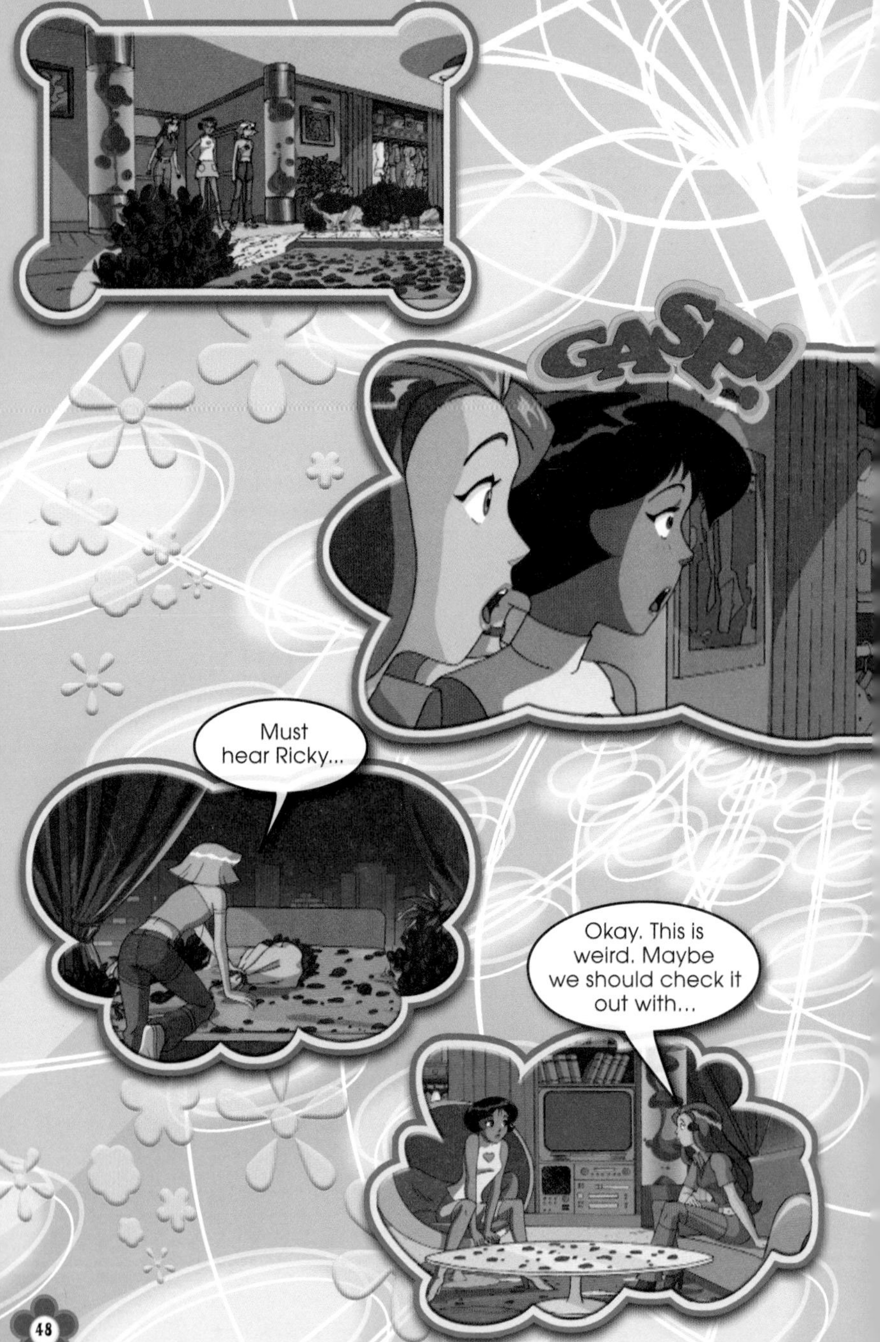
GASP!
Must hear Ricky...
Okay. This is weird. Maybe we should check it out with...

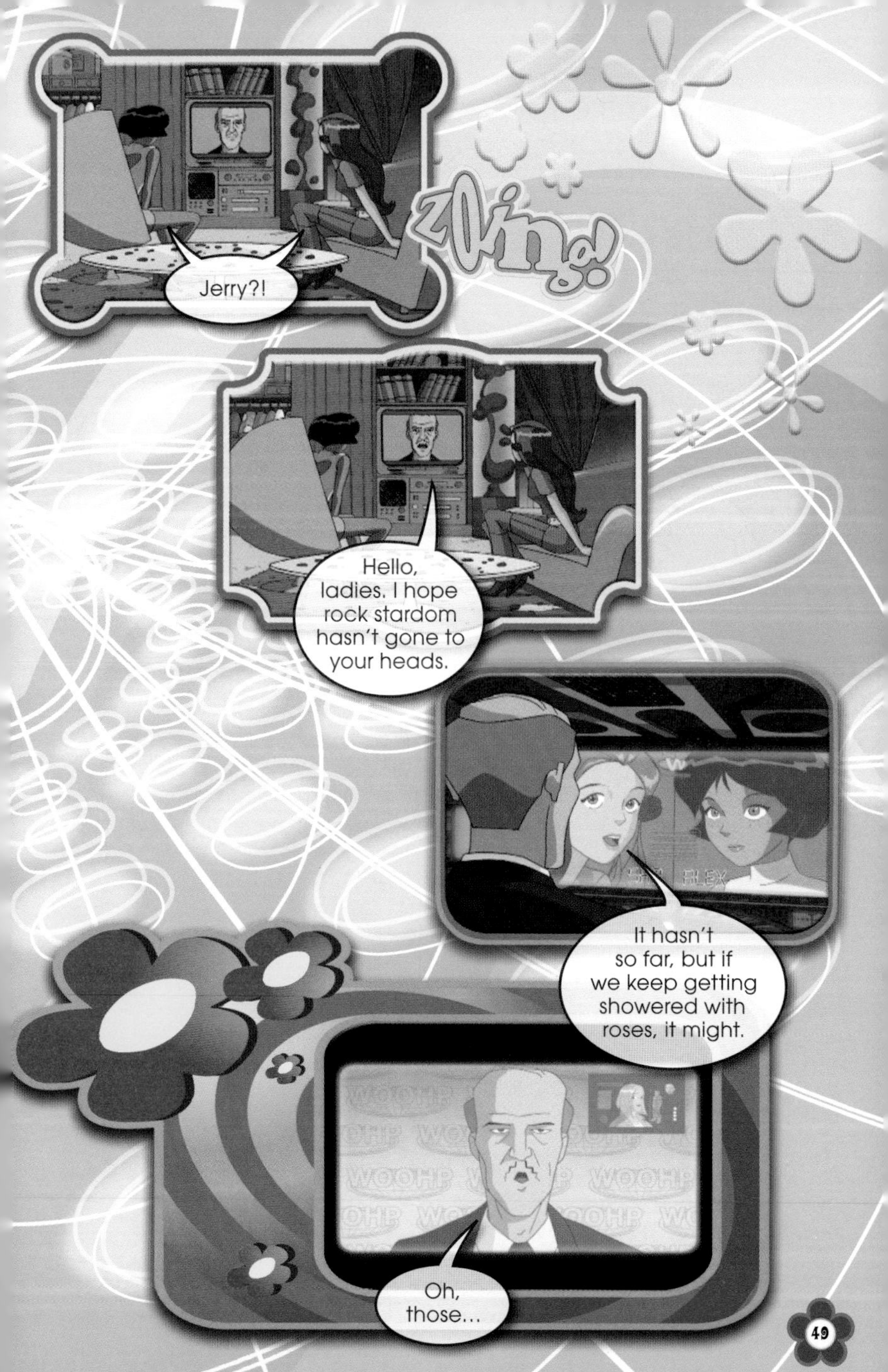
Jerry?!
zling!
Hello, ladies. I hope rock stardom hasn't gone to your heads.
It hasn't so far, but if we keep getting showered with roses, it might.
Oh, those...

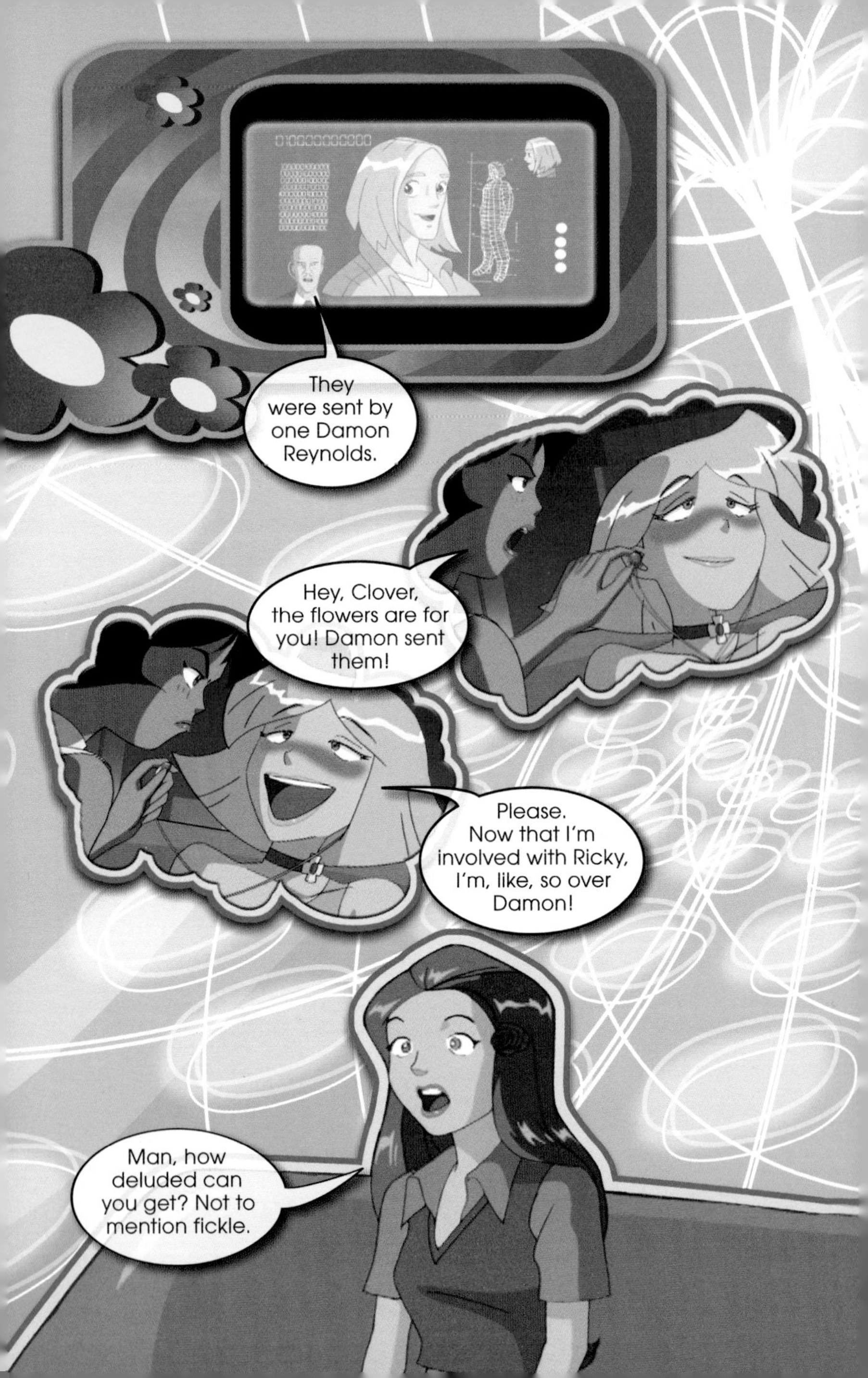
They were sent by one Damon Reynolds.
Hey, Clover, the flowers are for you! Damon sent them!
Please. Now that I'm involved with Ricky, I'm, like, so over Damon!
Man, how deluded can you get? Not to mention fickle.

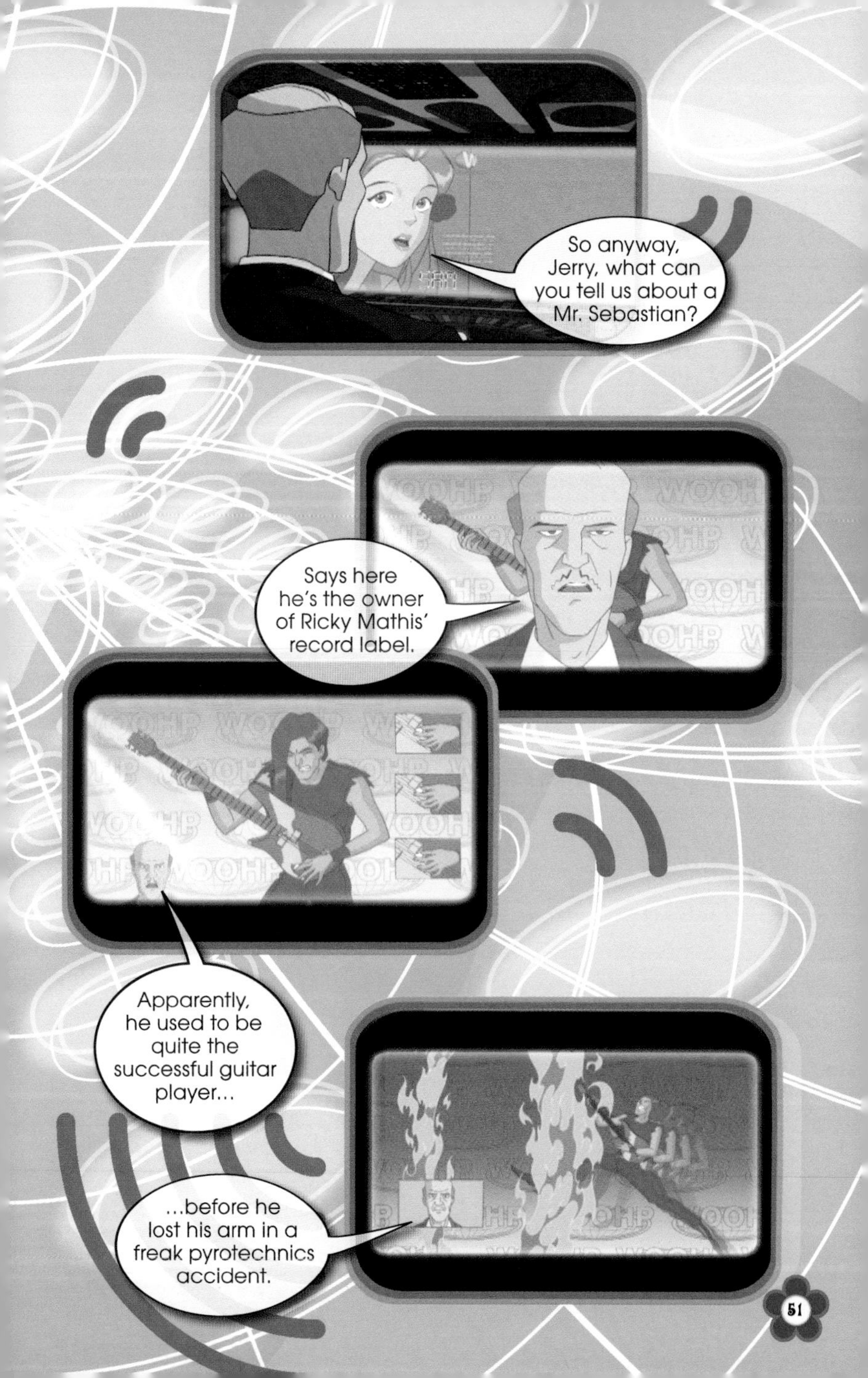

So anyway, Jerry, what can you tell us about a Mr. Sebastian?
Says here he's the owner of Ricky Mathis' record label.
Apparently, he used to be quite the successful guitar player...
...before he lost his arm in a freak pyrotechnics accident.

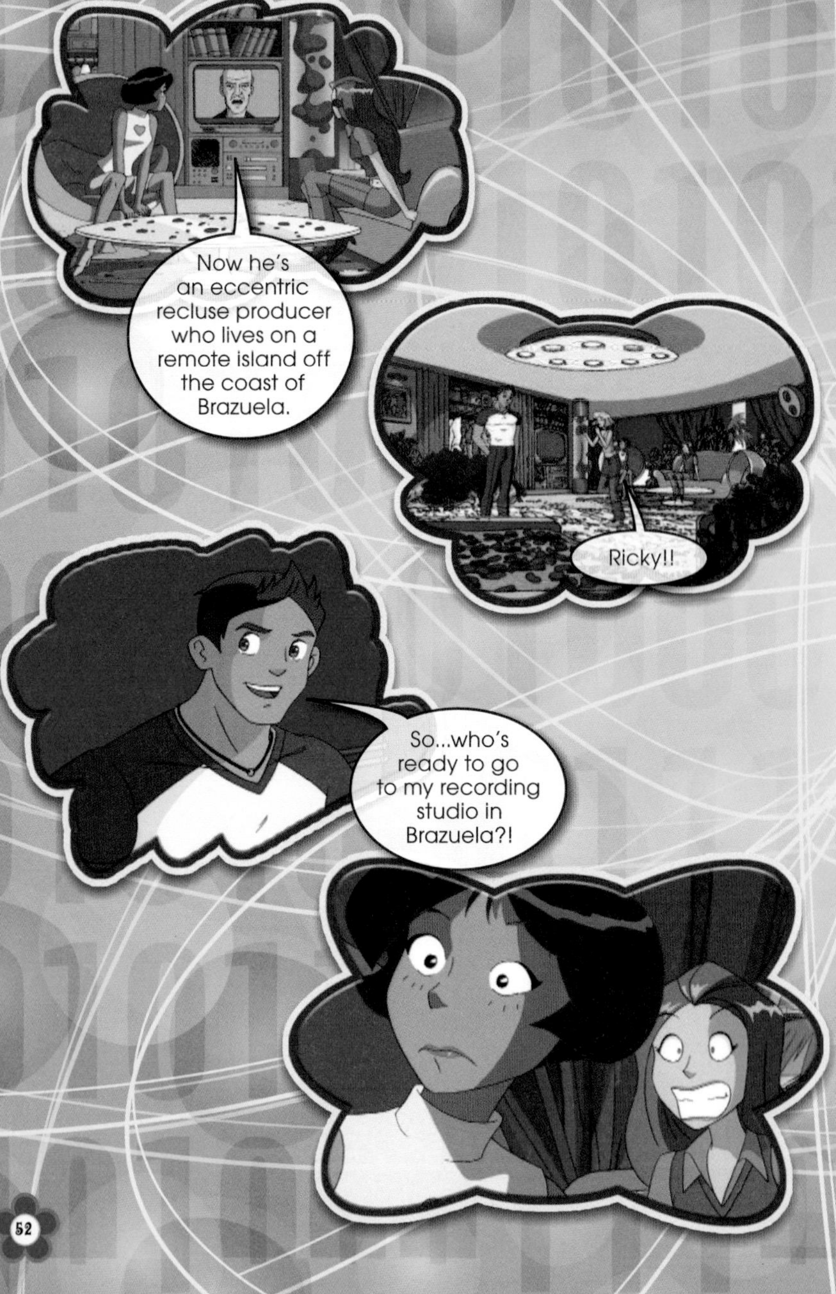
Now he's an eccentric recluse producer who lives on a remote island off the coast of Brazuela.
Ricky!!
So...who's ready to go to my recording studio in Brazuela?!

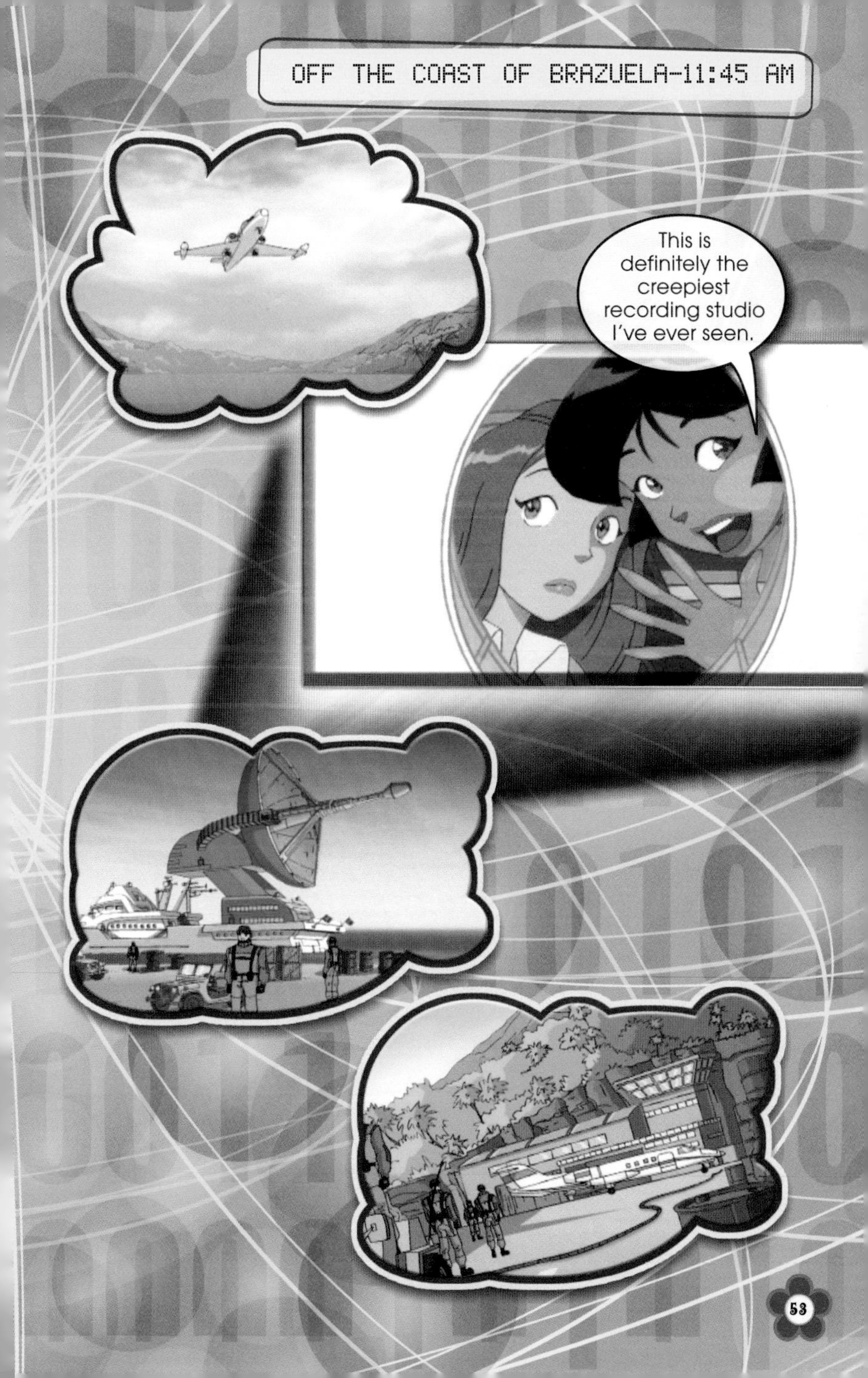
OFF THE COAST OF BRAZUELA-11:45 AM
This is definitely the creepiest recording studio I've ever seen.

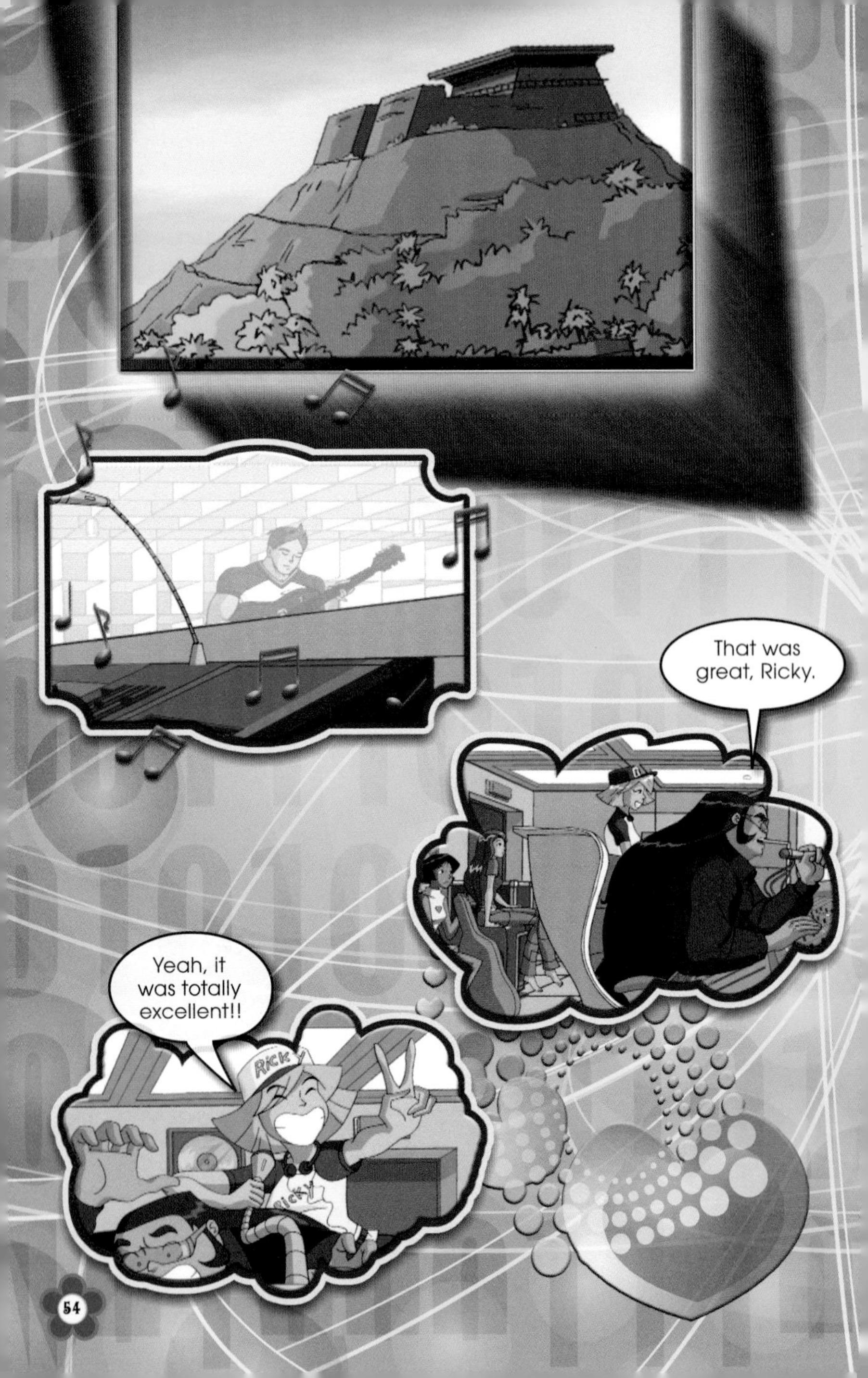
That was great, Ricky.
Yeah, it was totally excellent!!
RICKY

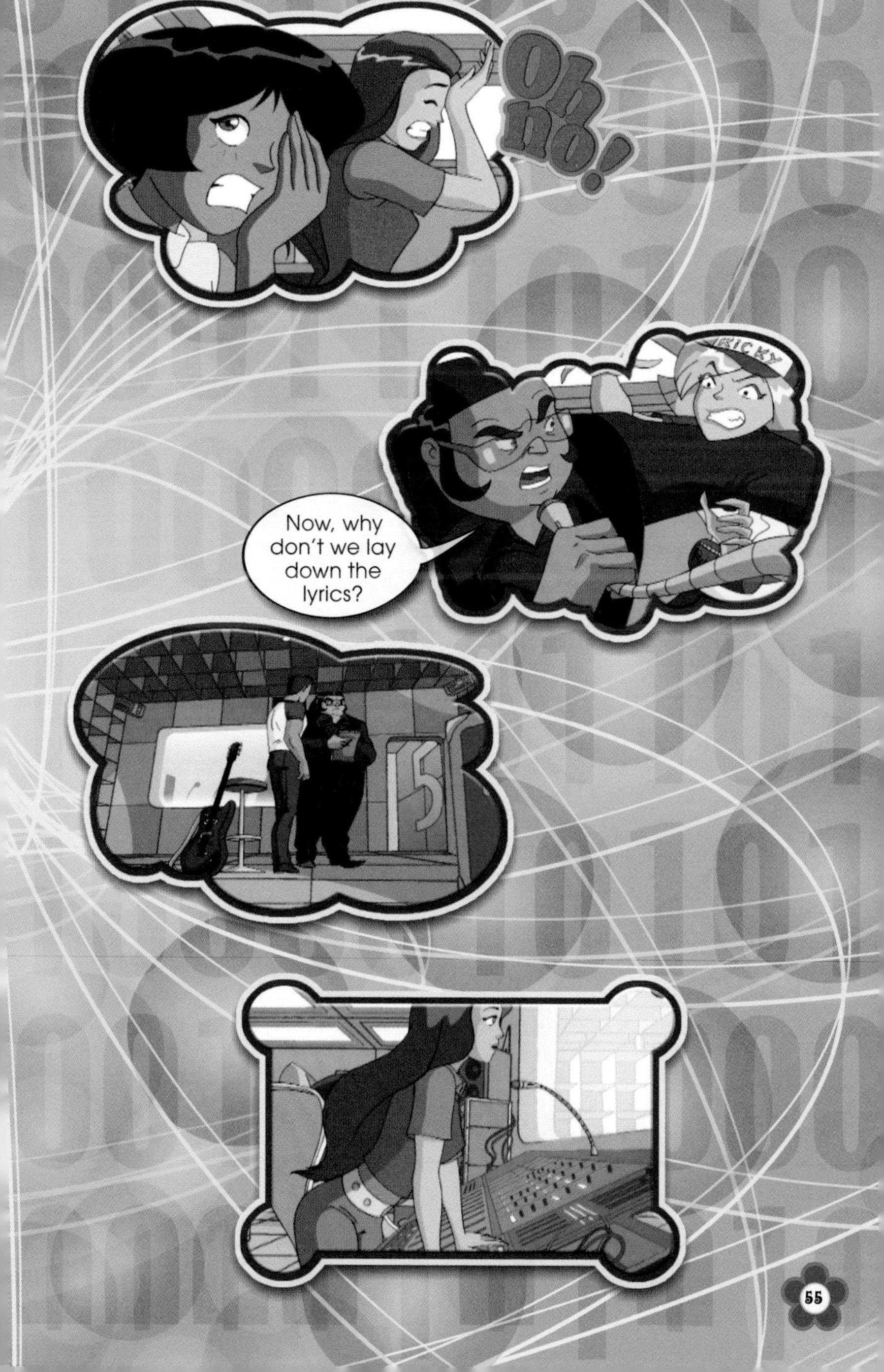
Oh no!
RICKY
Now, why don't we lay down the lyrics?

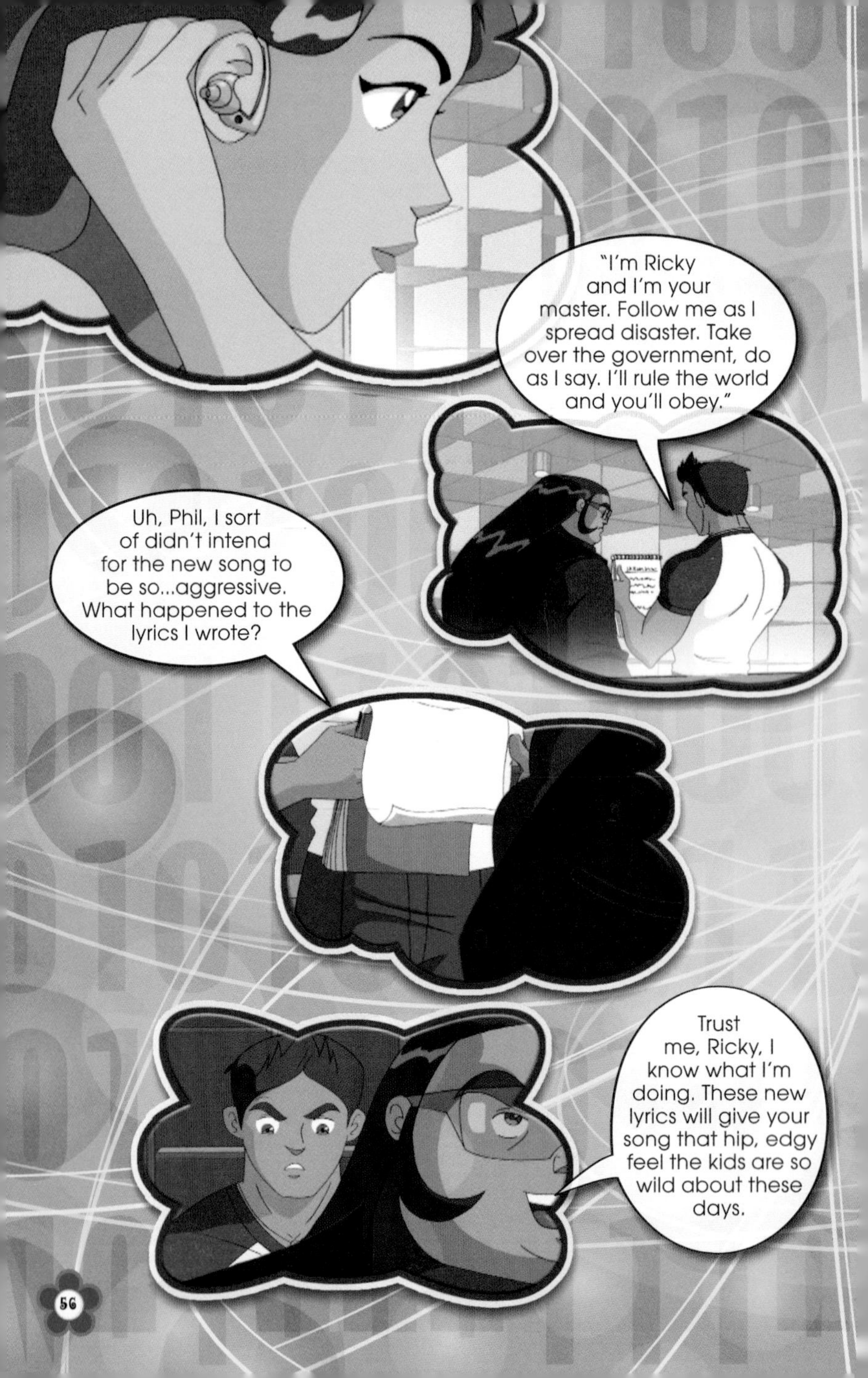
"I'm Ricky and I'm your master. Follow me as I spread disaster. Take over the government, do as I say. I'll rule the world and you'll obey."
Uh, Phil, I sort of didn't intend for the new song to be so...aggressive. What happened to the lyrics I wrote?
Trust me, Ricky, I know what I'm doing. These new lyrics will give your song that hip, edgy feel the kids are so wild about these days.

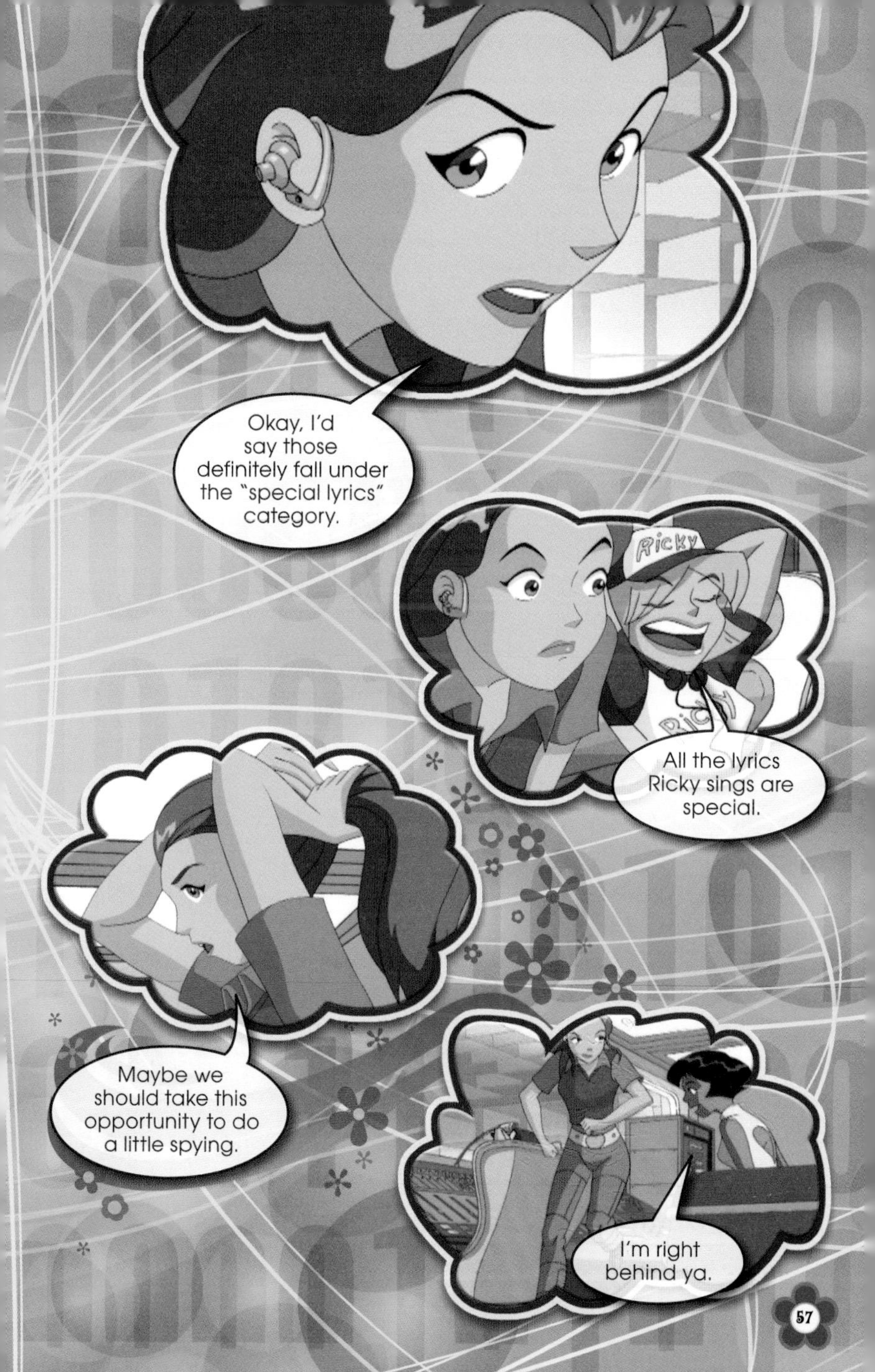
Okay, I'd say those definitely fall under the "special lyrics" category.
RICKY
RICKY
All the lyrics Ricky sings are special.
Maybe we should take this opportunity to do a little spying.
I'm right behind ya.

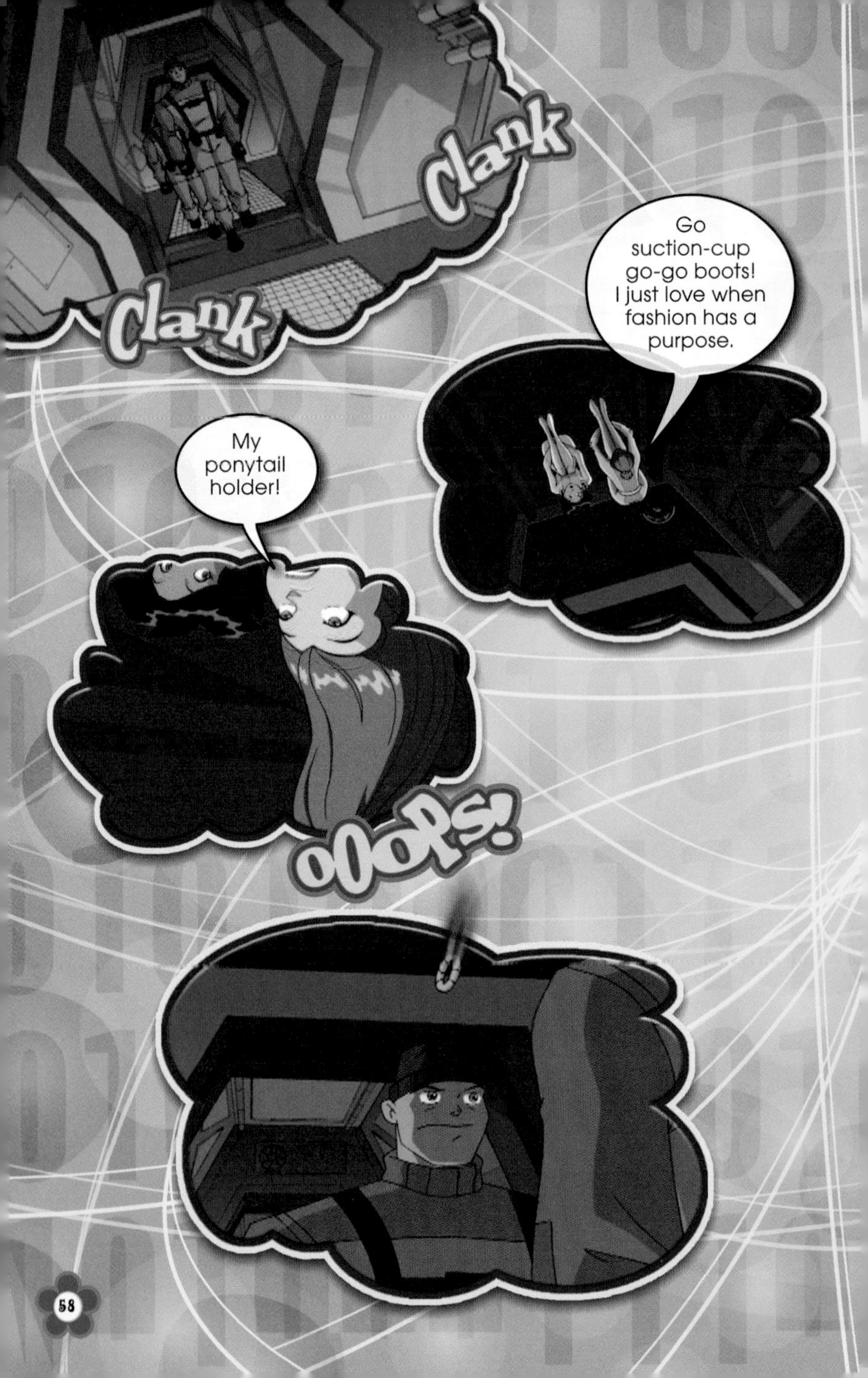
Clank
Clank
Go suction-cup go-go boots! I just love when fashion has a purpose.
My ponytail holder!
OOOPS!

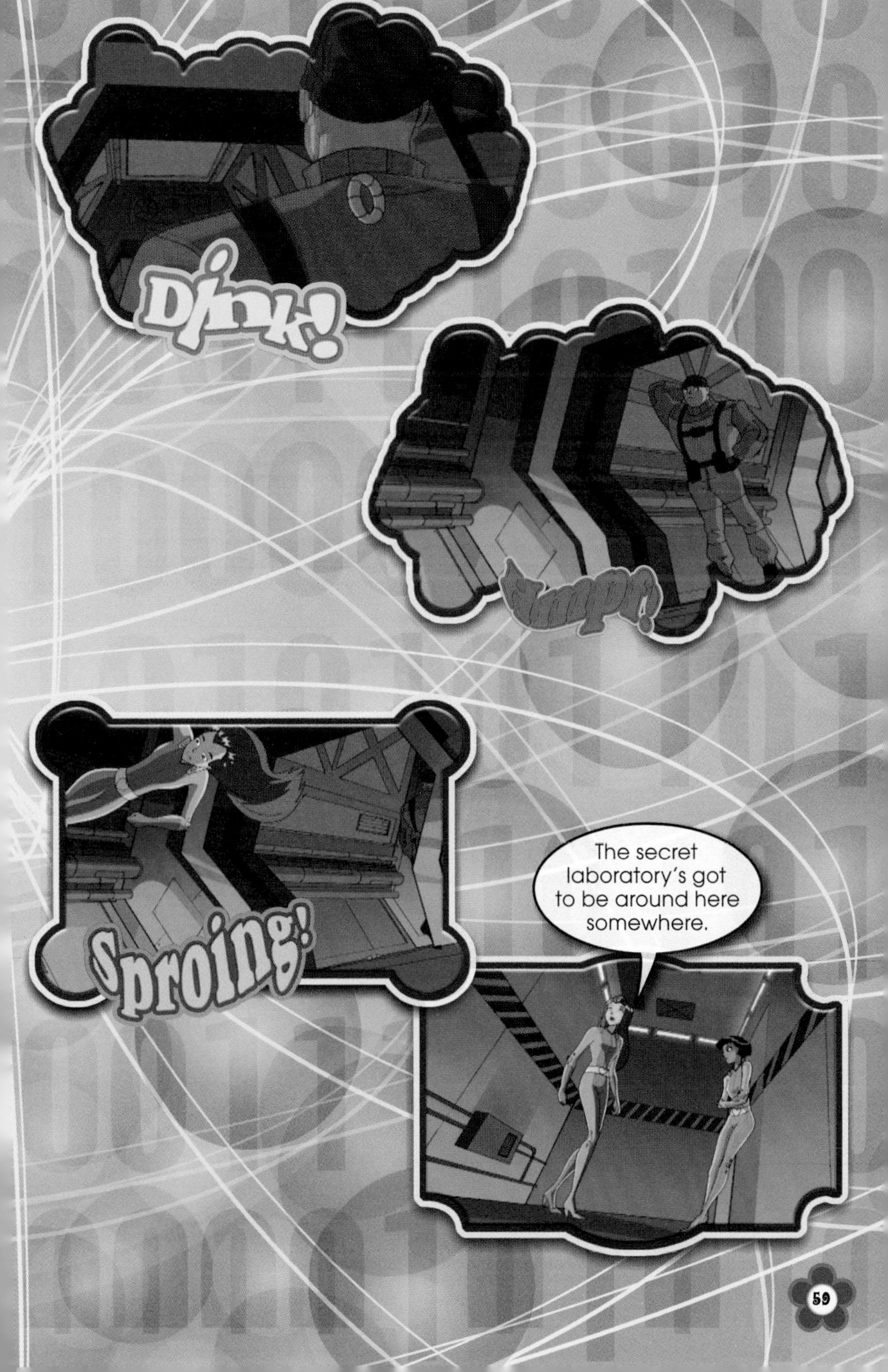
Dink!
Sproing!
The secret laboratory's got to be around here somewhere.

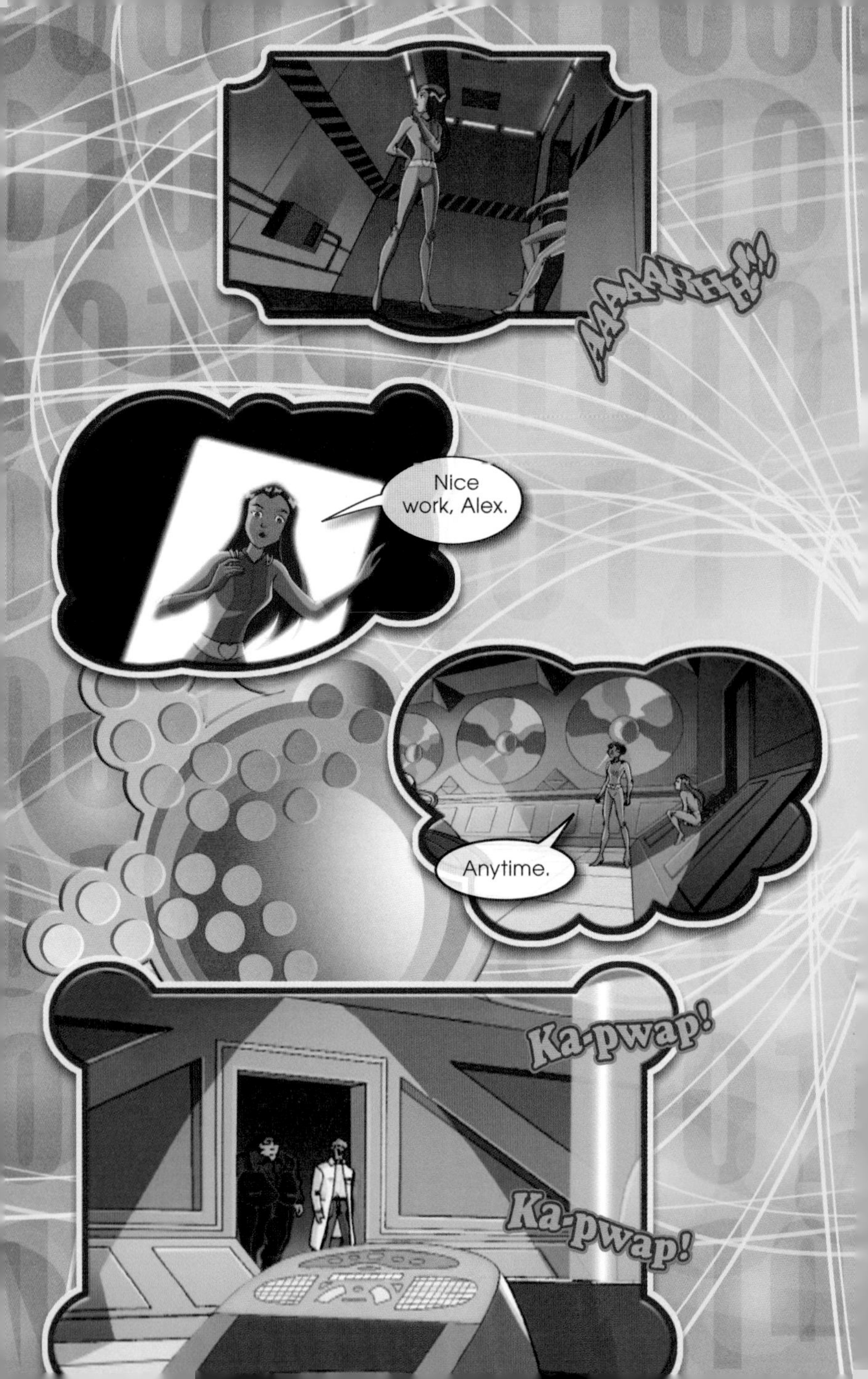
AAAAARHH!!
Nice work, Alex.
Anytime.
Ka-pwap!
Ka-pwap!

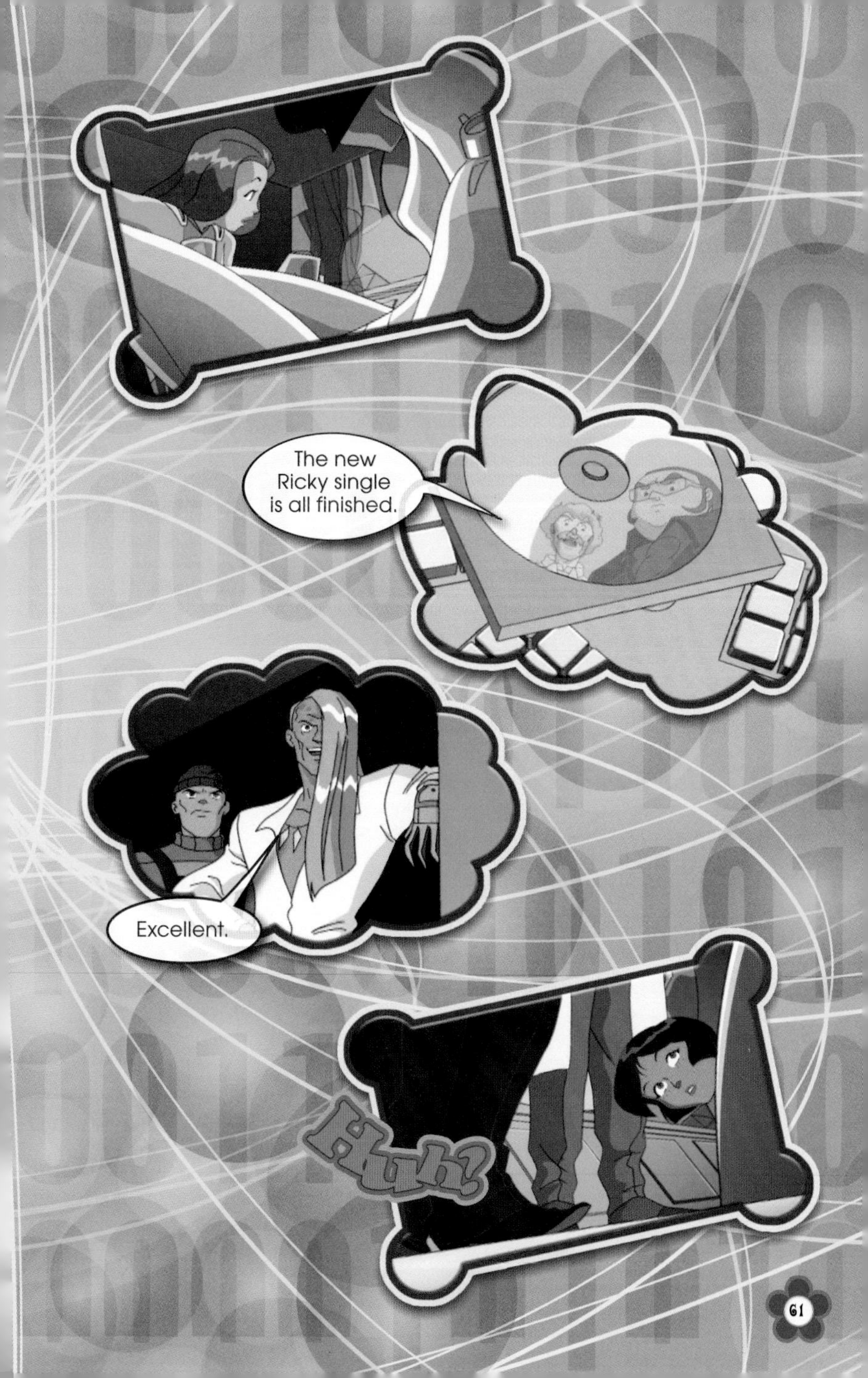
The new Ricky single is all finished.
Excellent.
Huh?

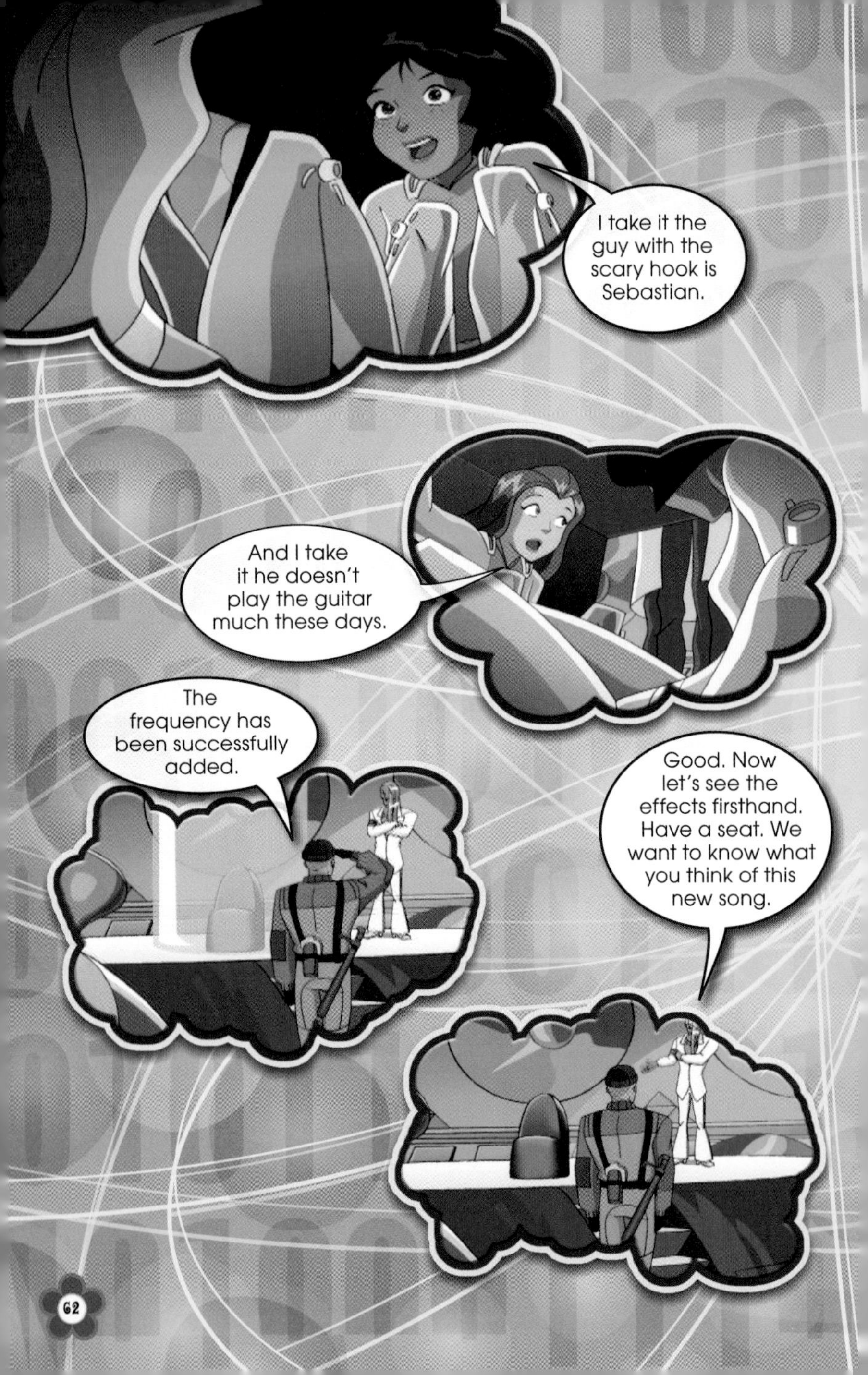

I take it the guy with the scary hook is Sebastian.
And I take it he doesn't play the guitar much these days.
The frequency has been successfully added.
Good. Now let's see the effects firsthand. Have a seat. We want to know what you think of this new song.

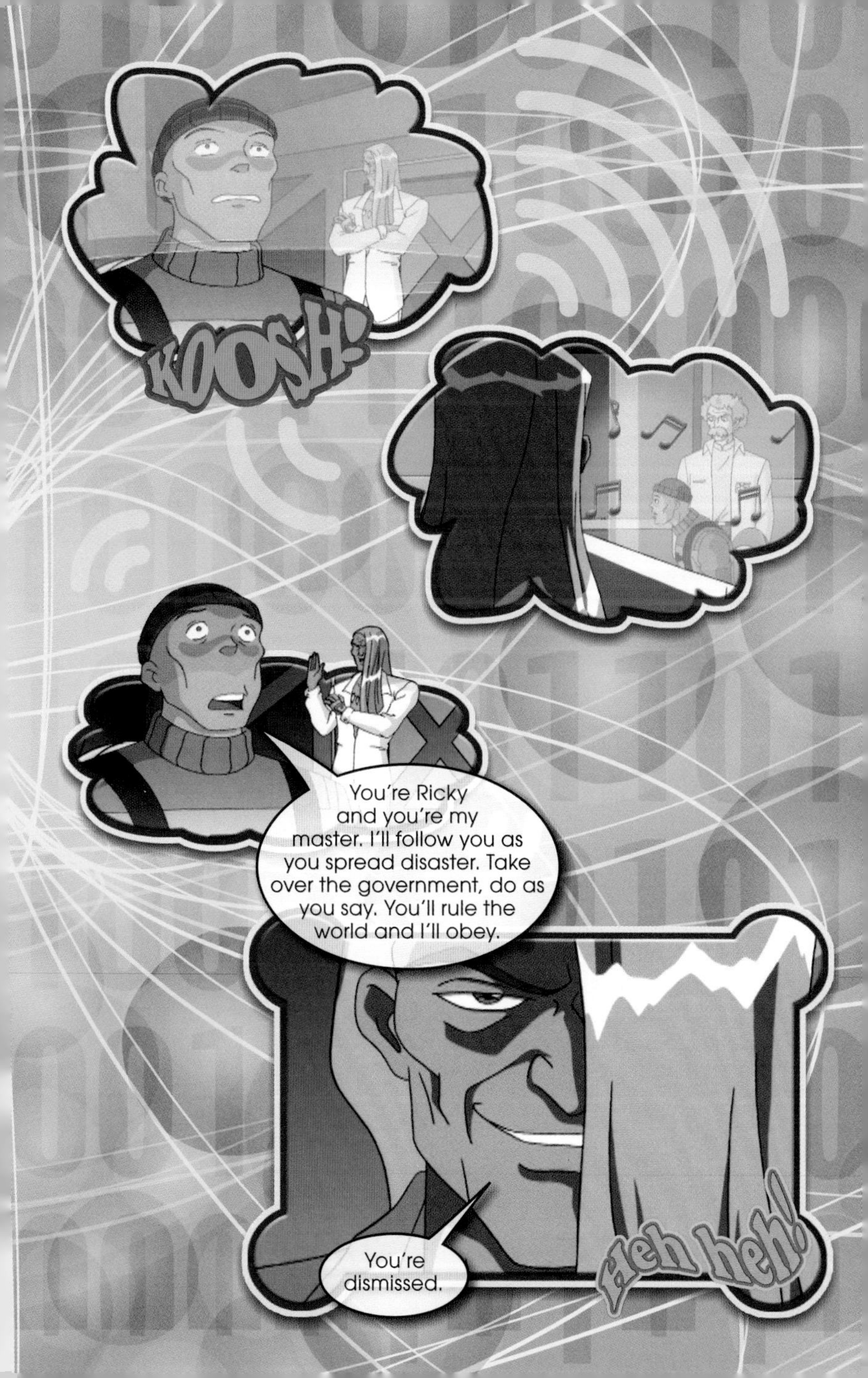
KOOSH!
You're Ricky and you're my master. I'll follow you as you spread disaster. Take over the government, do as you say. You'll rule the world and I'll obey.
You're dismissed.
Heh heh!

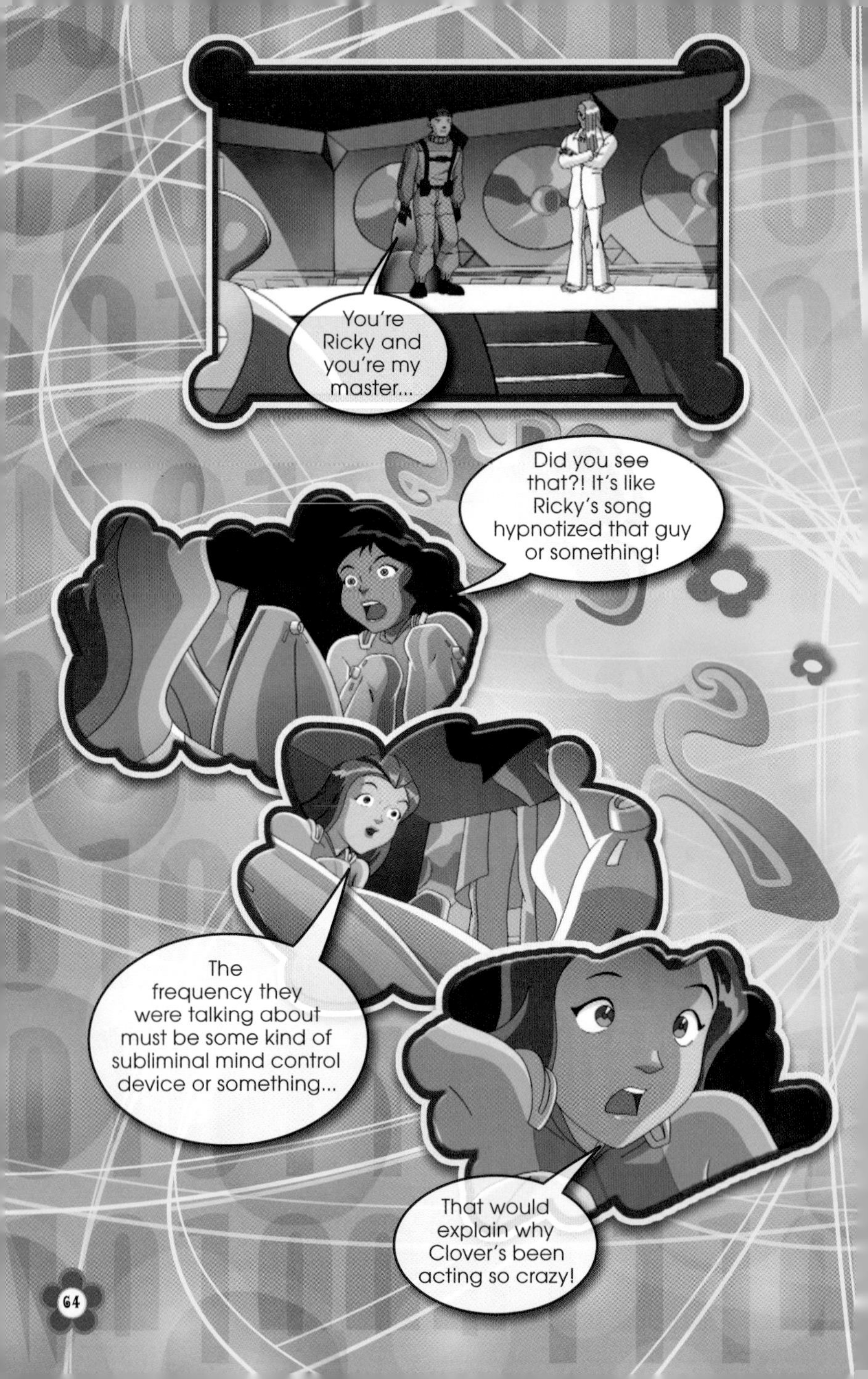
You're Ricky and you're my master...
Did you see that?! It's like Ricky's song hypnotized that guy or something!
The frequency they were talking about must be some kind of subliminal mind control device or something...
That would explain why Clover's been acting so crazy!

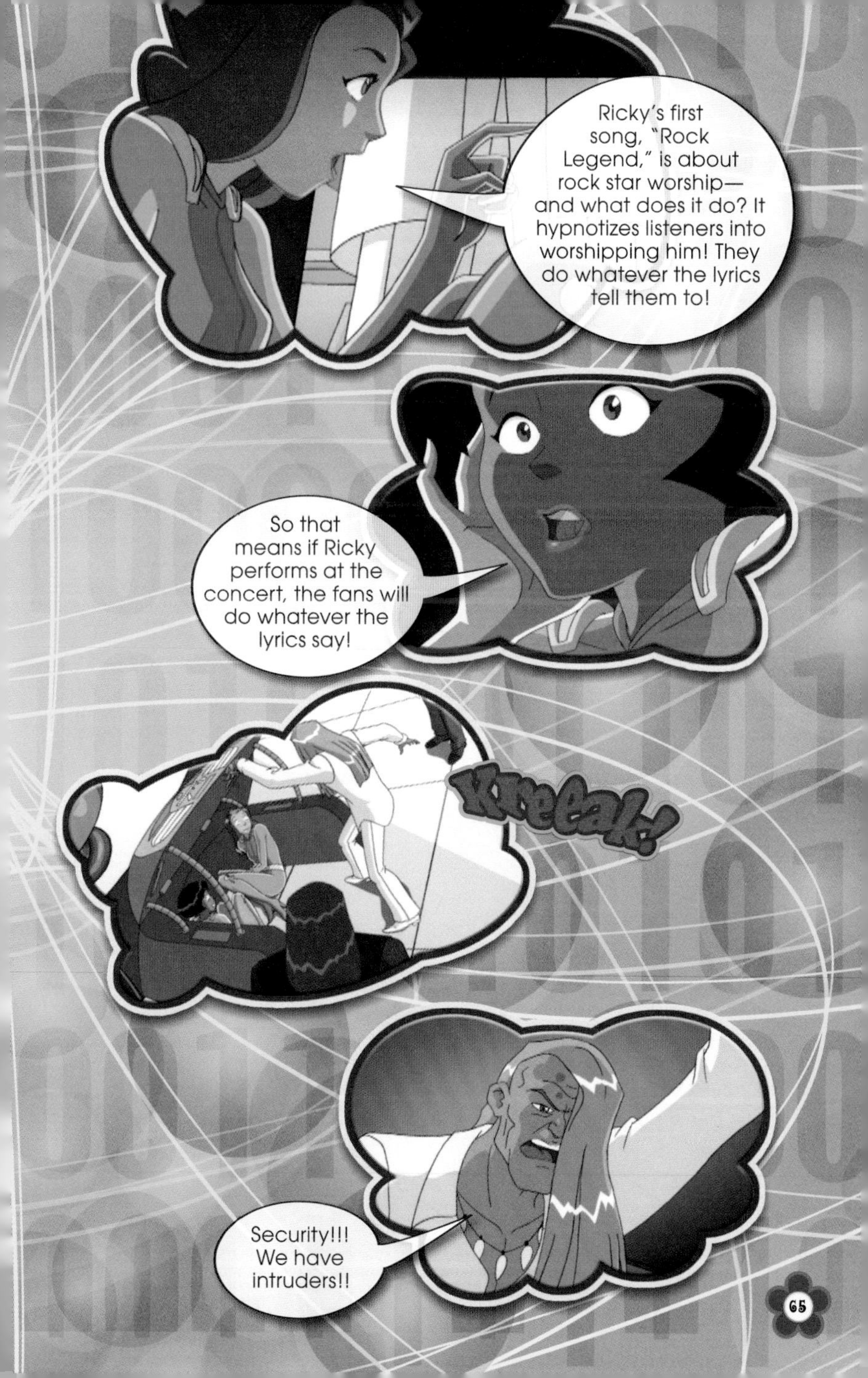
Ricky's first song, "Rock Legend," is about rock star worship—and what does it do? It hypnotizes listeners into worshipping him! They do whatever the lyrics tell them to!
So that means if Ricky performs at the concert, the fans will do whatever the lyrics say!
Krreak!
Security!!! We have intruders!!

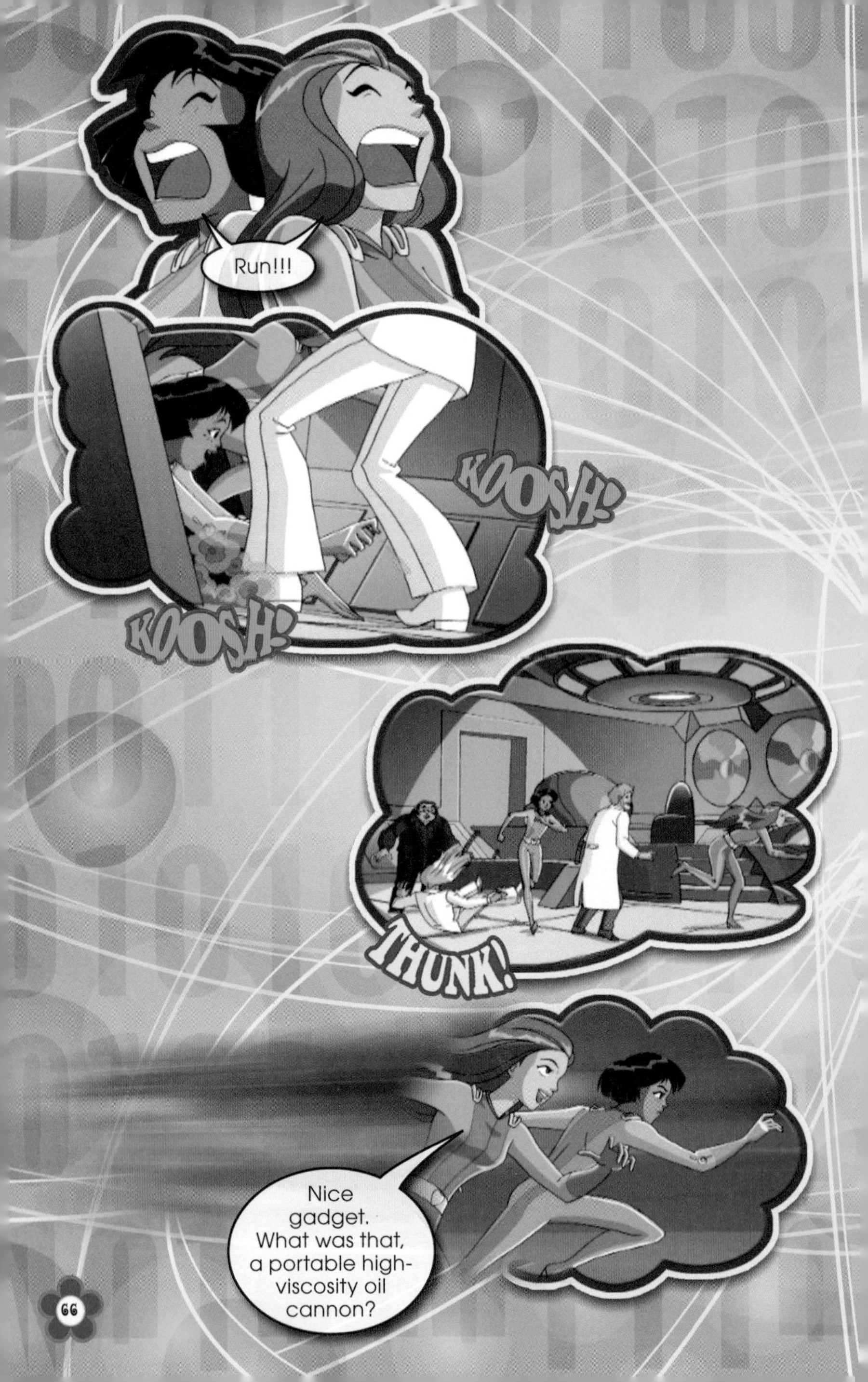
Run!!!
KOOSH!
KOOSH!
THUNK!
Nice gadget. What was that, a portable high-viscosity oil cannon?

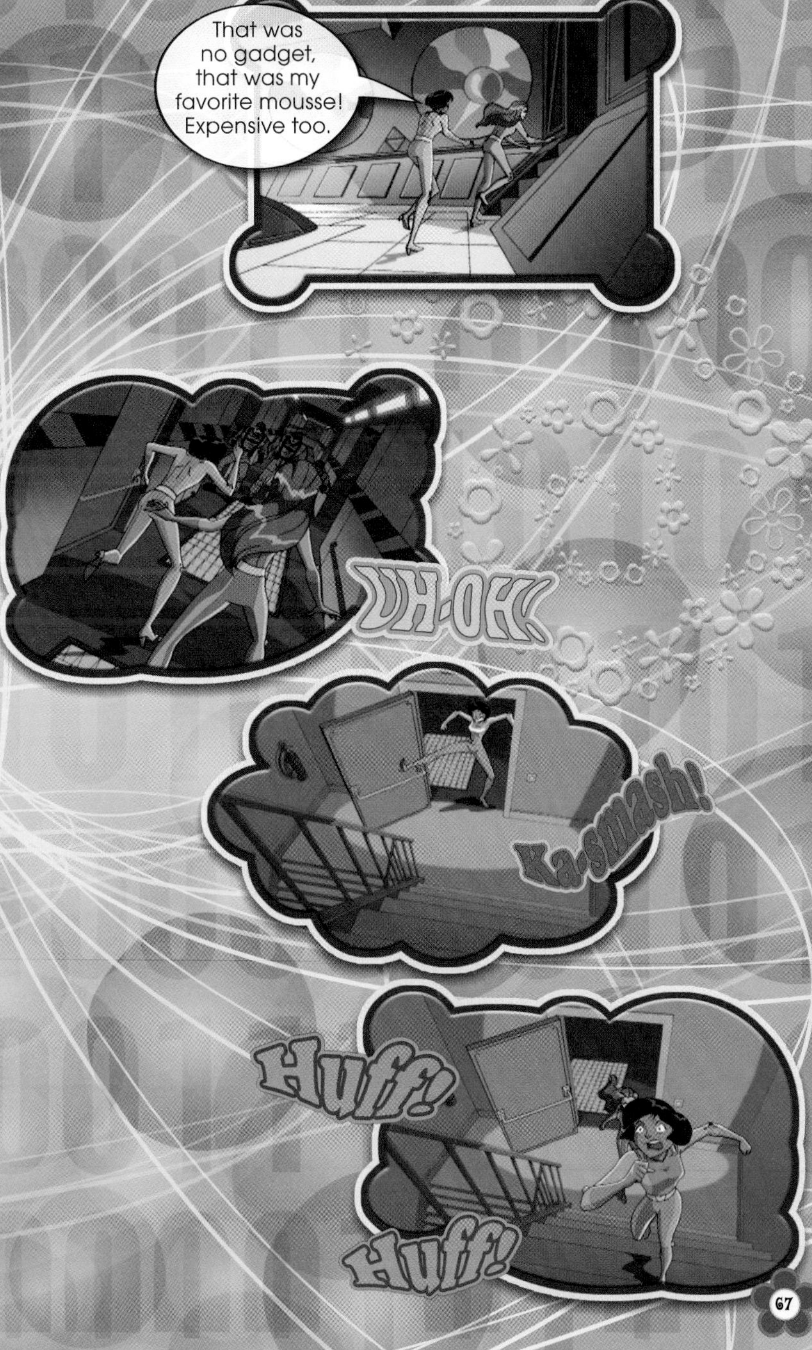

That was no gadget, that was my favorite mousse! Expensive too.
UH-OH!
Ka-smash!
Huff!
Huff!

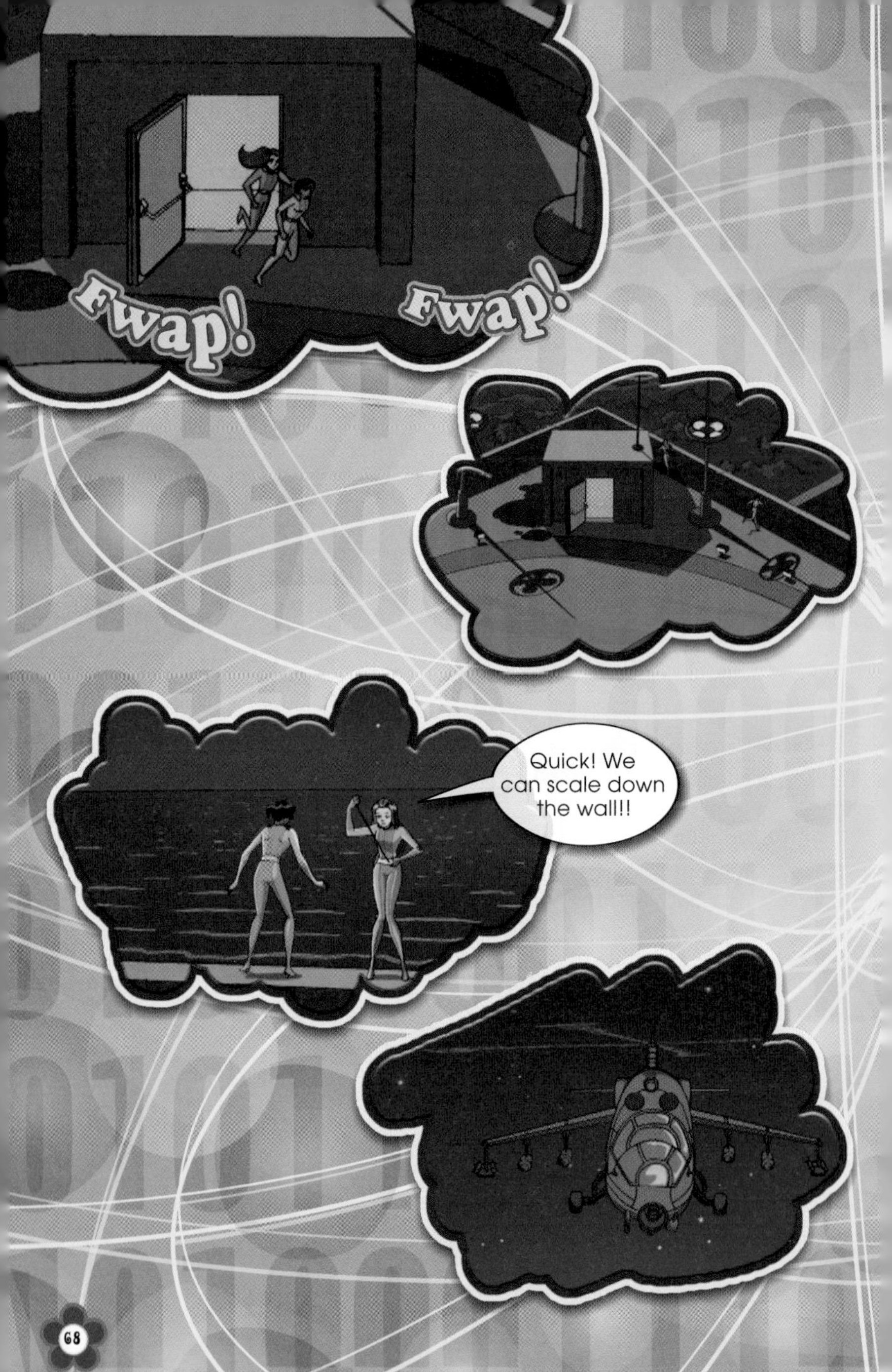
Fwap!
Fwap!
Quick! We can scale down the wall!!

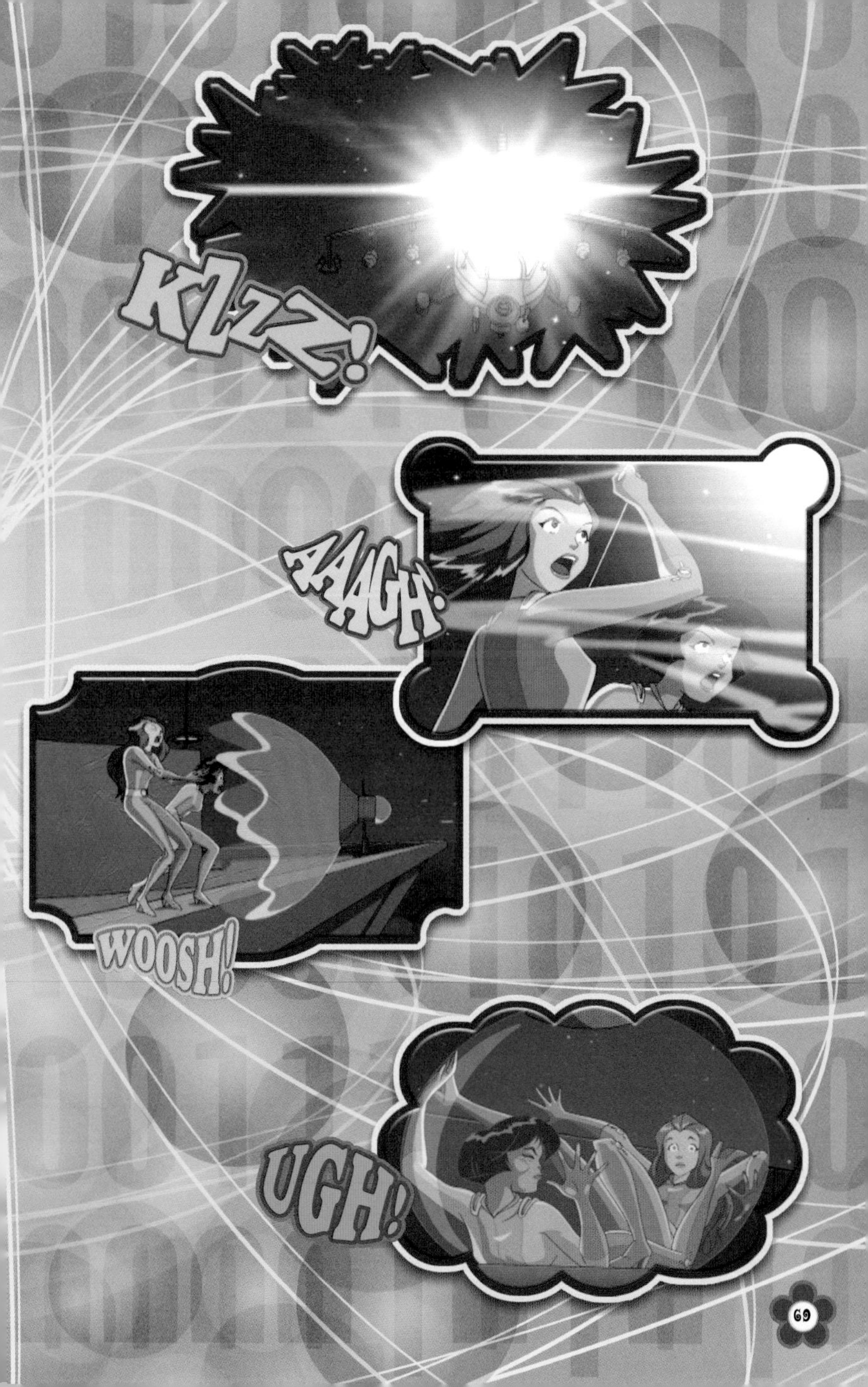
KZZZZ!
AAAGH!
WOOSH!
UGH!

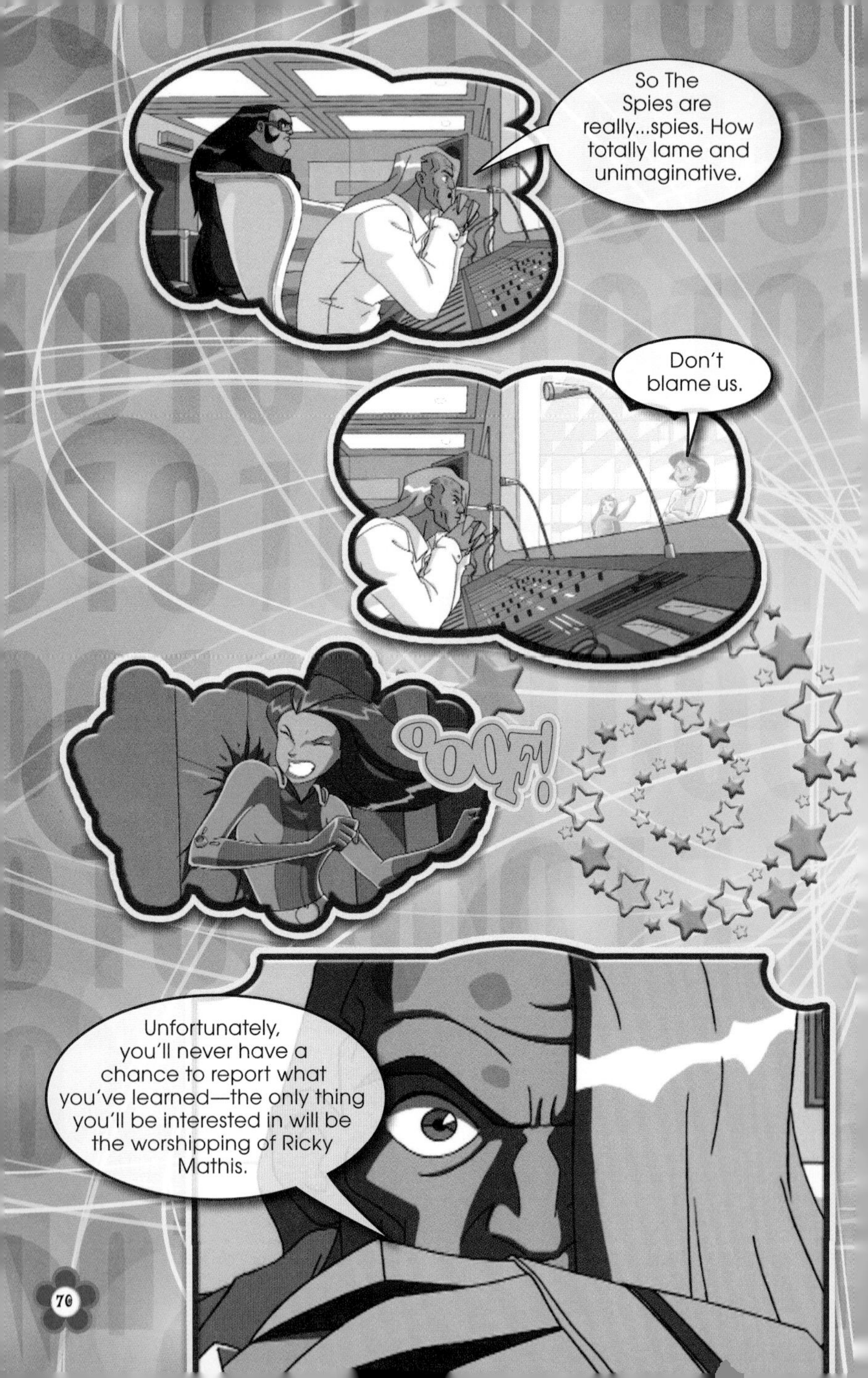
So The Spies are really...spies. How totally lame and unimaginative.
Don't blame us.
OOOF!
Unfortunately, you'll never have a chance to report what you've learned—the only thing you'll be interested in will be the worshipping of Ricky Mathis.

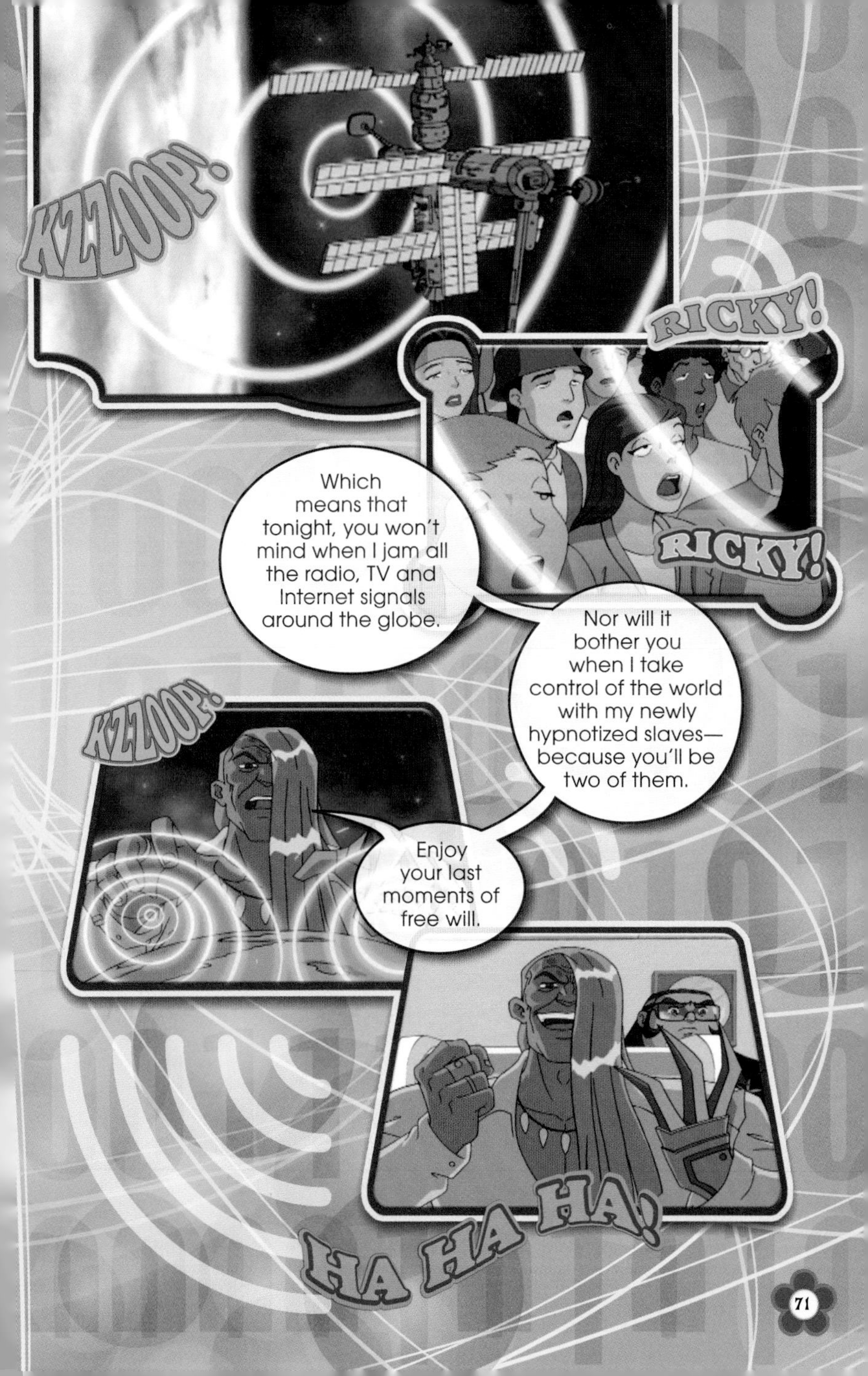
KZZOOP!
RICKY!
RICKY!
Which means that tonight, you won't mind when I jam all the radio, TV and Internet signals around the globe.
Nor will it bother you when I take control of the world with my newly hypnotized slaves—because you'll be two of them.
KZZOOP!
Enjoy your last moments of free will.
HA HA HA!

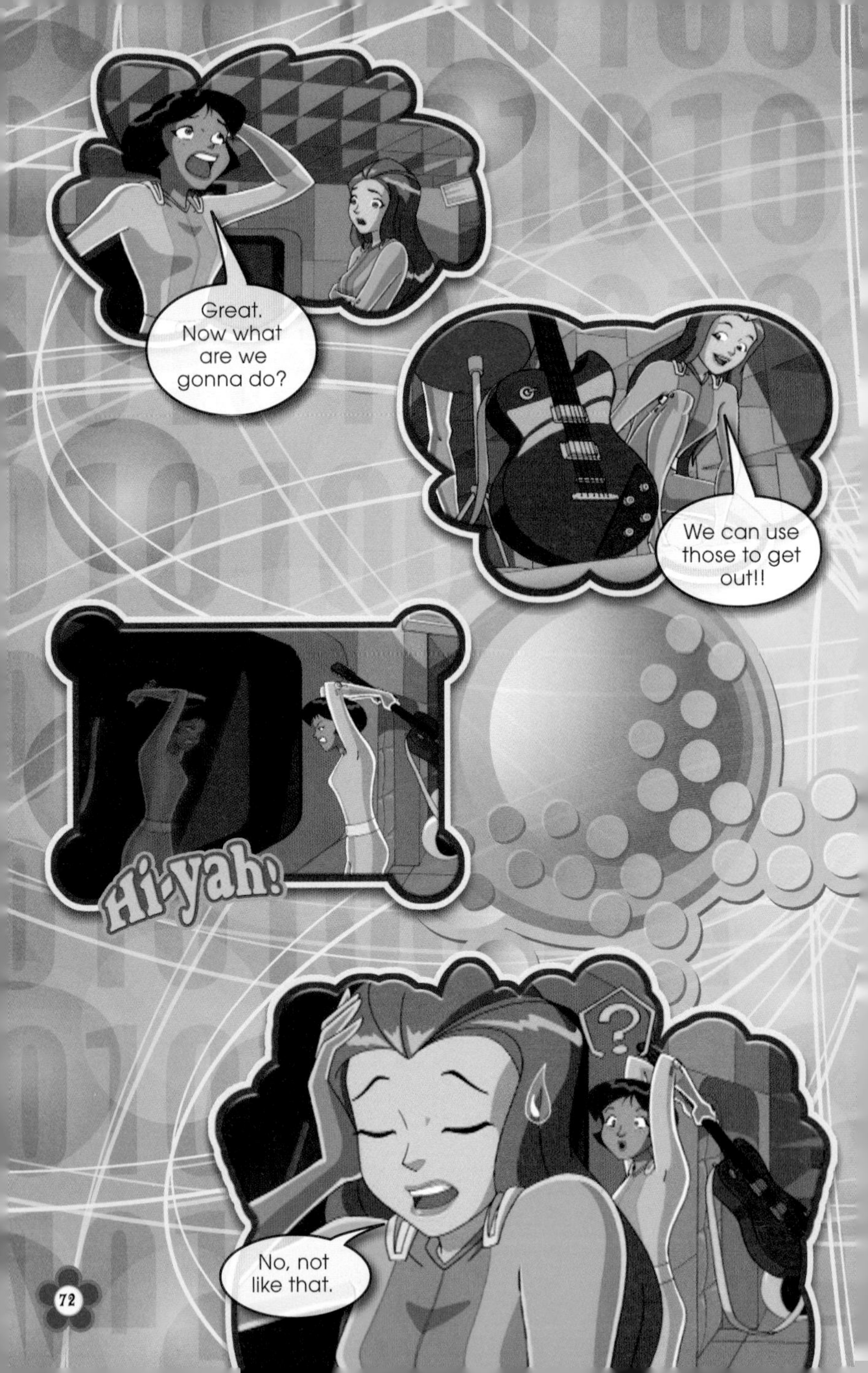
Great. Now what are we gonna do?
We can use those to get out!!
Hi-yah!
?
No, not like that.

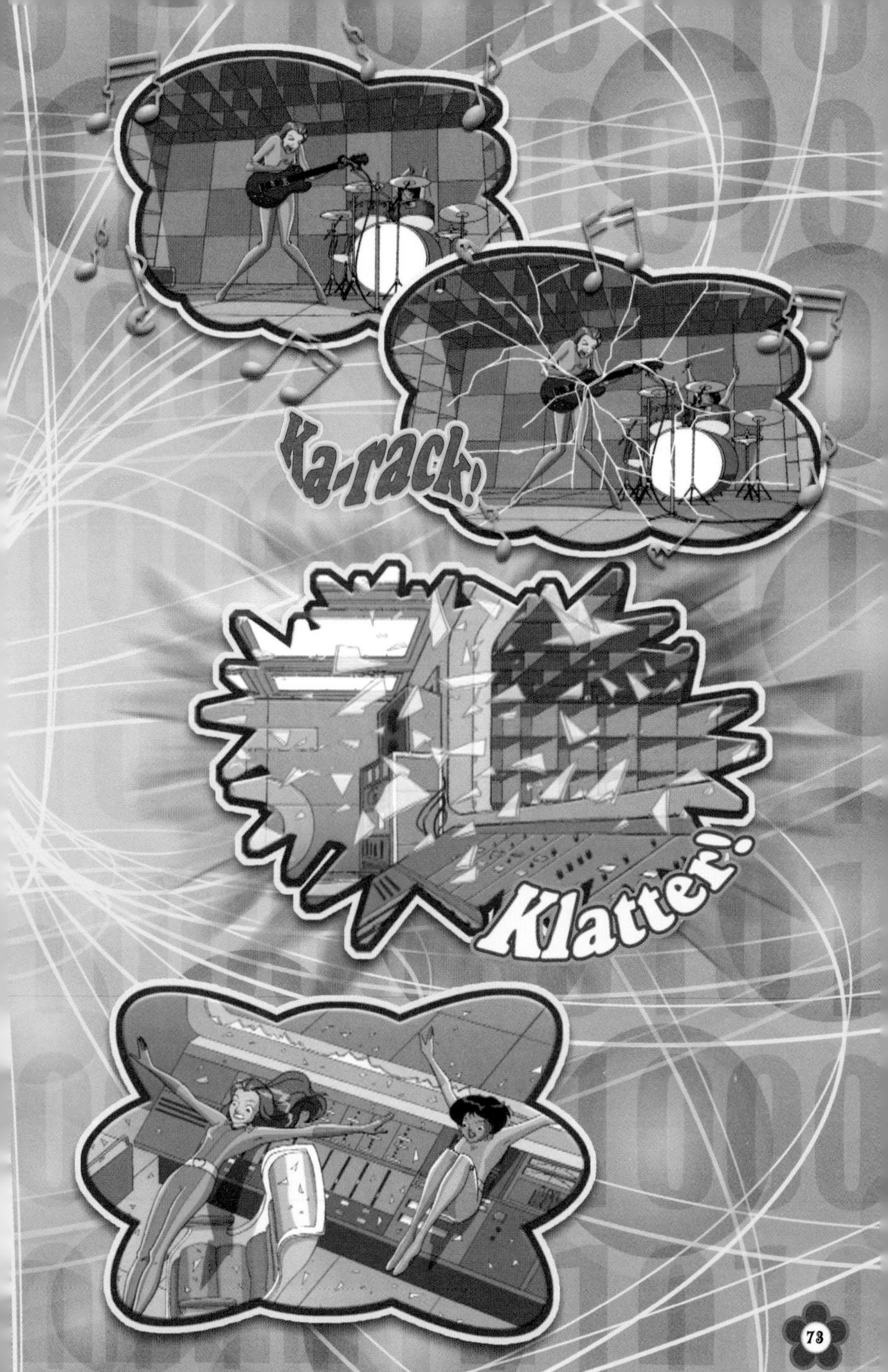
Ka-rack!
Klatter!

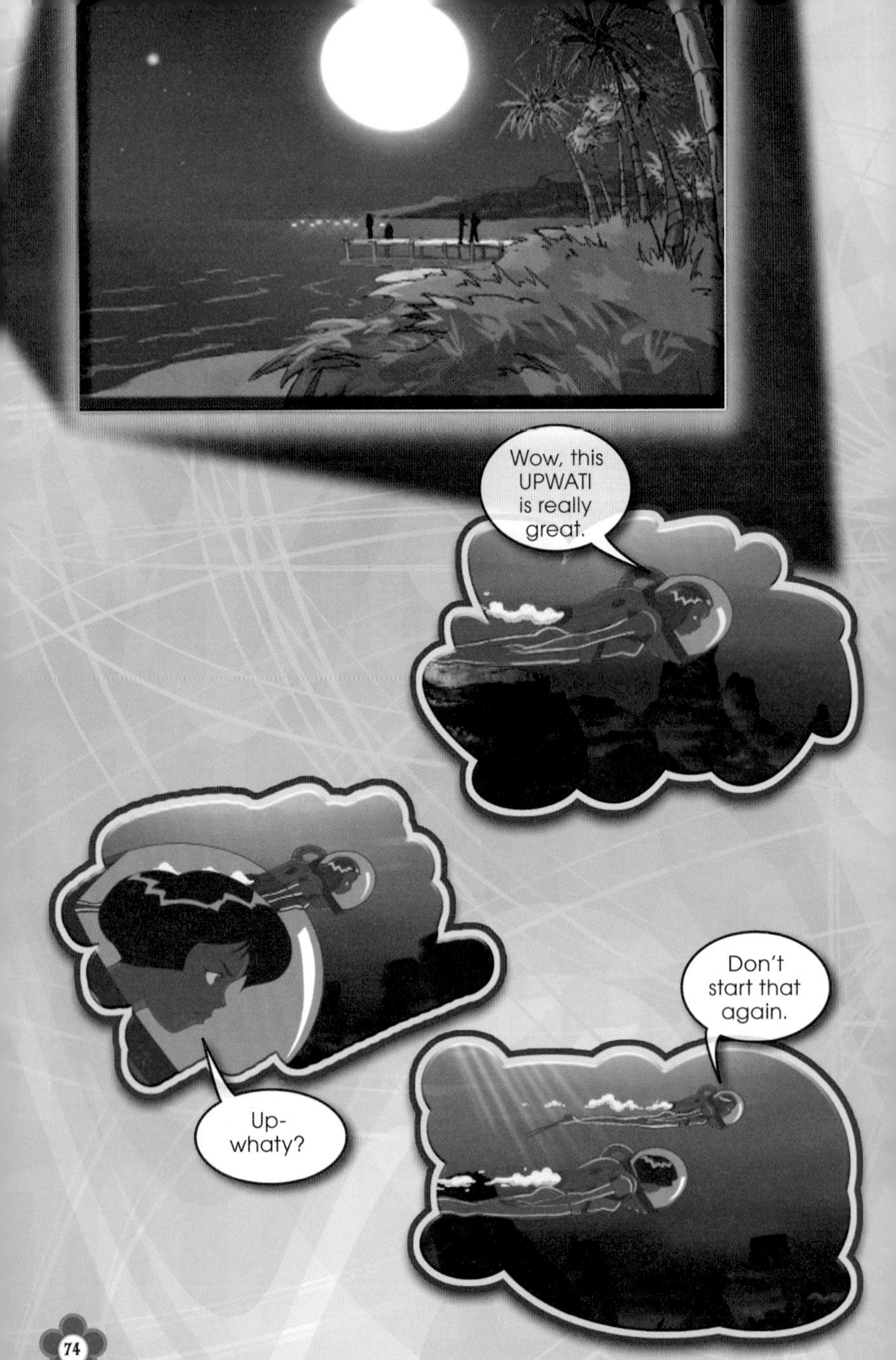
Wow, this UPWATI is really great.
Up-whaty?
Don't start that again.

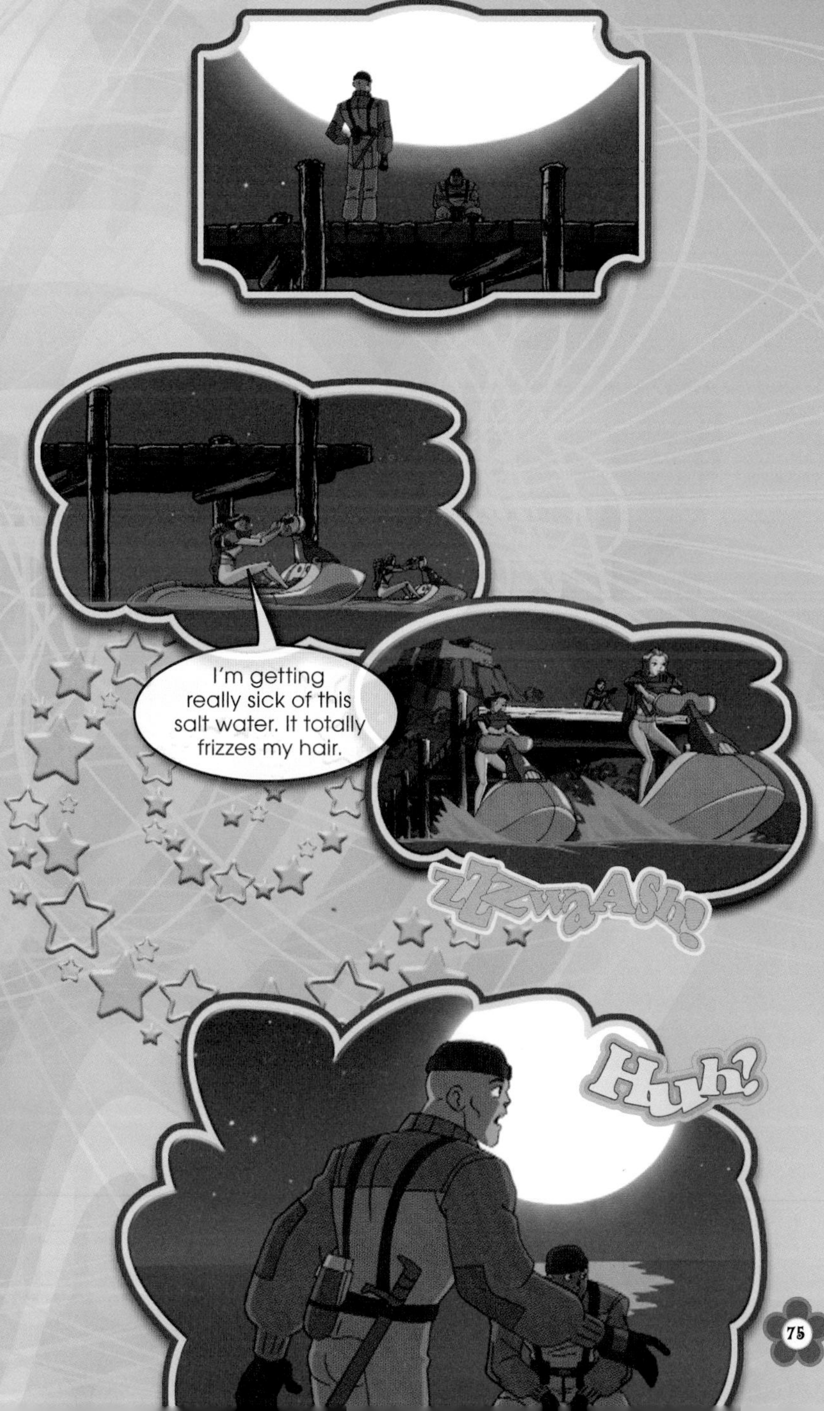

I'm getting really sick of this salt water. It totally frizzes my hair.
ZZZWAASH!
Huh?

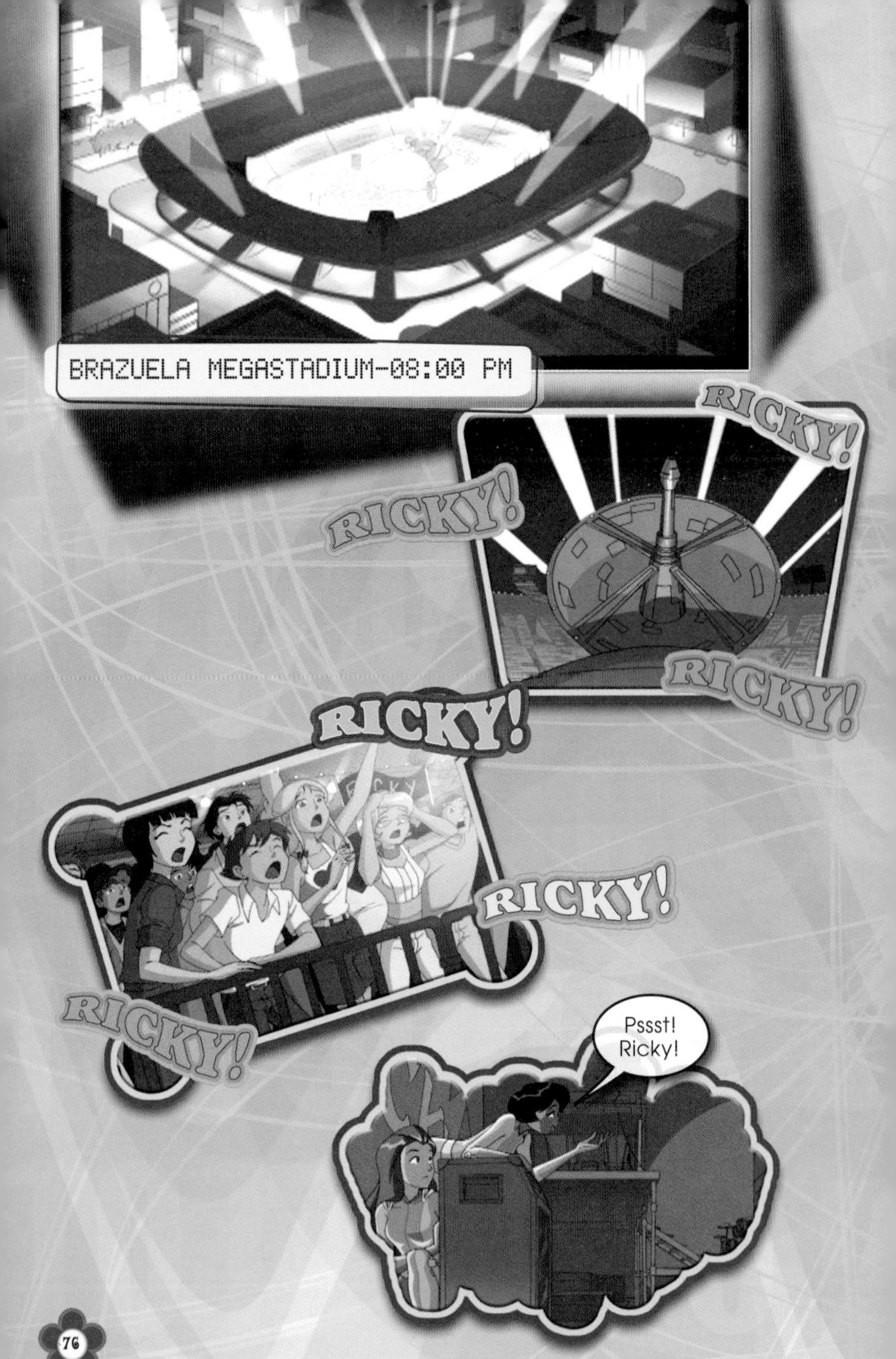
BRAZUELA MEGASTADIUM-08:00 PM
RICKY!
RICKY!
RICKY!
RICKY!
RICKY!
RICKY!
Pssst!
Ricky!

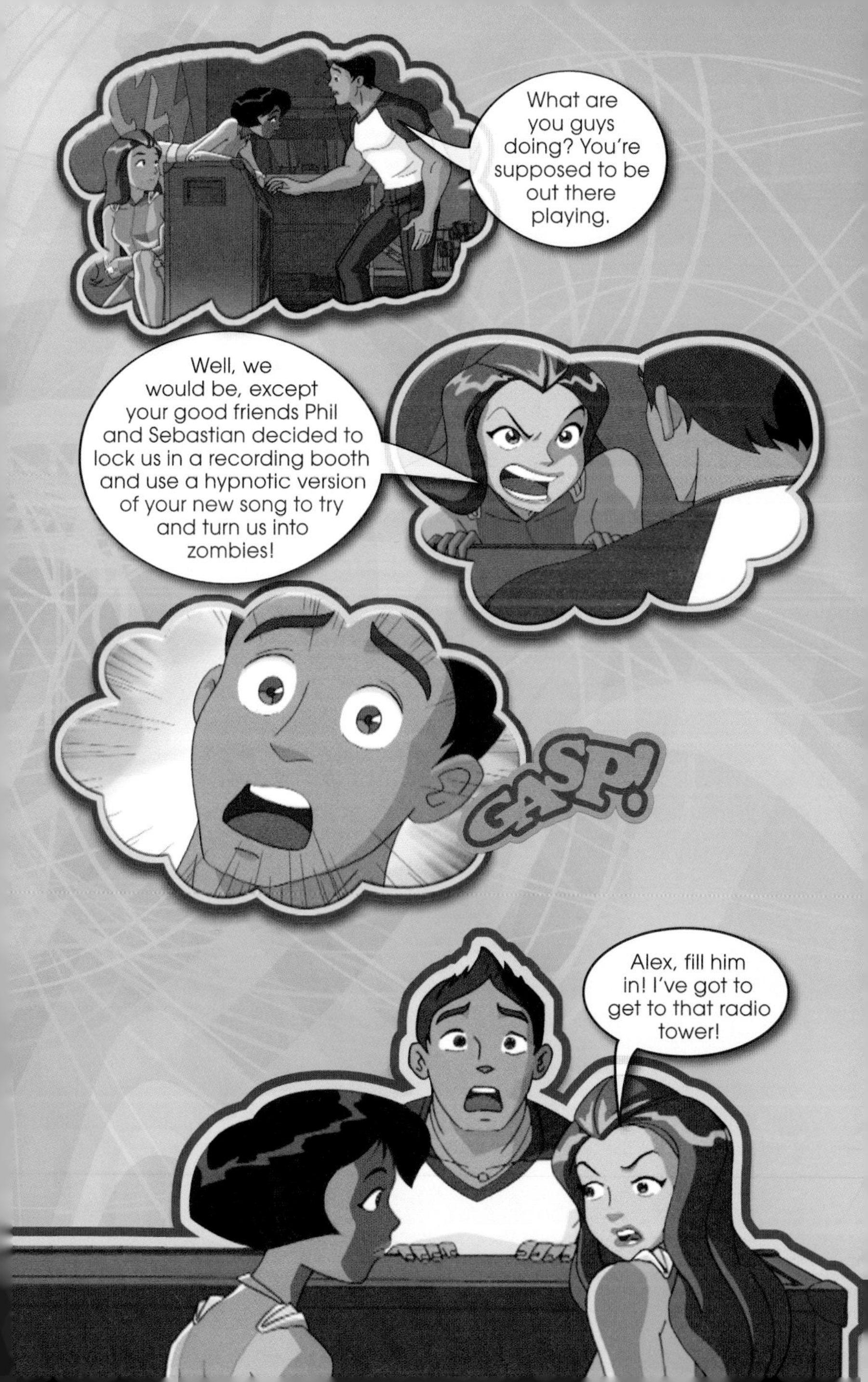
What are you guys doing? You're supposed to be out there playing.
Well, we would be, except your good friends Phil and Sebastian decided to lock us in a recording booth and use a hypnotic version of your new song to try and turn us into zombies!
GASP!
Alex, fill him in! I've got to get to that radio tower!

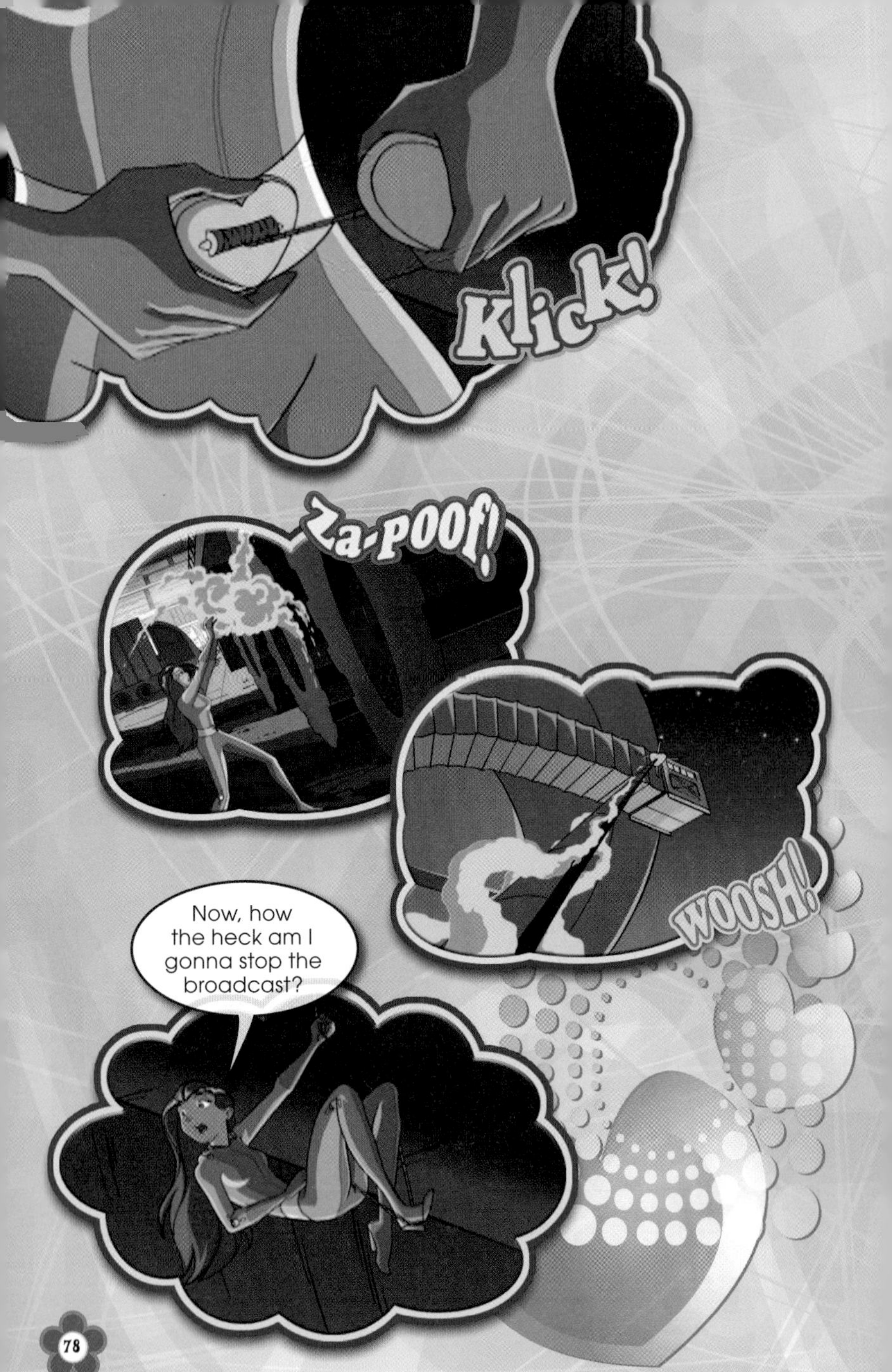
Klick!
Za-POOF!
WOOSH!
Now, how the heck am I gonna stop the broadcast?

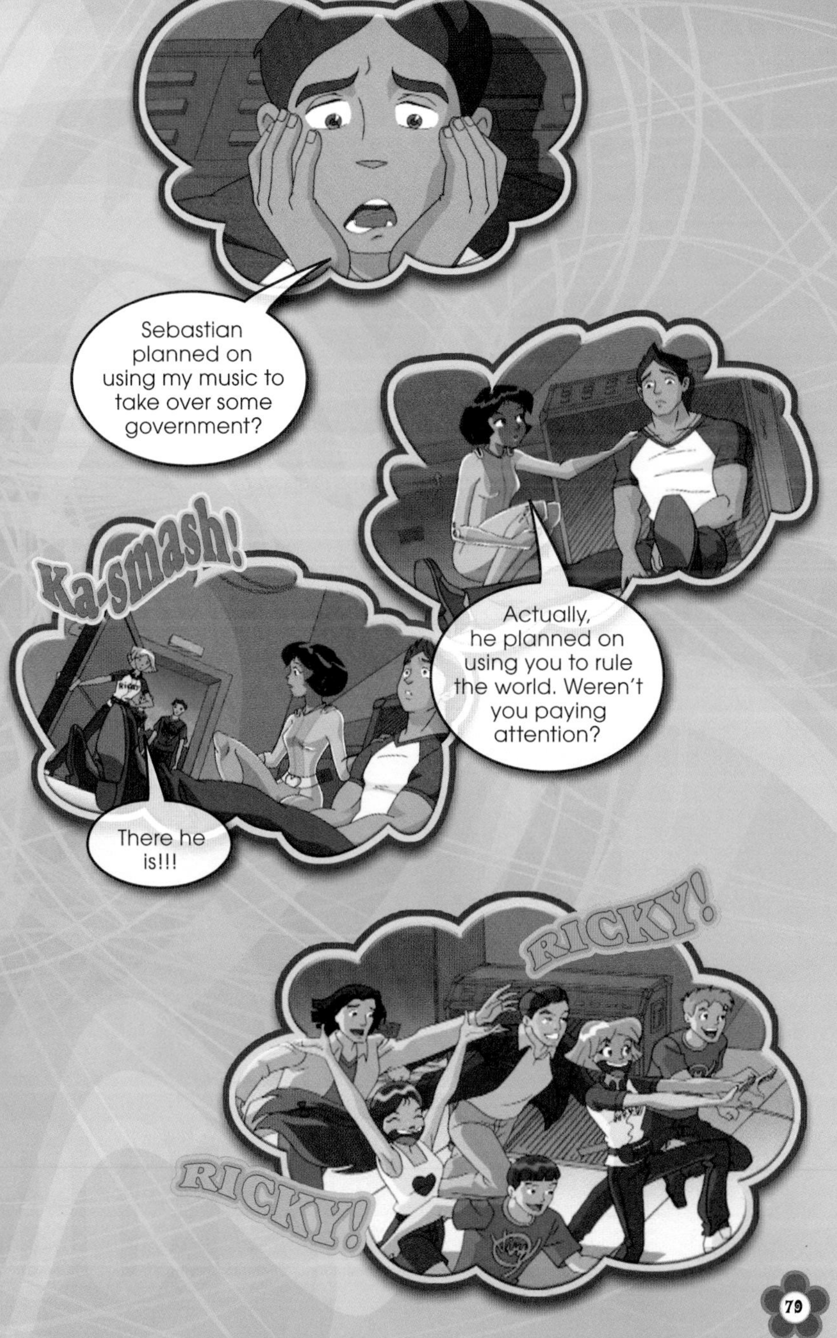
Sebastian planned on using my music to take over some government?
Actually, he planned on using you to rule the world. Weren't you paying attention?
Ka-smash!
There he is!!!
RICKY!
RICKY!

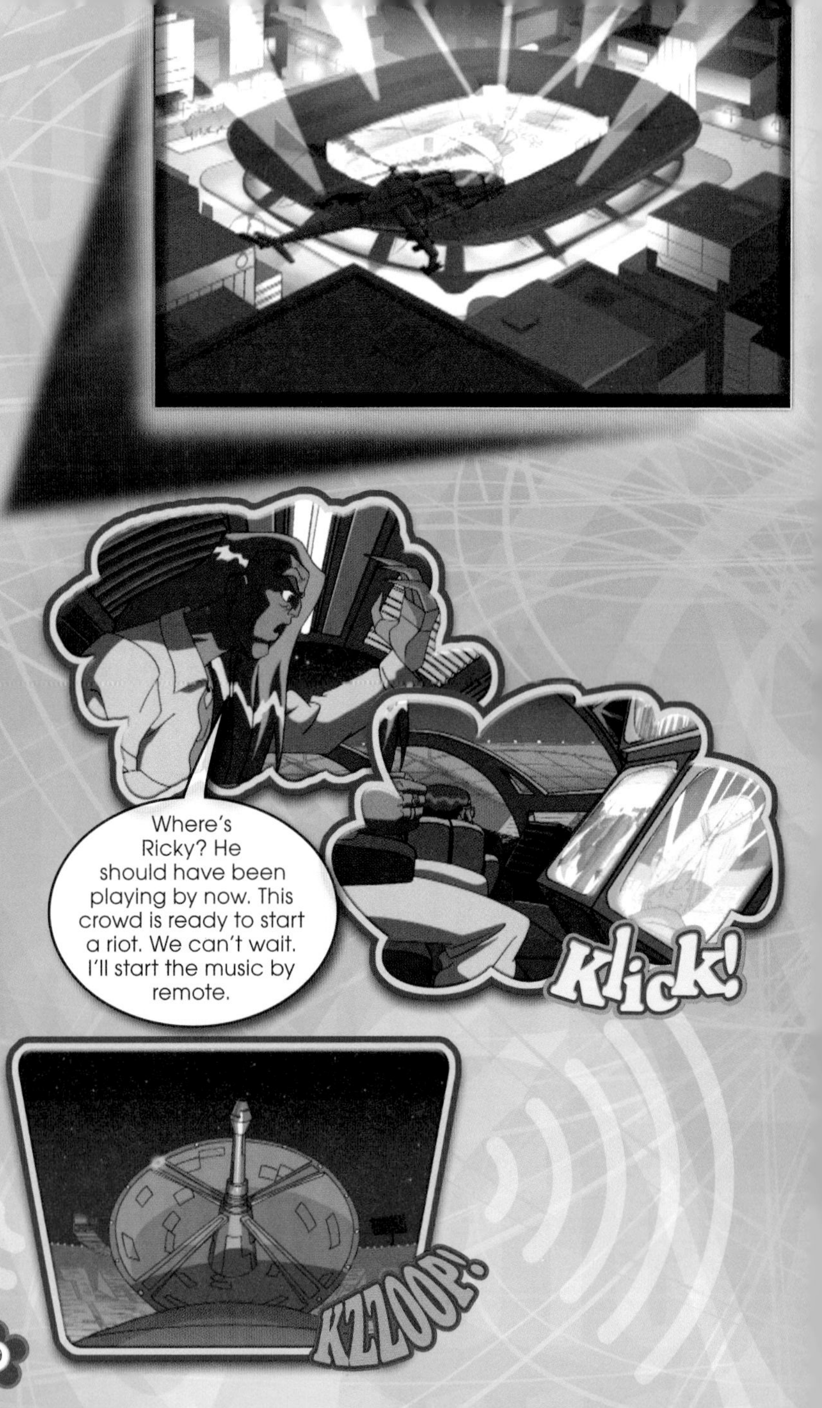
Where's Ricky? He should have been playing by now. This crowd is ready to start a riot. We can't wait. I'll start the music by remote.
Klick!
KZZOOP!

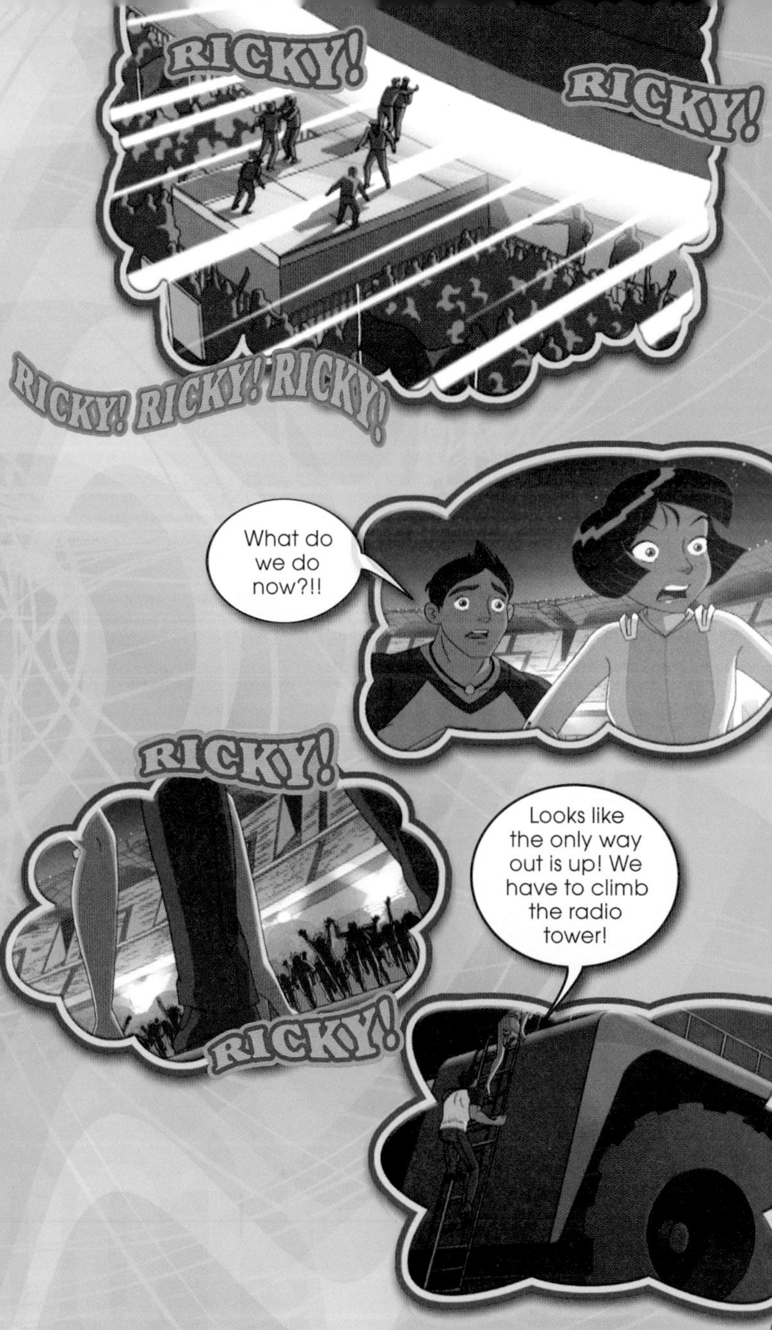
RICKY!
RICKY!
RICKY! RICKY! RICKY!
What do we do now?!!
RICKY!
RICKY!
Looks like the only way out is up! We have to climb the radio tower!

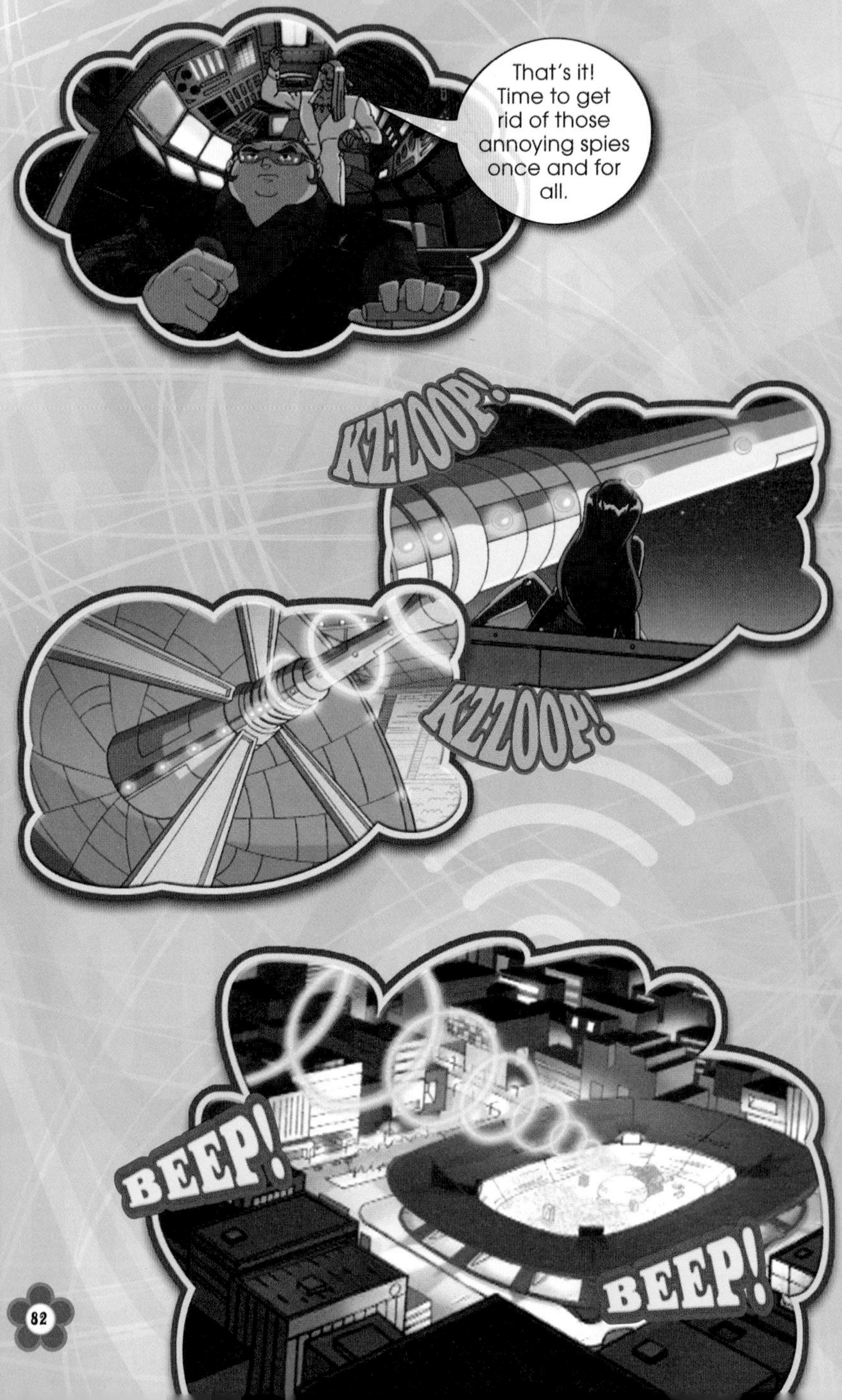
That's it! Time to get rid of those annoying spies once and for all.
KZZOOP!
KZZOOP!
BEEP!
BEEP!

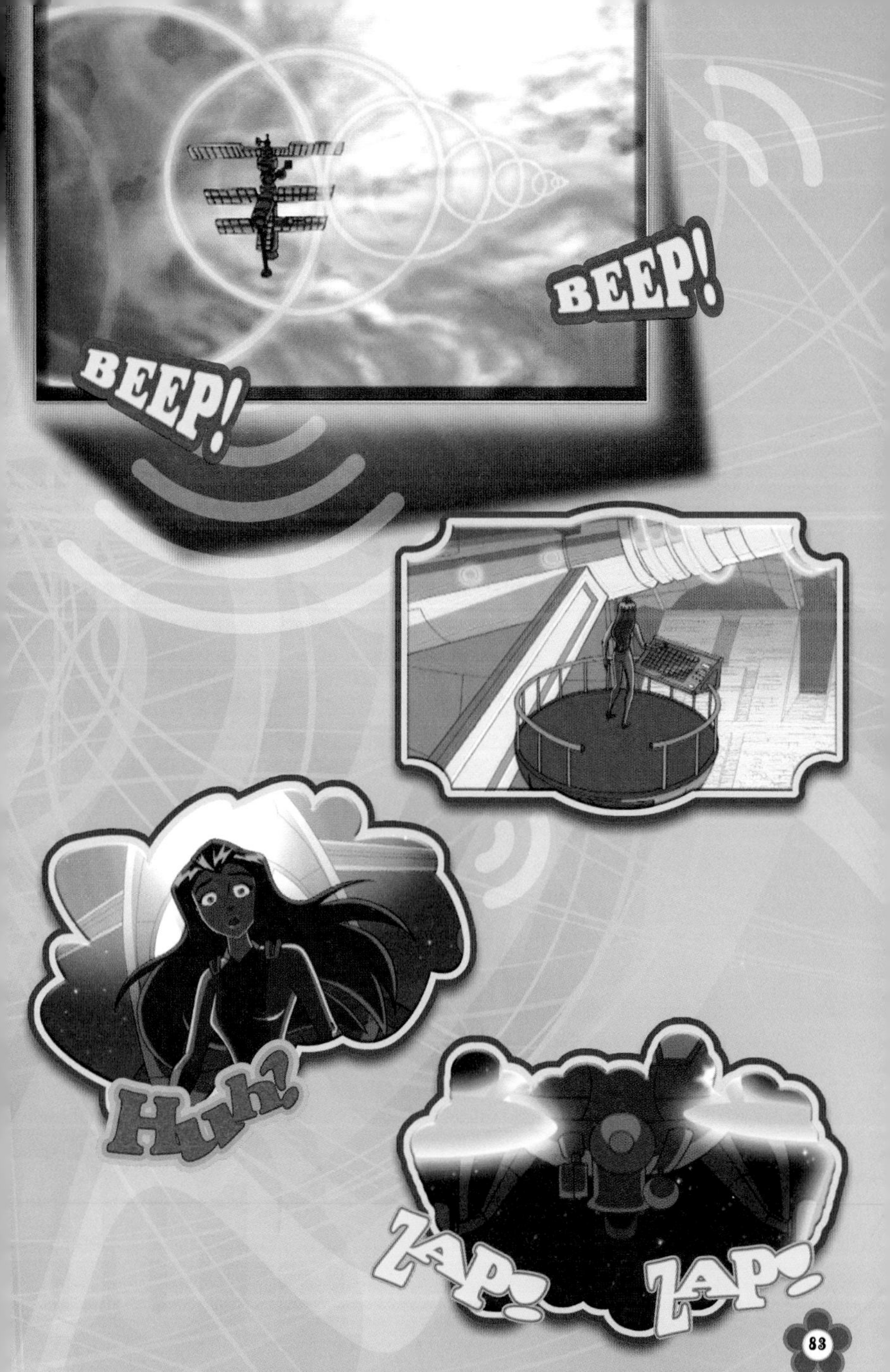
BEEP!
BEEP!
Huh!
ZAP!
ZAP!

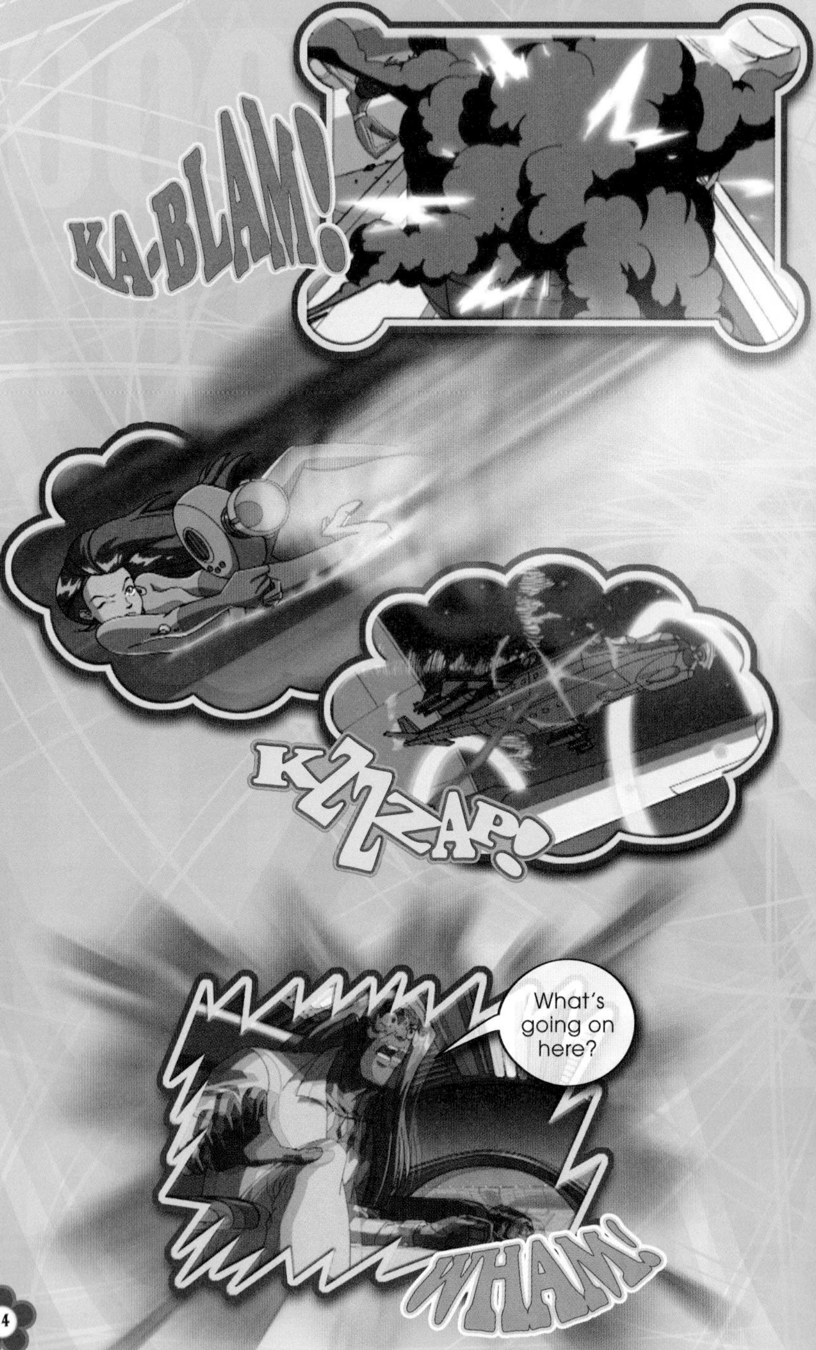
KA-BLAM!
KZZZAP!
What's going on here?
WHAM!

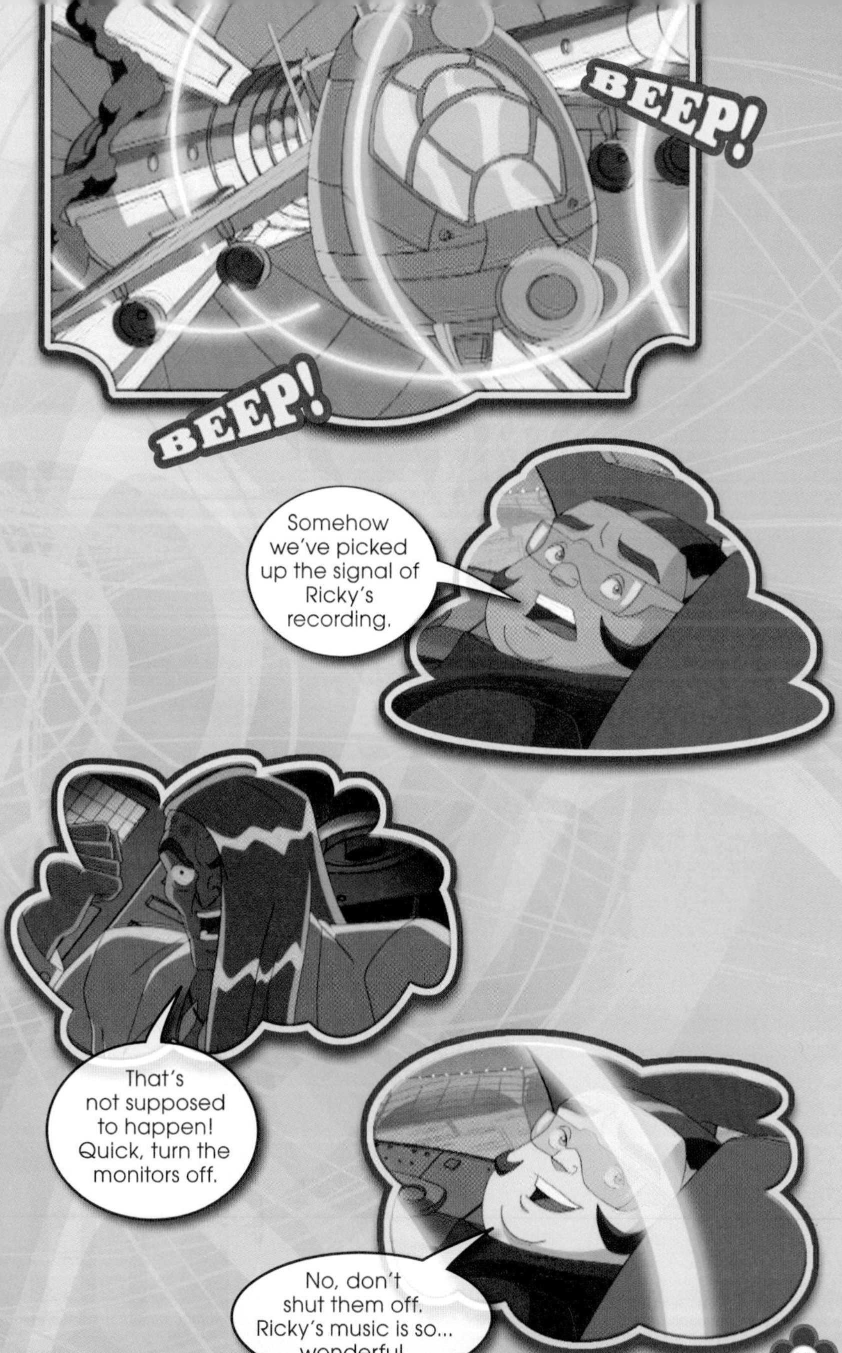
BEEP!
BEEP!
Somehow we've picked up the signal of Ricky's recording.
That's not supposed to happen! Quick, turn the monitors off.
No, don't shut them off. Ricky's music is so... wonderful.

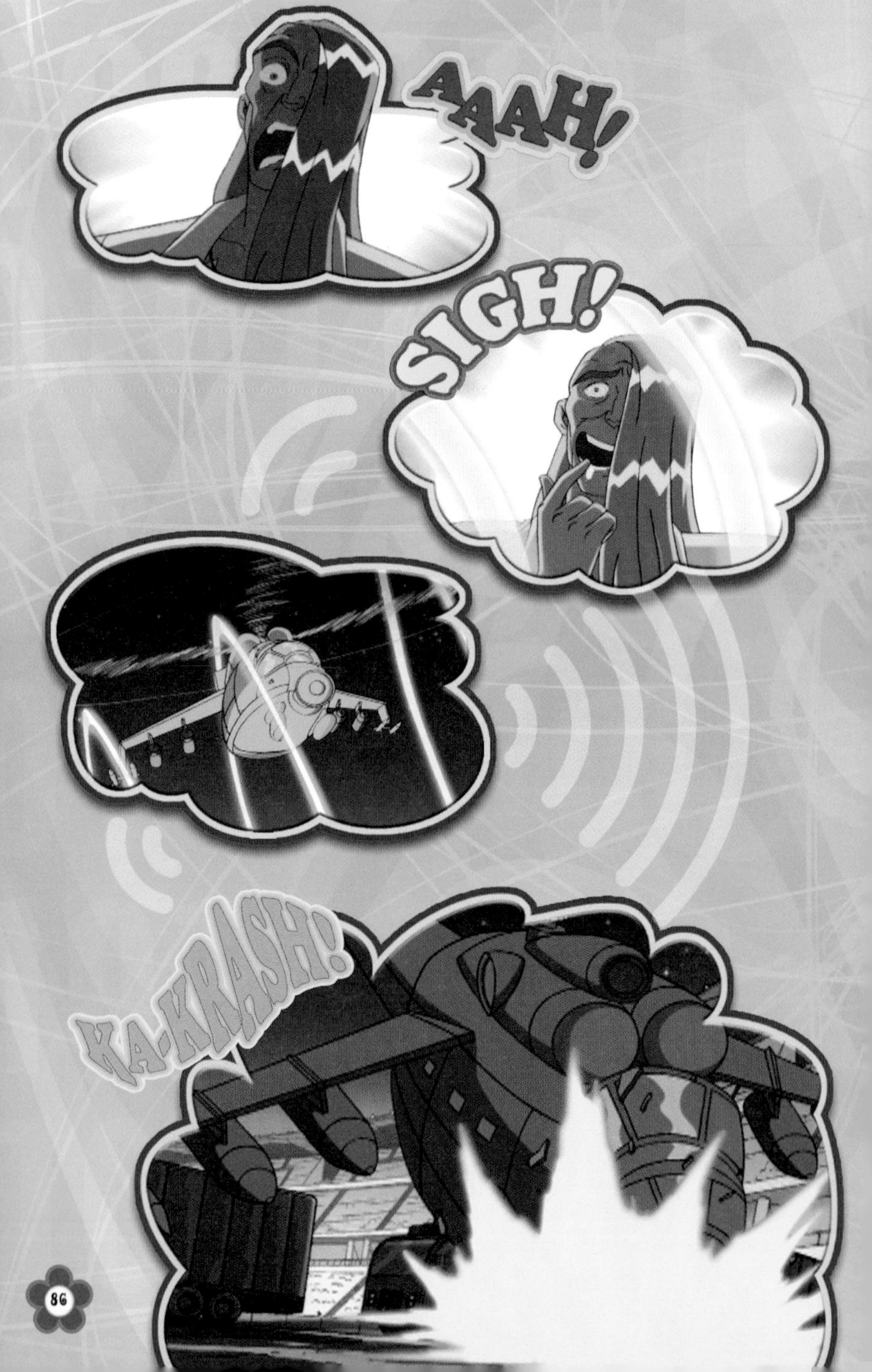
AAAH!
SIGH!
KA-KRASH!

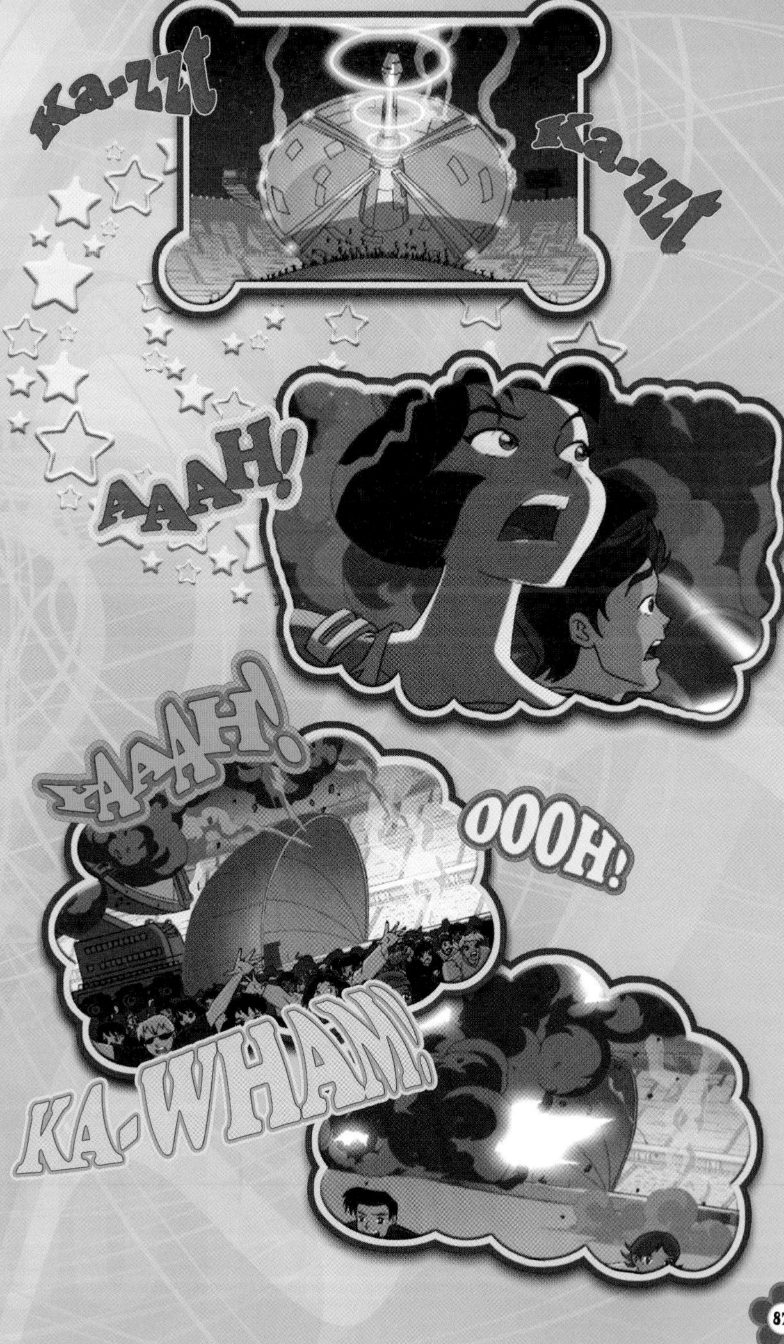
Ka-zzt
Ka-zzt
AAAH!
YAAAH!
OOOH!
KA-WHAM!

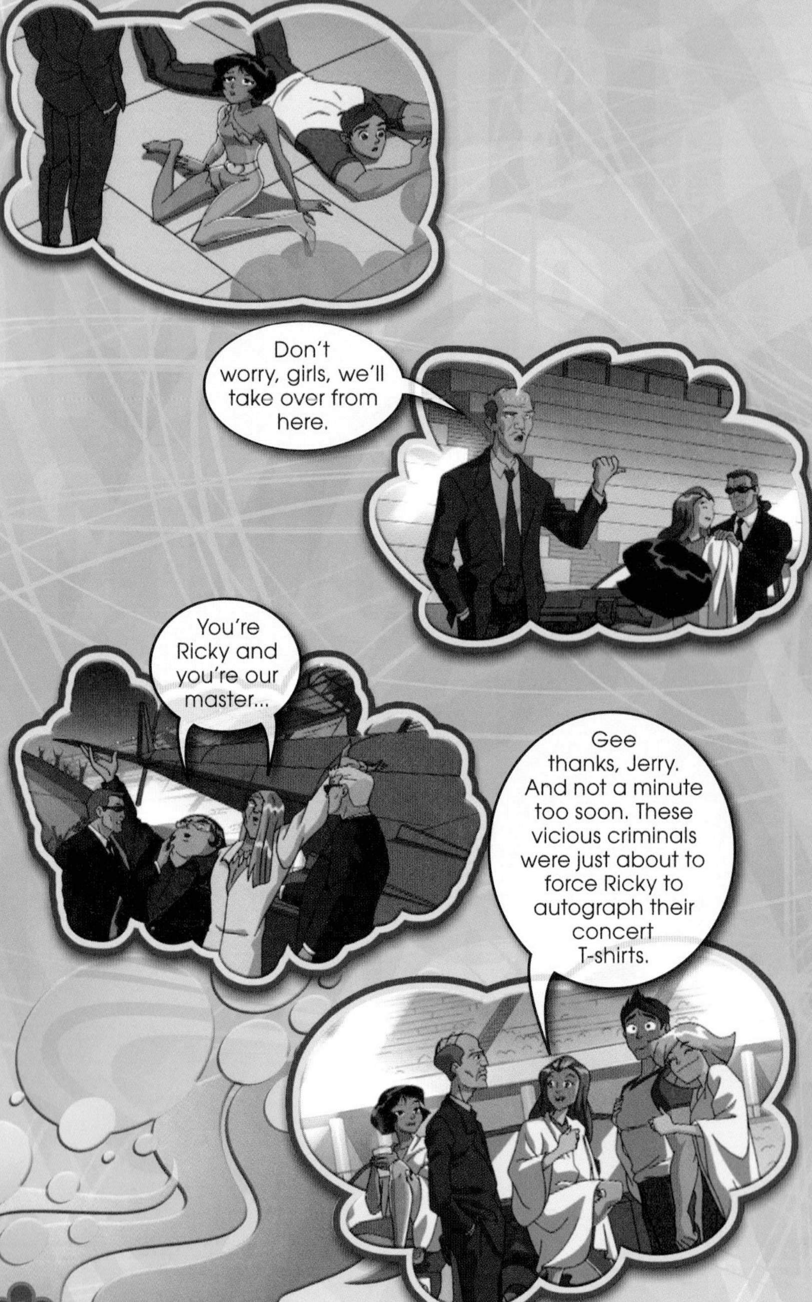
Don't worry, girls, we'll take over from here.
You're Ricky and you're our master...
Gee thanks, Jerry. And not a minute too soon. These vicious criminals were just about to force Ricky to autograph their concert T-shirts.

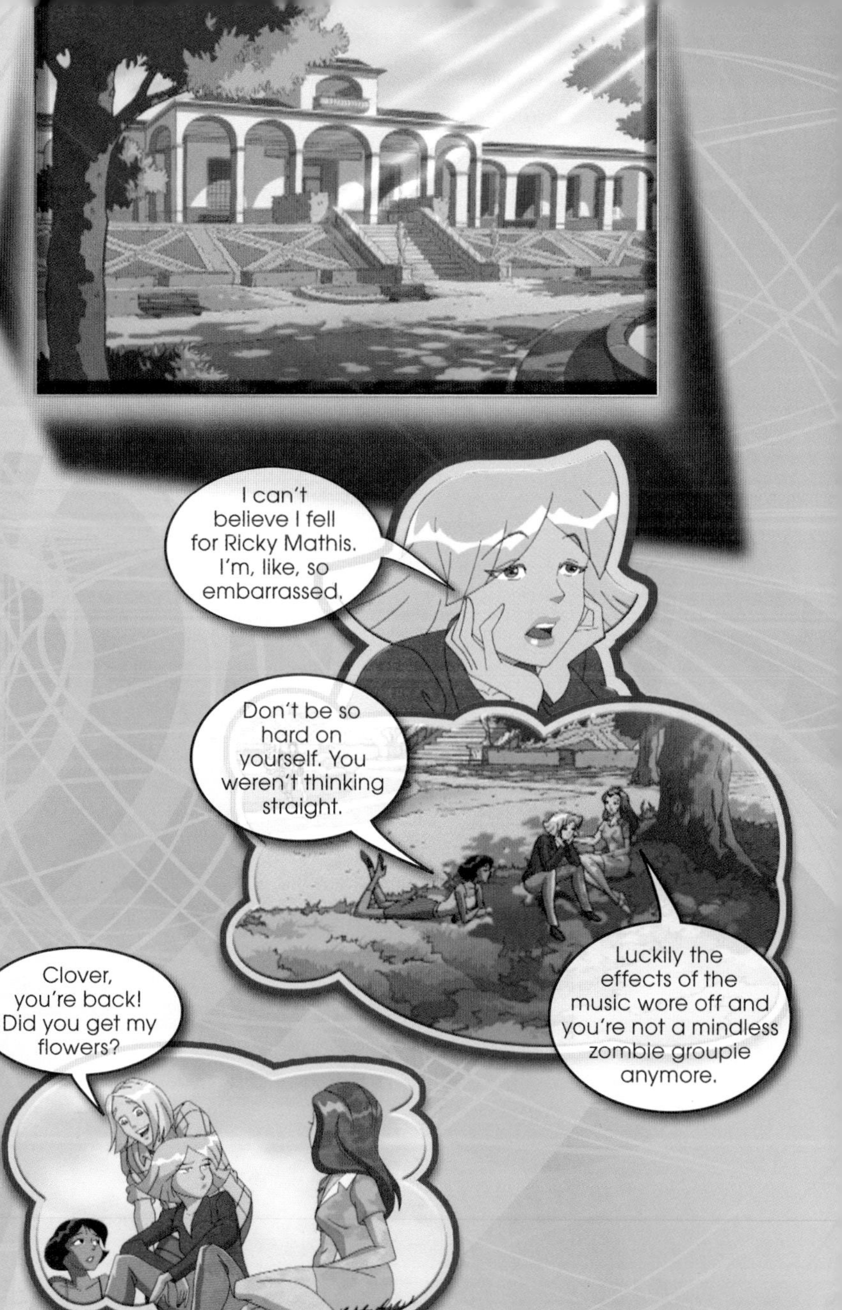
I can't believe I fell for Ricky Mathis. I'm, like, so embarrassed.
Don't be so hard on yourself. You weren't thinking straight.
Luckily the effects of the music wore off and you're not a mindless zombie groupie anymore.
Clover, you're back! Did you get my flowers?

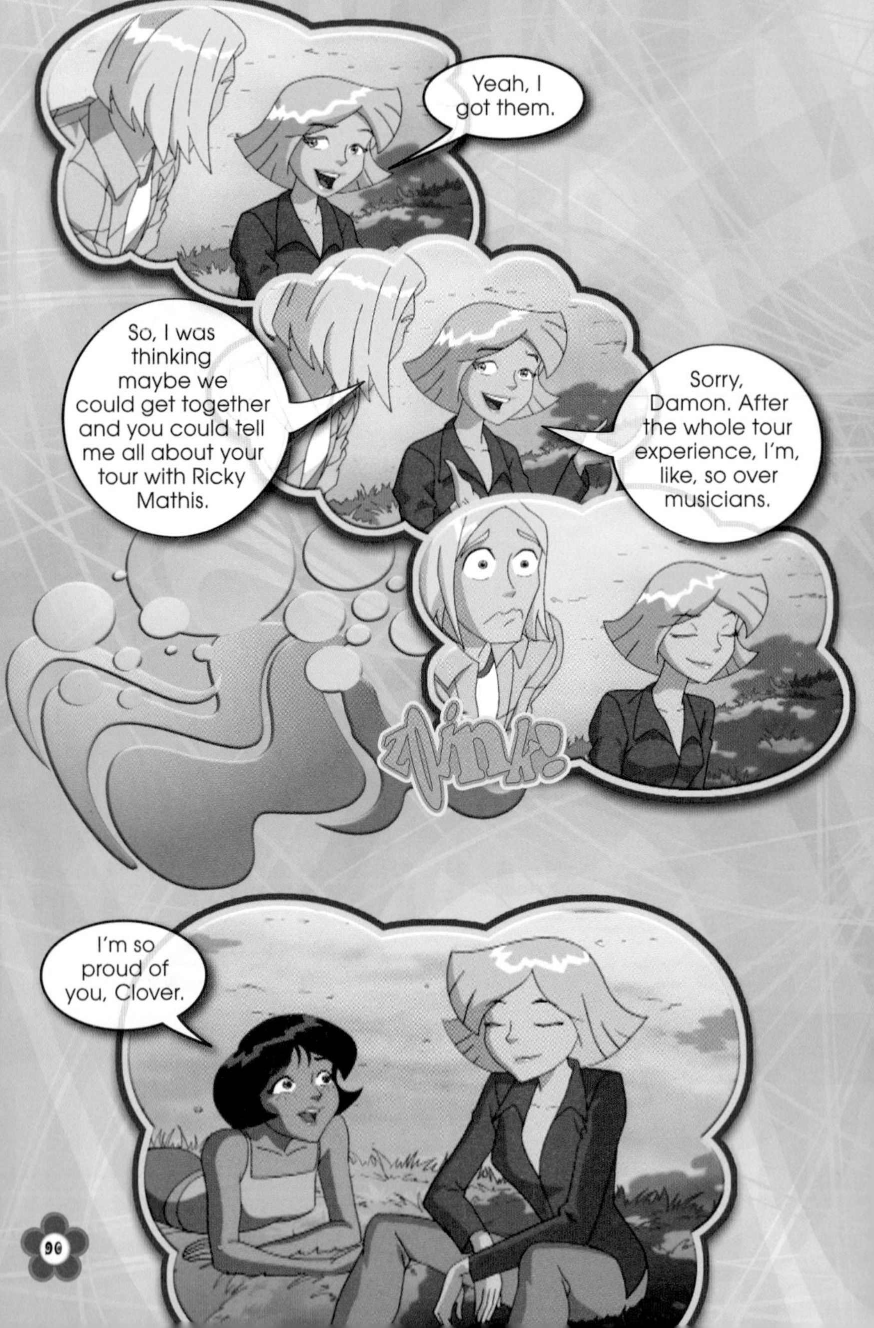
Yeah, I got them.
So, I was thinking maybe we could get together and you could tell me all about your tour with Ricky Mathis.
Sorry, Damon. After the whole tour experience, I'm, like, so over musicians.
zlink!
I'm so proud of you, Clover.

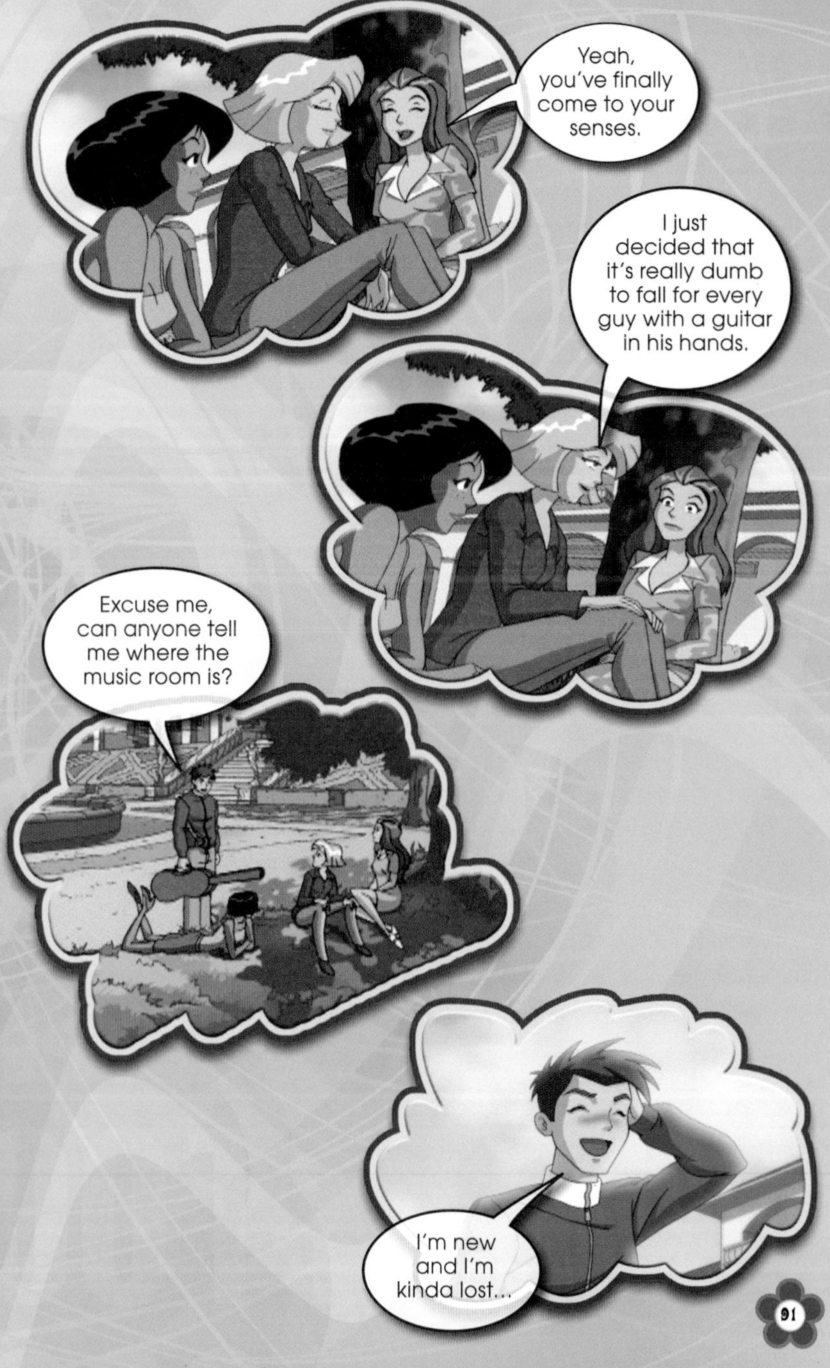
Yeah, you've finally come to your senses.
I just decided that it's really dumb to fall for every guy with a guitar in his hands.
Excuse me, can anyone tell me where the music room is?
I'm new and I'm kinda lost...

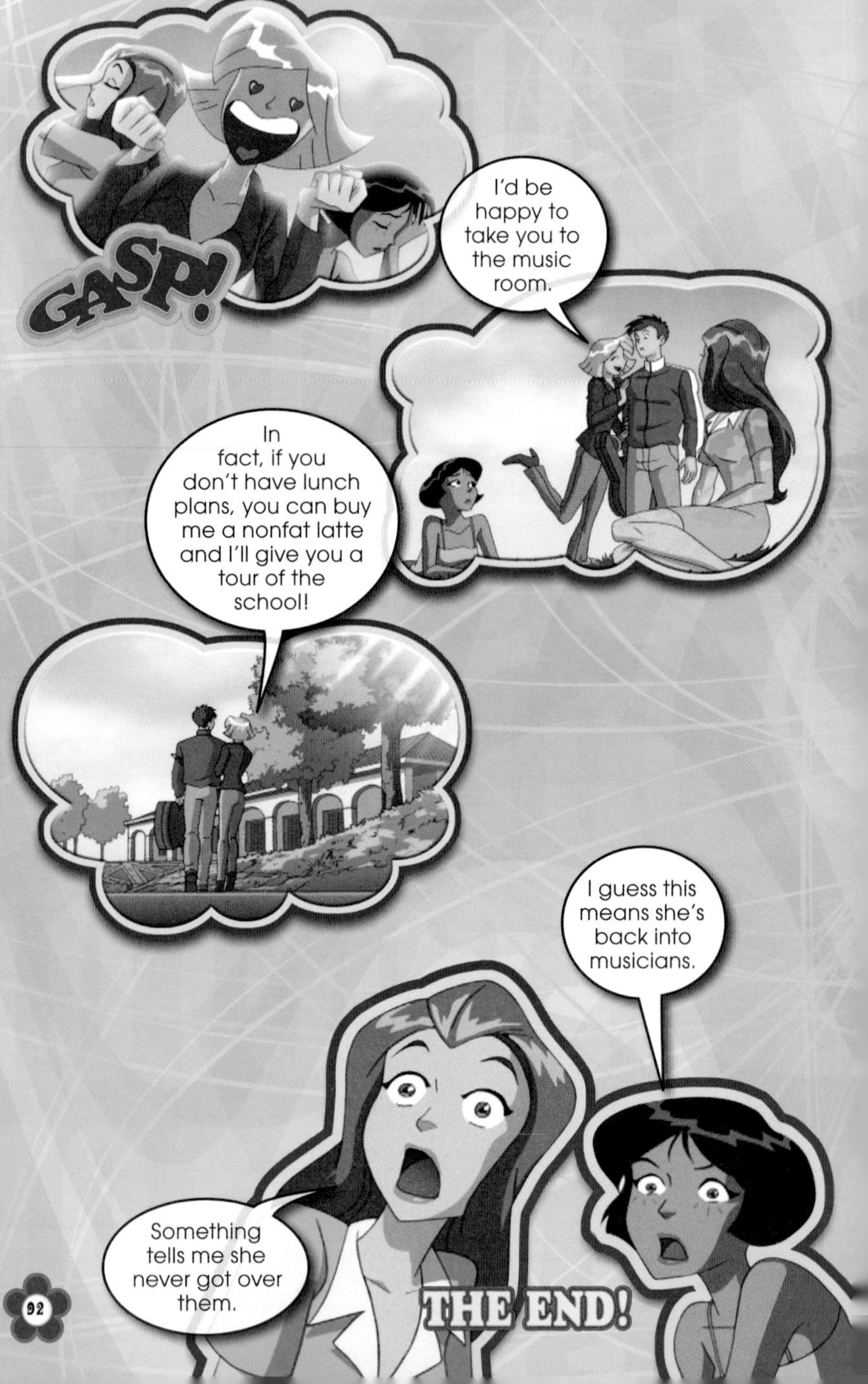
GASP!
I'd be happy to take you to the music room.
In fact, if you don't have lunch plans, you can buy me a nonfat latte and I'll give you a tour of the school!
I guess this means she's back into musicians.
Something tells me she never got over them.
THE END!

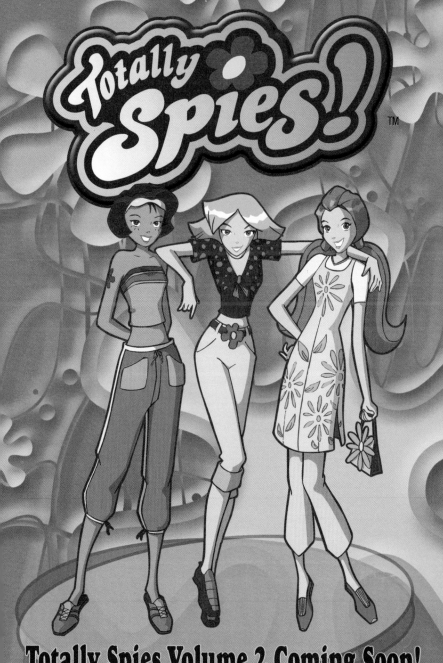

Totally Spies Volume 2 Coming Soon!

ALSO AVAILABLE FROM TOKYOPOP®

MANGA

.HACK//LEGEND OF THE TWILIGHT
ANGELIC LAYER
BABY BIRTH
BRAIN POWERED
BRIGADOON
B'TX
CANDIDATE FOR GODDESS, THE
CARDCAPTOR SAKURA
CARDCAPTOR SAKURA - MASTER OF THE CLOW
CHRONICLES OF THE CURSED SWORD
CLAMP SCHOOL DETECTIVES
CLOVER
COMIC PARTY
CORRECTOR YUI
COWBOY BEBOP
COWBOY BEBOP: SHOOTING STAR
CRESCENT MOON
CROSS
CULDCEPT
CYBORG 009
D•N•ANGEL
DEMON DIARY
DEMON ORORON, THE
DIGIMON
DIGIMON TAMERS
DIGIMON ZERO TWO
DRAGON HUNTER
DRAGON KNIGHTS
DRAGON VOICE
DREAM SAGA
DUKLYON: CLAMP SCHOOL DEFENDERS
ET CETERA
ETERNITY
FAERIES' LANDING
FLCL
FLOWER OF THE DEEP SLEEP, THE
FORBIDDEN DANCE
FRUITS BASKET
G GUNDAM
GATEKEEPERS
GIRL GOT GAME
GUNDAM SEED ASTRAY
GUNDAM WING
GUNDAM WING: BATTLEFIELD OF PACIFISTS
GUNDAM WING: ENDLESS WALTZ
GUNDAM WING: THE LAST OUTPOST (G-UNIT)
HANDS OFF!
HARLEM BEAT

HYPER RUNE
I.N.V.U.
INITIAL D
INSTANT TEEN: JUST ADD NUTS
JING: KING OF BANDITS
JING: KING OF BANDITS - TWILIGHT TALES
JULINE
KARE KANO
KILL ME, KISS ME
KINDAICHI CASE FILES, THE
KING OF HELL
KODOCHA: SANA'S STAGE
LEGEND OF CHUN HYANG, THE
LOVE OR MONEY
MAGIC KNIGHT RAYEARTH I
MAGIC KNIGHT RAYEARTH II
MAN OF MANY FACES
MARMALADE BOY
MARS
MARS: HORSE WITH NO NAME
MINK
MIRACLE GIRLS
MODEL
MOURYOU KIDEN: LEGEND OF THE NYMPHS
NECK AND NECK
ONE
ONE I LOVE, THE
PEACH GIRL
PEACH GIRL: CHANGE OF HEART
PITA-TEN
PLANET LADDER
PLANETES
PRESIDENT DAD
PRINCESS AI
PSYCHIC ACADEMY
QUEEN'S KNIGHT, THE
RAGNAROK
RAVE MASTER
REALITY CHECK
REBIRTH
REBOUND
RISING STARS OF MANGA
SAILOR MOON
SAINT TAIL
SAMURAI GIRL REAL BOUT HIGH SCHOOL
SEIKAI TRILOGY, THE
SGT. FROG
SHAOLIN SISTERS
SHIRAHIME-SYO: SNOW GODDESS TALES

07.15.04Y

ALSO AVAILABLE FROM TOKYOPOP

You want it? We got it!
A full range of TOKYOPOP
products are available now at:
www.TOKYOPOP.com/shop

07.15.04Y